IN WARTIME EAST [...]
an isolated Jewish vi[...]
ing ground for a Naz[...]
beyond even the Final Solution

IN A GERMAN CONVENT
a novice nun is forced by a brilliant and
sadistic S.S. colonel to reveal a secret that
will damn her soul forever

**IN A DYING PENNSYLVANIA STEEL
TOWN**
a sexually abused young girl whose beauty
is her curse discovers she is blessed by a
mysterious saving grace

**IN A SMALL CONNECTICUT
COMMUNITY**
an aging survivor of the Holocaust finds he
is heir to a hellish legacy of the Nazi past
in the form of a miraculous gift from his
dead father

**In Nazi Germany, Operation Brimstone had
been abandoned in error. Now, in 1990s
America, it was being revived in deadly earnest ...**

THE
BERLIN
COVENANT

THE
BERLIN
COVENANT

CELESTE PAUL

A SIGNET BOOK

SIGNET
Published by the Penguin Group
Penguin Books USA Inc., 375 Hudson Street,
New York, New York 10014, U.S.A.
Penguin Books Ltd, 27 Wrights Lane,
London W8 5TZ, England
Penguin Books Australia Ltd, Ringwood,
Victoria, Australia
Penguin Books Canada Ltd, 10 Alcorn Avenue,
Toronto, Ontario, Canada M4V 3B2
Penguin Books (N.Z.) Ltd, 182–190 Wairau Road,
Auckland 10, New Zealand

Penguin Books Ltd, Registered Offices:
Harmondsworth, Middlesex, England

First published by Signet, an imprint of New American Library,
a division of Penguin Books USA Inc.

First Printing, June, 1992
10 9 8 7 6 5 4 3 2 1

PUBLISHER'S NOTE
This is a work of fiction. Names, characters, places, and incidents either
are the product of the author's imagination or are used fictitiously, and
any resemblance to actual persons, living or dead, events, or locales is
entirely coincidental.

This book is dedicated to my parents,
Roy and Eleanor Paul,
who raised me to believe that I could accomplish
anything I set my mind to.
Thanks, Mom and Dad.

Acknowledgments

Though a novel is conceived in solitude, there are many people who contribute their time and talents to the birthing process. Many thanks to my editor, Christopher Schelling, and my agent, Donald Maass, for their patience and expertise.

Thanks to my husband and family for putting up with all the hurried meals eaten off of paper plates.

A special thank-you to Raianne Hodges Melton, for reading the final draft and giving helpful suggestions.

Chapter One

The morning was gray, the air dense with a light, misting rain that beaded on the slick wax shine of the staff car. Droplets formed silver runnels down the windshield, then pooled where the glass met the cold, black steel, forming rivers that ran off the fenders into the mud of the roadbed.

The driver sat at attention behind the wheel, his cap pulled low, his face expressionless, his eyes fixed dead ahead. His business was driving—only that—and he tried to keep his mind away from anything else. In these times it was best not to see too much, not to hear, to be as hard and indifferent as the stones of the wall that bordered the road. Stones survived.

The two men standing beside the car ignored the rain, save to pull the upturned collars of their raincoats more firmly about their ears. They were an odd pair: one tall, slim, and so straight that a rod seemed to have been driven down his spine; the other short, with a roll of fat about his middle that even the bulk of the raincoat could not disguise.

The tall man was clothed in the sleek uniform of an SS colonel, his boots as gleamingly black and highly polished as his auto. He held a pair of binoculars to his eyes, more in an effort to ignore his companion than out of any real interest in the scene before him. If this grubby, pompous little man was any reflection of his work, the morning promised to be a waste of valuable time.

The short man's raincoat was a mass of creases and wrinkles. On his round head was perched a battered fedora, so old and crushed that its shape was barely recognizable. The hat was too small. It kept slipping, and every few moments the little man would reach up and jam it more tightly around his skull. Standing on tiptoe, he strained his short neck and squinted through the rain at the valley below.

"Can you see it? Is it time?" His voice was high and nasal. It irritated Colonel Klaus Brauer like the whine of an insect. He lowered his binoculars and looked down his nose at the disgusting little man. When he answered, the disdain in his tone was barely concealed.

"A few moments, *Herr Doktor*. You are sure that we are at a safe distance?"

"Yes, yes. I've calculated the mass and the forces involved. We are quite safe, *Standartenfuhrer*. There is nothing to fear."

Anxious for any excuse to cut short the conversation, the colonel raised the binoculars to his eyes and focused them on the village nestled in the valley's heart. Breshkov was a small settlement, a farming town with a population of under three hundred. There was nothing noteworthy about it, save that it was a Jewish village. Inoffensive and remote, it had, so far, escaped the pogroms and actions that were decimating the Jewish population of Germany and its conquered neighbors.

His eyes searched and found the small postal van, parked now in the town square. He watched the driver unload the single sack of mail and sling it over his shoulder. Children were in the square, despite the rain. A little girl ran up to the driver. She was small, with dark hair, and her thin body was clad in a red coat. Brauer watched the driver stop and reach into his pocket. He gave the girl something, patted her head affectionately, then continued about his business. The child stood very still, looking down at the treasure in her hand.

She raised her head.

Brauer flinched as her dark eyes seemed to meet his. They were full of condemnation. Two thousand years of suffering stared back at him accusingly. Confused, he let the binoculars slip. Panic seized him, but he used reason to force it down. It was impossible, of course. Hundreds of meters separated them. Through the veil of rain the girl could make out, at most, two figures on the crest of a faraway hill, outlined against the sky. Brauer brought the binoculars back to his eyes again. The child was gone.

He searched in vain among the milling children in the square, but there was no sign of the red coat. At last he turned his attention back to the original subject of his surveillance, just in time to see the postal driver carry his burden into the Town Hall.

A smile of satisfaction twitched the corners of the colonel's mouth. If the postmaster opened the sack, he would find nothing irregular. The letters were all there. Nothing had been removed. But there was one very important addition. Among the envelopes and postal cards was a small package, wrapped in brown paper. It was addressed to the village rabbi, a touch that Colonel Brauer had been unable to resist. The package had been added to the sack this morning, just before the daily pickup. They could jostle it, even open it; inside was a music box, seemingly harmless. But if a tenth of what had been promised him was true, the small box held the fury of Hell itself . . . or the power of Heaven, depending on how you looked at it. He let the binoculars fall and glanced at his watch. It was one minute to nine.

"Soon," he whispered.

The seconds ticked by interminably. Brauer became acutely aware of the rain as a cold stream of water evaded the protecting collar of his raincoat and trickled down his back. The men waited in silence. The only sounds were liquid: the soft patter of the raindrops, and the steady drip and swish of water as it ran off their bodies and that of the car.

At precisely 9:00 A.M., the music box began to play. The sound was not audible to human ears. It was ethereal, the music of the spheres. Neither the postmaster, busy sorting his mail, nor the driver, intent on a hot cup of coffee, heard it. The postmaster's aging bassett hound, curled before the coal stove in the center of the room, slept on, oblivious. But within the body of the music box, something heard and responded to the summons.

Success came as a flash, brightening the gray morning with the light of a thousand suns. Before Brauer's dazzled eyes the valley seemed to rise up silently, like a giant animal awakening. It was several seconds before the sound reached them. A great enveloping roar battered at their ears, threatening to crush their skulls. The force of it drove the little man to his knees. His hat tumbled into the mud. With a cry of alarm, he flung one arm up to shield his eyes and wrapped the other about his head to cover his ears.

The tall man started, but he held his ground. He disdained weakness of any sort. As the sound faded, he squinted through the rain and watched the floor of the valley settle in a soft hail of debris. Heat like that of a blast furnace seared his face as a gigantic pillar of black smoke rose to merge with the gray sky. Around them, the misty rain turned to steam. The tiny dot on the map that had been Breshkov was no more.

Exhilaration filled him, and he breathed slow, careful breaths through his nose until the excited pounding of his heart had slowed. He prided himself on control in all things. With proper discipline, even the capricious functions of the human body could be brought into subjection to the will. He turned grudgingly to the smaller man, who had scrambled to his feet and was uselessly trying to brush the mud from his hat.

"You have done a great service to the Fatherland, Doktor Meintz. The Führer will be pleased when I inform him that Project Brimstone is a success. You'll find that the rewards of his pleasure are more than generous."

The little man came to attention and bowed, the gesture ludicrous when combined with his dishevelment. "I am most grateful to the Führer for his interest and his support. I—"

Whatever else he was going to say was cut short,

as the door to the staff car was suddenly flung wide. The driver staggered from it, his face the gray of the mist, one shaking hand pressed to his lips. Without explanation he ran to the rear of the car, where he doubled over and began vomiting onto the road.

Brauer ignored him. With an impatient jerk of his head, he motioned Dr. Meintz into the car. The doctor climbed into the rear seat and Brauer, eager to avoid conversation at any cost, took the front. Impatiently, he leaned over and pressed the horn, signaling the driver. As he straightened up, his eyes flickered across the rain-streaked windshield. Behind him, he heard Meintz gasp.

A hand lay upon the glass—a child's hand, the small fingers slightly curled, still clutching a sweet wrapped in bright yellow cellophane. Red rivulets of blood flowed from the severed wrist, turning a deeper red as they soaked into the scrap of scarlet cloth that had snagged on the splintered ends of bone, protruding from the ravaged flesh. Unbidden, Brauer's mind served up the memory of the little girl in the village square. He felt his gorge rise and forced it down. Control was everything.

Averting his eyes and breathing deeply, he reached over and switched on the windshield wipers. They swept the offending thing aside. With a soft thump, the hand fell to the fender and then bounced silently to the ground.

The chauffeur resumed his seat and put the engine in gear. As he turned the car around, the rear wheels ground the hand deep into the mud, until no trace remained.

Breshkov was dead and buried.

Brimstone lived.

Berlin, Germany
Two weeks later

In his quarters, Colonel Klaus Brauer stripped off his uniform. He bathed and toweled his lean body until his skin tingled. He didn't stop until he was certain that all trace of contact with Dr. Frederick Meintz had been expunged. If only he could as easily rid himself of the knot of anger that had formed in his stomach at the thought of Meintz, or the fiery pain of the peptic ulcer that the anger had ignited. Brauer strode to the bureau and took a brown bottle of powder from the top drawer. He mixed some of its contents with water and downed the chalky mixture in a single gulp. Gradually, the pain in his stomach eased.

The little man was a blemish on the flawless features of the Reich. He was soft, undisciplined. His indulgence was evident in his slovenly manner of dress, in the way he had allowed his body to run to fat. There was no room for weakness in Germany's future. Like the mental defectives and the racially impure, men of Meintz's kind were dross, to be burned away. Unfortunately, for now, the man was useful. His Project Brimstone had proved an unexpected success. When the process was finally refined, when it had given up all its secrets ... Frederick Meintz would become expendable.

Brauer folded the towel and hung it neatly on the rack on the back of the lavatory door. Naked, he padded into the bedroom and sat on the threadbare rug beside the bed. For the next twenty minutes he engaged in a series of calisthenics: sit-ups, push-ups, leg raises. When he had finished, he strode across the room to stand before the full-length mirror. He was satisfied with what he saw.

The man in the mirror was blond and blue-eyed, with the aristocratic, Nordic features that the Reich found desirable in its officers. There was strength in that face, and if an unbiased observer had chosen to call that strength hardness, well, so be it. These were hard times. The war would be won by those who could see what needed to be done and who could find the strength within themselves to do it.

Standing sideways, he ran a hand over the ripple of muscle that covered his broad rib cage, then pressed his palm into the rock-hard hollow of his belly. Here was the Aryan ideal: a being disciplined, superior in mind and body. Was it any wonder that, at only twenty-seven, he had already earned the rank of colonel? Brauer smiled. He was the elite of the elite, a wearer of the coveted dagger.

For many men that would have been enough, but for Klaus Brauer it was a mere stopover on his climb to power. Brimstone, if it proved to be as successful as its initial test had indicated, would be the boost that he needed to send him on his way. By the next year's end he planned to be numbered among the twelve generals of Himmler's inner circle. His name and coat of arms would grace the proud walls of Castle Wewelsburg. From there, under the Führer's guidance, he would help to determine Germany's future. Such was his destiny.

He took a fresh uniform from the wardrobe and dressed quickly, then returned to the mirror once more. He straightened the black tie. Tonight was important, for he would be dining with Greta

Ernst. Not so unusual an occurrence, but tonight he would ask her to be his wife.

Their relationship had been cool and passionless. Passion—love, if you wished to call it that—had had very little to do with his decision to marry the woman. The SS expected its men to marry and establish a family as part of their duty to the Reich. True, if Greta accepted him, there would still be the formality of the questionnaires and the health exams. But Brauer had no fears on that score.

He'd already had her background meticulously investigated. Greta Ernst, tall and blond, had no taint of foreign blood in her ancestry. She was racially pure. Within the next two months, if all went according to his plans, they would be married in the Registry Office and receive the traditional bread and salt. Together they would produce exceptional children, children who would be leaders in the future their father was even now helping to create for them.

Brauer placed his cap upon his head and tugged on the brim until it was at the proper angle. The light glinted off the silver death's-head framed against the black cloth. Before turning away Colonel Brauer smiled in satisfaction at the picture he made, unaware how closely the cold lines of his face were beginning to resemble the silvered features of the visage that stared mockingly above it.

Berlin
The next morning

Dr. Frederick Meintz sat at his desk, hunched over the report of Brimstone's test. The results were all he'd hoped for. The blast had leveled everything for a distance of fifteen square kilometers. The amount of compound required to produce such destruction was only slightly larger than an egg.

His chubby face took on a smirk of satisfaction, as he closed the cover of the official-looking folder. The report he'd prepared for Colonel Brauer encompassed seventeen pages, but to Frederick Meintz it could all be boiled down and condensed into one single, sweet word: success!

How long it had been in coming! The work had been slow and tedious, and further hampered by the meager funding given to it. Physics was in fashion these days. The Reich was investing thousands of deutsche marks in Heisenberg's atomic project. Uranium and heavy water supposedly would decide the war. Such foolishness.

He leaned back in his chair and stared affectionately at the periodic table tacked to the far wall, as a father watches a favorite child. Chemistry would determine man's future, just as it had determined his past. Hadn't life itself begun in some primordial cauldron—molecules combining and recombining until they'd achieved animation? The combinations that could be produced were virtually infinite. Any fool could carry that reasoning a step further and see that limitless energy could be produced as well.

Unfortunately, it was new ideas that attracted the funds. Heisenberg's talk of self-sustaining chain reactions had captured the Führer's imagination. The expense and potential danger of the process had only served to make it more appealing. Uranium was scarce and, in the powdered form, highly pyrophoric. Just a few months past, Heisenberg's Leipzig lab had gone up in smoke when his crude atomic pile had gone out of control. Still, that had done nothing to quell the Reich's enthusiasm. Evidence that the British and Americans also were working on an atomic bomb clinched it. The chemists and their old-fashioned theories were shunted aside, like poor relations.

Meintz's round face crinkled into a sly smile. The lack of funds had proven to be an unexpected advantage. It had forced him to produce an explosive that could be made cheaply and plentifully, from common materials. He had used the bones they'd tossed him, testing and discarding one approach after another. Purely by accident, he'd discovered Brimstone.

He frowned. If the truth were told, the actual discovery had been made by his assistant, Isaac Kauffman. But Kauffman was an unknown, a mere graduate student. He had needed Meintz's professional standing within the academic community to lend credibility to the project. It was a shame that credit for the discovery had to be shared. By rights, Meintz should have stumbled upon it first.

The formula, once grasped, was childishly simple. So simple, in fact, that he had passed the last few months in inner terror, fearful that someone else might claim the discovery first. The successful test, with Colonel Brauer as a witness, had at last laid that fear to rest.

He had no illusions about Klaus Brauer. He knew the colonel detested him, and the feeling was mutual. The man was a dangerous fanatic, an imbecile who actually accepted the Reich's ridiculous racial purity doctrine as gospel. Still, he was useful. Brauer was an opportunist, and ambitious. He would extol the virtues of Brimstone, and use its success to further his career. He would see that Project Brimstone received all the attention due it.

Meintz looked around the cramped office, really seeing it for the first time. It was an ugly place, its shelves crammed to capacity, the rug on the wooden floor dirty and threadbare, pockmarked with chemical burns and stains. The single window faced the brick wall of another building, and it was so thick with accumulated grime that, even if there had been a view, Meintz would have had to strain to see it. The laboratory in the adjoining room was comparatively larger, but its equipment was equally ugly and outdated. The lab tables themselves were mere planks thrown across wooden sawhorses.

No more. Soon he would be moved to larger quarters. The latest equipment would be at his fingertips, to be used as he saw fit. Gone would be the flimsy, makeshift shelves, with their dusty clutter. He would insist on a work place that was bright and airy. He would do away with the leaky wood stove that had been the only source of heat in the winter. His new lab would be properly lighted, properly heated, properly ventilated. It would be a showplace, a center of learning for the students his success inevitably would attract.

A knock sounded on the office door precisely as the small, dust-covered cuckoo clock on the far wall sounded ten o'clock. Meintz started guiltily from his chair, his daydream giving way to reality. As always, Colonel Brauer was on time. The doctor quickly straightened the report and stuffed it into a folder, then made a hasty if futile effort to neaten his desk: aligning books just so, throwing stray papers into the top drawer. He gave a cursory glance around the room, knowing that the cleanup fell far short of what was required. It was not good policy to keep Colonel Brauer waiting. He straightened his lab coat and ran a nervous hand through his thinning hair.

"Enter."

Isaac Kauffman opened the door and stood back to allow the colonel to enter. Meintz's chief assistant kept his eyes downcast, the picture of humility. Brauer swept by him as if the man did not exist. Kauffman withdrew, pulling the door closed silently behind him.

"*Guten Morgen, Standartenfuhrer.* I was just putting the finishing touches on your report." Meintz came to attention, trying to suck in his pot belly. The younger man's haughty demeanor always unsettled him. It was galling to have to defer to someone half his age. He was suddenly conscious of the coffee stain on his coat, as he stared at Brauer's immaculate black uniform. In the colonel's presence he always felt dirty, and he had not yet determined whether the feeling came from comparison or association. Awkwardly he offered his hand, and was further chagrined when Brauer ignored it.

Reaching past him, the colonel picked up the folder of papers from the desk and tucked it under his arm. "*Sehr gut*, Doktor Meintz. I trust everything is in order?"

"Oh. Yes, sir."

"Tomorrow, my aide will see that you are moved to larger quarters—somewhere in the country, where you can accomplish your work in peace. My men are securing a suitable building. In the meantime, make a list of any equipment you will need in order to begin full-scale production. Have your people, and all files and materials relating to Project Brimstone, ready for transport by morning."

"Yes, sir. Thank you, sir."

"Heil Hitler!"

"Heil Hitler!" Meintz returned the salute, for the first time feeling pride in the words. His dream was becoming a reality.

Brauer turned to leave, then paused, his hand on the door knob. He turned back to Meintz, the slight flicker in his eyes making the little chemist uneasy.

"One more thing. Kauffman—your assistant. Did you know that the man is a Jew?"

Meintz felt his knees turn to jelly. "That cannot be. His background was thoroughly investigated at the time I took him on as my assistant."

Brauer's lips drew back in a sneer. "You examined his papers and found them all in order. That is not a thorough investigation. You're sloppy, Meintz, sloppy and lazy. If you had dug a bit deeper, as I did, you would have uncovered the truth. Or perhaps you did know the truth, and chose to ignore it because the rotten little Jew had something you wanted, something that would give you the prestige that you could not earn on your own. Brimstone is Kauffman's brainchild—not yours. Do you know the penalty for harboring a Jew?"

Meintz swallowed hard, his throat suddenly tight and dry. "I did not know he was a Jew, Herr Colonel. I swear to you, I did not know."

"For your sake, I hope that you are telling the truth. As for Kauffman—I've ordered his family picked up for resettlement. Say nothing of this. Allow him to pack his things along with the others. This afternoon, when his usefulness is completed, my men will come for him. Understood?"

Meintz nodded. When Colonel Brauer turned on his heel and casually took his leave, the little man began to shake uncontrollably. He understood all too well.

He sank heavily into the chair at his desk and poured himself a glass of brandy, downing it in a single, burning gulp, then refilled the glass. As the brandy took effect, the shaking gradually subsided.

The thought formed slowly, its edges blurred by the alcohol. When it came into clear focus in his mind he sat up straighter, his small, piggy eyes widening at the realization. He grinned.

By the time this day was over, the credit and glory of Brimstone would be his alone.

In the laboratory supply closet, Isaac Kauffman stealthily slipped a single brick back into its place in the wall. He had discovered the loose brick two years ago, when taking an inventory. As this particular wall adjoined Dr. Meintz's office, Kauffman had immediately perceived its usefulness. On Meintz's side the opening was concealed by a huge, unwieldly set of bookshelves. With the brick removed, it was possible to hear with absolute clarity everything that was said in that office. Isaac rested his forehead on the shelves, struggling to hold back tears of despair. What he had just heard amounted to his own death sentence.

Chaya . . .

Little Dov . . .

Thoughts of his wife and infant son drove him to the border of madness. Chaya had trusted him, when he'd chosen to stay. Blond and blue-eyed, they'd hoped their physical appearance and the false papers that Isaac had paid so dearly for would be enough to hide their true identities until this terrible war had ended. Both had grasped at Brimstone as a means to salvation.

Isaac bit his lips, fighting for control. He'd been a fool to think the Nazis could be so easily deceived. Chaya . . . What terror had she felt when Brauer's monsters came for her? No lies about resettlement would have soothed her—both of them had known the truth for a long time now. They'd watched others disappear, one by one.

And Isaac had seen more tangible proof. Once, on a drive through the country with Dr. Meintz, the air suddenly had been filled with a terrible stench. There, by the roadside, in a farmer's field, they came upon a mass grave, less than twenty-four hours old. He would never forget the smell of death, or the sight of pale arms and legs protruding from the thin covering of sand, or the lake of blood bubbling up from the horror below ground. Was Chaya, even now, standing at the brink of one of those pits . . . naked . . . Dov in her arms . . . a gun at her head?

For long moments he stood, head bowed, paralyzed by grief. Then the instinct of self-preservation took over. Perhaps it was not too late. There was still Dr. Meintz. The man was his personal friend. He'd sent gifts to both Chaya and the baby at their son's birth, and he was often a guest at their table. He knew the fate that awaited them at Brauer's hands. Surely, he would help.

With shaking hands, he shifted several racks of beakers back into place to hide the brick from sight. The fragile glass rattled at his touch, the sound seeming very loud in the confined space. Footsteps approached the closet, so he hastily picked up his clipboard and pretended to list supplies, the printed forms a blur before his eyes.

"Ah, Isaac. There you are." Meintz's round form filled the closet doorway. He beamed a false smile, and the young chemist felt hope die within him. Meintz went on, his eyes darting guiltily, unable to look his assistant in the face. "Colonel Brauer brought good news. Tomorrow, we will all be moved to larger facilities in the countryside. Clear your desk. Pack all your notes and equipment. . . ."

As the doctor continued, Isaac barely heard the rest of his lies. Hatred acted as a restorative. Calm filled him, and his mind became as crisp and clear as a winter's morning. He knew what he would do.

"All this will have to be packed, too. See to it."

"Yes, sir. Right away."

He waited until Dr. Meintz had gone back into his office, then went to his own desk and slowly began to empty the drawers of notes and papers. Other members of the research team bustled around him, packing up their belongings. An air of celebration filled the drab laboratory.

Kurt Geller, one of the lab technicians, clapped him on the back and thrust a glass of wine into Isaac's hand.

"Don't look so glum, Kauffman! Tomorrow, it's off to the country—fresh air, sunlight, and no more worries about the British bringing this roof down upon our heads! Drink up, my friend!"

Isaac forced a smile and the young man went on his way. *When I am taken away, my friend, you will not lift a hand to stop them*, he thought. *By tomorrow, you will have forgotten my name*. He downed the glass of wine.

It tasted bitter.

He continued on through the rest of the morning as if nothing were wrong, while behind his eyes danced pictures of Chaya with blood on her lovely face, of Dov dashed against the ground, his small cries still and silent. At noon, Meintz and the rest of the personnel went out to have their lunch. As was his custom, Isaac stayed behind. When they all had gone, he opened the empty middle drawer of his desk. With the ease of long practice, he pushed a bit of wire under the false bottom and lifted the thin piece of wood, placing it on the desk. From the hollow space beneath it he took a sealed envelope and a small, round, china box.

He tucked the envelope into his vest pocket and smiled bitterly. Dr. Meintz kept the formula for Brimstone in a safe in his office. The doctor had no idea that Isaac secretly had made a copy from memory. No other copies existed, and Meintz's copy soon would be no more.

He placed the box atop the piles of notebooks covering his desk. A soft cry of anguish escaped him as he looked at it. The box had been Chaya's, used to hold rings and other trinkets. He swallowed hard, and squeezed his eyes tightly closed for a moment to force back the tears that threatened to spill over. Time was passing. He had to work quickly.

He opened the box and set the lid aside, the ceramic cool and smooth in his hands. Inside, affixed to a small wooden base, was a pocket watch. The back had been removed, exposing the works. From the gear that controlled the hour hand, a tiny lever extended to a row of miniature tuning forks mounted in the wooden base. One other item was crammed in the confined space: a lump of the compound he and Frederick Meintz had nicknamed "Brimstone." The latter was an ugly gray-brown, the size of a hazelnut. More than adequate to do the job.

Isaac set the time and wound the watch, careful not to set the tuning forks in motion. Then he carefully replaced the lid. He put the box back into the drawer and set the false bottom in place on top of it. He'd fashioned the crude bomb months ago, against just such a day, hoping he would never need to use it. Now that evil day had arrived. . . .

He snatched his coat from the hook by the door and pulled it on as he hurried into the hallway, taking the stairs two at a time until he'd reached the street. He had feared that Brauer might place a guard at the door, but such was not the case. He continued on his way unmolested.

His feet automatically took him to the right. Toward Chaya and Dov, and all that was dear to him. Toward home.

Chapter Two

Mother of Mercy Abbey
Berlin
Noon, that same day

"The Jews are not the monsters that these evil men would have you believe."

Mother Abbess raised her great Bible and patted its worn cover affectionately. Her gentle face, surprisingly unlined for that of a woman fast approaching seventy, was radiant. "God's Word reveals the Jews as his chosen people, a race much beloved by Him. He singled them out from among all the barbaric tribes of their time, and deigned to reveal Himself to them and through them. Through the simple obedience of a young Jewish maiden, He gave us the gift of His Son. We owe a debt to the Jews that we can never repay. Do not forget that." She lowered the Bible, holding it against her heart. Her voice trembled with emotion as she continued. "These are times of contest—of good and evil locked in mortal struggle. We will be judged by these times, and by our response to them."

She opened the Bible on her lap and paged

quickly to the verse she wanted. She looked up at the group of nuns, who sat with their chairs pulled close to hers. There were the older sisters, sitting with an almost military straightness, and with a serenity about them that came only with years of prayer. Then there were the novices, their young faces rapt and attentive. Thin faces—too thin—a product of too much work, too much fear, and too little food. For a moment, the trust shining in all those pairs of eyes terrified her into silence. As always, she drew strength from the Word.

"Matthew tells us: 'And one of them, a doctor of the law, asked him, tempting him: "Master, which is the great commandment in the law?" Jesus said to him, "Thou shalt love the Lord thy God with thy whole heart and with thy whole soul and with thy whole mind. This is the greatest and the first commandment. And the second is like to this: Thou shalt love thy neighbor as thyself." ' "

She looked around the small circle. Her gentle face hardened. "The Nazis would have us think that in sheltering Jews, we break the law. Always remember that, as Christians, we obey a higher Law. Our duty is to God, and we are not bound by laws that are in direct conflict with His." She closed the Bible, and her smile returned. "That is enough for today. As you work, meditate on the parable of the good Samaritan. Go in peace, my children."

She watched them file out. How she loved them. She knew the sacrifices that she asked of them, the dangers, the risks. Yet they accepted them willingly. These were the children of her heart, and no true mother could have looked at them with more pride. At the doorway, the last girl hesitated. It was Sister Margarethe, the youngest novice, barely sixteen.

"May I speak with you, Mother?"

"Certainly, Sister. Would you prefer here, or in my office?"

"Here is fine." The girl moved closer, close enough for Mother Abbess to see that her hands were shaking.

"What's troubling you?"

"Mother . . . Mother, what if you are wrong?"

"Love is never wrong, child."

"But I'm so afraid. What if the authorities discover what we're doing?" She peered earnestly into the older nun's face, her blue eyes so wide that the whites showed at the edges. "Aren't you ever afraid?"

"Of course I'm afraid—all the time. The risk of discovery is always with us. We accept it willingly, as a cross that must be borne." She smiled compassionately. "None of this is binding on you, Margarethe. You've not taken your final vows. If you are having second thoughts, I can release you and send you home. I trust you to keep our secret. No one will condemn you."

"Oh, no. Please. It's only that my faith isn't as strong as yours."

"Faith is a gift that we can all use more of." She reached out and patted the girl's wan cheek. "Ask God for it, and He will hear you." The girl nodded and turned to go. The Abbess laid a staying hand on her arm. "Remember what I have said, Sister. The religious life is not for everyone. So long as you live your life according to God's law of love, it doesn't matter whether you're within these walls or outside them. There is no shame in admitting a mistake."

The girl's chin set stubbornly. "There's been no mistake."

"Very well. Go in peace, my child."

The girl hurried from the room, closing the door behind her. The Abbess stared for a long time at its ornately carved surface. Her own peace had fled, replaced by a deep feeling of uncertainty. The girl was so young. Perhaps she was asking more of her than the girl was capable of giving.

This was not a time of persecution against the Jews alone, but against any who tried to follow God's will. Many other orders had been closed altogether, their members sent to the camps ... to their deaths. Two years ago, their own parish priest, Father Heiser, had been taken after the morning mass ... supposedly for questioning. They'd never seen him again.

Theirs was a nursing order and, with so many nurses called away to serve in field hospitals near the front, they were needed to staff the local hospital. That need had formed a protective buffer for the sisterhood. Before her life as a religious figure, Mother Abbess had been a member of the aristocracy. She had many friends among the upper classes and, thus far, their influence had kept the small convent open. However, if they were caught sheltering Jews, no amount of influential pressure would be able to help them.

Her policy of sheltering Jews had not been the result of any conscious decision. It had simply happened. Now and then, always at night, they would come: singly, in pairs, sometimes whole families, their pitiful belongings stuffed into a single suitcase. Despite the danger, her heart would not let her turn them away. She hid them in the crypt beneath the chapel altar, until her sources in the underground could obtain papers for them and get them safely out of the country. In this way she and her sisters had saved over one hundred lives.

She passed a hand wearily over her eyes. Life and death—sometimes the responsibility nearly overwhelmed her. She had no worries about the older sisters. She'd lived under the same roof with them for so long that she knew their hearts as fully as she knew her own. It was the novices who concerned her. Sister Ingrid, the Mistress of Novices, had advised her against accepting new vocations until this trouble had passed, but she felt that the call of God was not something to be denied. She screened the girls carefully, accepting only those whom she felt could be trusted. So far, her luck had held. Perhaps, in young Margarethe, that luck was running out.

They were all afraid, but they didn't let it show. Fear was an unwelcome companion they lived with on a daily basis, and each dealt with it in her own way. Through work, laughter, song, and prayer, they pushed the dark thoughts aside and managed to go on with their daily routine. But in this girl the fear showed: raw, barely controlled. Fear made people do strange things. If she kept the child on, the girl might betray them out of mistaken patriotism. If she sent her home, she might do the same out of spite.

What worried her most was that fear was the only emotion the girl exhibited. Sympathy and compassion seemed either dormant or lacking in her. She'd spoken fervently enough in her entrance interviews. Only now that the girl was part of the order and privy to its secrets had Mother Abbess begun to suspect that a terrible mistake had been made.

She sighed. If only she knew the child better . . . If only there was someone to tell her what to do . . . The beginnings of a headache began to throb behind her eyes as her thoughts chased round and round, like a puppy after its own tail.

She gathered up her Bible and prayer book. The faint swish of her skirts was the only sound as she silently switched off the lights and secured the door. She shifted the books to her left hand and took up her rosary. The soft clicking of the beads struck a counterpoint of worry to her measured footsteps, as she made her way down the dim hallway to her cell.

His street.
His home.
Isaac knew the danger. This was the first place they would look for him. But he had to see. He had to know. At the corner he slowed his pace, careful to do nothing to draw attention to himself. There was no need. All eyes were fixed on the commotion at the center of the block.

An army truck stood at the curb in front of his building. With a terrible feeling of dread knotting his stomach, Isaac crossed to the other side and walked slowly past the rows of shops until he was directly across the street, anonymous among a crowd of onlookers. He raised his eyes to the second floor.

Gone were the white lace curtains that Chaya had taken such pride in. The windows were smashed. For the first time he noticed the sheen of broken glass that sequined the street. Laughter filtered down from overhead, and he watched as a soldier came to the window and took a crowbar to the wooden frame. The wood gave way with a tortured groan, leaving only a ragged, rectangular hole where the window had been. Moments later, Chaya's spinet came hurtling through the hole to shatter on the street below.

Isaac closed his eyes, fighting for control. His first impulse was to rush across the street, to beat their ugly faces and break their bones—to make them tell him where Chaya was. Instead, he leaned in close to a man in the crowd. He tried to make his voice sound casual, curious.

"What is happening?"

"They are just evicting some Jews. Imagine them living here, under our very noses!"

"Are there many?"

"I saw only two, a Jewess and her brat."

"What happened to them?"

"What happens to all Jews? They are gone."

Isaac felt a hand pull gently at his sleeve. He turned to find Elise Wendel, a neighbor. She took his arm and drew him away from the crowd.

"You must get out of here, quickly, before someone else recognizes you." Her voice was low. As she spoke, her eyes darted nervously toward the others.

"I must find Chaya and Dov!"

"They're dead." The words came in a rush, striking him with the force of a hurricane. The girl took his arm, steadying him. "I saw them die. You'll die too, if you don't get away from here." Taking his hand, she tried to lead him farther down the street.

Isaac held his ground. "How did they die? I must know how!" He gripped her hand so tightly she winced in pain.

The girl tried to pull away, but he held her fast. Her face hardened. "All right, I'll tell you. Two of the soldiers started tossing the baby in the air, and when Chaya tried to stop them they shot her. The captain caught the baby on his bayonet." She pulled free. "There! Is that really what you wanted to know? Now get out of here! Go, before you bring trouble down on all of us!" She wrenched free and crossed the street to her house. For a moment she paused in the doorway to stare at him, then she ducked inside, closing the door quickly behind her.

Isaac barely noticed. He stared numbly across the street, saw the dark stains on the pavement beneath the broken glass. His mind rejected both the sight and the meaning behind it. He turned away from the destruction and continued along the street. Unshed tears blurred his vision. Rage and grief mingled in him, spreading a dark mist through his mind. He moved by instinct alone.

It was some time before his mind had cleared and he'd become aware of his surroundings once more. He found himself shuffling, bent over like an old man, barely able to lift one foot after the other. Immediately he straightened up and put more purpose into his steps. He knew that shambling, defeated walk. He'd seen it in the bewildered crowds, as the Nazis herded them through the streets to the trains. It was the walk of the victim, and now it marked him, as clearly as if he'd worn the Star of David on the sleeve of his coat.

He looked around. The neighborhood was unfamiliar. He had no clue as to where he was, no plan as to where he was going. Yesterday's rain had given way to blue sky, but the air was cold. He pulled the collar of his coat more firmly about his neck. In doing so, he felt the crisp firmness of the envelope where it lay against his breast.

Here was purpose, a means of revenge, if nothing else. If he could get the formula to Samuel, in America, it might bring about the end of this evil war. Thoughts of Sam filled him with guilt. Why hadn't he listened to his brother and taken his family to safety while there was still time? Sam had seen the way the wind was blowing and had taken his wife and fled. Now he was making a good living as a chemist in Boston. Isaac could have done the same, but in his naiveté he'd thought things could never get this bad. By the time he'd realized the truth, there was no escape. Recognizing the futility of such thoughts, Isaac switched them off. It was too late for Chaya and Dov, but thousands of other lives could be saved. To the Allies, the papers in his pocket were valuable beyond price. If he could get in touch with the underground, the papers would surely gain him passage to Britain and, ultimately, the United States.

In his excitement, Isaac found himself almost running. Quickly he slowed his pace, watching for street signs, trying to get his bearings. He had to decide what to do, where to go. It had to be done quickly. Every moment on the streets he was in danger of search and interrogation. By now they would be looking for him. They would find the envelope in his pocket, and it would all have been for nothing.

The Abbey. Even as his eyes came to rest on the distant steeple and its cross, silhouetted against the sky, the memory surfaced. Blindermann, the tailor, had told him of a link to the underground, of a place of hiding . . . just before he and his family had disappeared. Like so many other disappearances, Isaac had attributed it to the Nazis. But what if Blindermann had gotten away?

The place he had mentioned was the Mother of Mercy Abbey.

At the next corner, Isaac turned west. He moved surely, confidently. In spite of himself, he began to hope.

"He's gone! It was not my fault, I tell you! Not my fault!"

The voice on the phone was breathless, high with panic. Even so, Colonel Brauer recognized it. The man kept rambling, and Brauer broke in impatiently. "What are you talking about, Meintz? Slow down. Get hold of yourself."

"Kauffman—the Jew. We returned from lunch and he was gone. He never goes out during the workday. It has always been his habit to take lunch at his desk. He is gone, I tell you!"

Brauer considered. "Could he have gone home?"

"I don't know. I just don't know. The technicians were clearing out the supply closet. They discovered a loose brick in the wall adjoining my office. This morning, after you left, I found Kauffman taking inventory in there. It is possible he heard our conversation."

Brauer closed his eyes, feeling a twitch of pain in his stomach as the ulcer there reacted to the news. "And the formula?" he asked wearily.

"It is still in the safe in my office. That is the

first thing I checked. It is the only copy—for security reasons I allowed no others to be made."

"Whose security—the Reich's or your own? Kauffman has no need of a copy, you old fool. So long as he is alive, the formula is in danger of falling into the hands of the Allies." The ulcer flared again, and Brauer pressed his fist hard against the pit of his stomach, as if he could hold back the pain.

"I am sending some men over there. If Kauffman returns, they will take charge of him. In the meantime I will order a city-wide search. Damn you, Meintz! You had better pray that he turns up! If he gets away with the formula . . . if he gets it out of the country . . . your precious Project Brimstone will be finished!"

"It's not my fault! Not—"

Brauer slammed the receiver into its cradle. No, it was not Meintz's fault. Any fault here was his own, and the leadership would establish that fact pretty quickly. He should have had Kauffman picked up this morning, should have disposed of the wretched little Jew along with his wife and child.

The pain in his belly flared briefly. He ignored it. So much rested on the outcome of the next few hours. Everything had been going so well, following the design he had planned. Last night, as expected, Greta had accepted his proposal. The future was almost within his grasp. . . . But now Brimstone might be lost—and if it was, he was lost as well.

He put his hat on and called for his driver. Calm returned slowly as he made his way to the car. It was impossible, of course. The man was a Jew, racially inferior. It was unthinkable that such a man could be a threat. By the time he settled into the backseat, his confidence had returned. He would find this dirty Jew and make him pay for every moment of worry and inconvenience. As the car pulled away from the curb, he took his dagger from its sheath and absently tested the point against his thumb.

So close.

It was past two-thirty by the time Isaac reached the Abbey. Every passing moment made discovery and capture more likely. A sigh of relief escaped him as he rounded the last corner and made his way along the street toward the towering stone edifice at the opposite end. The street curved in a great U, leading to and from the Abbey. The inner part was taken up by a grassy park, dotted with stone benches. Although, over the years, stores and houses had sprung up along the sides of the street, it was obvious that the Abbey was its main purpose for being.

As Isaac moved into the shadow of the great church, he heard vehicles approaching swiftly along the main road. There was an urgency to the sound that made him quicken his steps. He ducked into a small alleyway between two houses just as a truck pulled into the mouth of the road. Soldiers poured from the canvas-topped bed and fanned out to cover both sides of the street. Starting at the open ends of the U, they began a methodical search of the shops and homes, working their way slowly inward, toward the center.

They were looking for him. Isaac knew it, as surely as he knew his own name or the prayers his mother had taught him as a child. He edged farther back into the shadows of the alley, his mouth dry with fear. He kept backing away, until he could go no further. Slowly, he turned around.

The alley was a dead end, a cul-de-sac terminating in a high stone wall. He could hear the soldiers' voices moving closer . . . closer. In desperation he leapt and got his fingers over the top of the wall. His feet scrabbled for a moment, then found a purchase on the rough stone. Pulling, pushing, he heaved himself up and over the wall, to drop heavily to his knees on the other side.

He was in a garden of some sort. Plants, dead from the recent frost, stood in rows, sagging limply against the wooden stakes meant to support them. Trees hunched along the wall, bare-limbed and sinister. At the garden's edge was a statue, winged, the head looking down, one arm cradling a book, the other stretched heavenward, the hand splayed, as if to ward off something. Behind it gray stone, identical to that of the wall, rose upward to meet the sky.

The Abbey. He was in the Abbey's grounds, in the Abbey's garden. This long building, angling off from the main church, must be the residence. Hurriedly, Isaac moved to the side of the great structure and worked his way along its face toward the nearest door. There was no sound of pursuit. He had not been seen. If the sisters would take him in, there was still a chance.

Gray stone steps rose before him to meet a massive wooden door. With a hasty glance over his shoulder, Isaac took the steps two at a time and raised the gleaming brass knocker affixed to it. The metal was cold in his hand, but not nearly so cold as the lump of terror, ice-hard around his heart. He let the knocker fall, and felt its summons vibrate through the stones beneath his feet. Behind him, on the other side of the wall, voices rose excitedly. A whistle began to shrill. He had been seen, after all.

Sister Margarethe sat in a tiny alcove, just inside the entrance door. Her knitting lay idle in her lap. She hated to knit. The long black woolen stockings worn by the order were scratchy and uncomfortable. The process of turning a heel on one was almost as bad as having to wear the finished product. She liked being assigned to answer the door. The work was minimal. In these times visitors were few, and the job afforded long hours of leisure, supposedly to be spent in prayer. Margarethe chose to spend them in daydreams of the silk stockings and other luxuries she'd owned before she'd taken up the religious life. She sighed wistfully.

The sound of the door knocker interrupted her reverie. Quickly, she stuffed her knitting into her workbag and jumped to her feet. She paused just before the door, to straighten her veil and arrange her face in what she hoped was a suitably pious expression. With as much dignity as she could muster, she opened the door.

Her pious mask vanished at the sight of the man on the other side. His clothes were old, the knees muddied. A cluster of dead leaves clung to the hem of one side of his tattered coat. But more than his clothes, the desperation in his eyes told her what he was and why he was here. He glanced worriedly over his shoulder as he spoke.

"Please . . . please may I come in? I was told I would find friends here . . . a place to stay. Please. It's urgent."

Whistles sounded from the other side of the garden wall, and Margarethe realized that he was the cause of them. Many a night she had lain sleepless on her narrow bed, picturing how it would be if they were found out. In those long nights death had come in a thousand ways, and she had met it with the unfailing courage of the martyrs. Now death was just outside the wall—and she was terrified. Instinctively, she began to close the door.

"Please." He moved closer. "If they find me, they'll kill me. There must be somewhere I can hide, somewhere you can shelter me until they've gone. You've got to help me."

His foot was between the doors and she couldn't close them. Spurred on by her fear, Margarethe tried to push him back. "There's no place to hide you. You don't belong here. Go away. Go away before they kill us all."

The voices had moved to the main gate now. The entry bell on the inner gate post began to ring frantically, and she could hear them pounding on the other side of the wooden gate. The man looked from her to the gate and back. The desperate hope in his face gave way to despair, then bitterness. He reached inside his coat and drew out an envelope, pressing it into her hands.

"All right, I'll go. But you must take this and see that it gets to my brother in America. The address is marked on the front."

"I can't. . . . I won't." She pulled her hands away from the envelope, as if its touch would burn. Leaning her shoulder against the door, she put all her strength into closing it.

The man's face set in anger. He threw himself against the door, jogging it open enough to grasp her wrist. His grip caused her to cry out in pain and brought tears pricking at the corners of her eyes. He shouldered the door open wider. As she whimpered in protest, he thrust the envelope into her hand and forced her fingers to close around it.

"You'll take this, or I'll call the soldiers myself and implicate you as my accomplice. I'm going to die anyway. I've no objection to taking you with me. You'll get that to the United States, but not through the mails. The Nazis will find it and trace it to you. Send it through the underground."

His eyes fell to the large gold crucifix she wore on a chain about her neck. He snatched it up and held it before her eyes. "Swear to me. Swear by your Christian God that you will do this." She was silent. He dropped the crucifix and took her by the shoulders, shaking her roughly. He shook her so hard that she bit her lip. Blood, salty and warm, filled her mouth. She began to grow faint. "Swear!"

Margarethe felt her knees going weak. The sounds in the background became a ringing in her ears, faraway and unreal. As if from a great distance, she heard her own voice say, "I swear."

He looked over his shoulder at the gate. Another Sister was crossing the grounds toward it from the direction of the church, her purposeful strides quickly eating up the distance. She did not see him. He turned back to Margarethe and, using the crucifix, yanked her close to him, so that her face was only inches away. "My name is Isaac Kauffman," he hissed. "Isaac Kauffman: Remember that name, *good* Sister, for you have murdered me."

Isaac released her and ran down the steps, just as the main gates were flung wide. He ran along the edge of the building, keeping low to the ground.

When he reached the corner of the residence, he made a break for the wall.

"Halten sie! Halten sie!"

He paid no heed to the shouts at his back or to the shots that followed. At the edge of the garden the first bullets caught him, spun him around. He fell.

Isaac lay on his back, staring upward at the stone statue. Its sightless eyes stared back at him, and his eyes followed its fingers skyward. Pain lanced through his chest and back. He tried to rise, but his legs refused to move. Blackness began to close in around his vision as the babble of excited voices grew closer.

Suddenly the sky brightened, the brilliance hurting his eyes. The voices became a loud roaring in his ears. As he watched, the stone statue softened, changed. He saw that it was not stone at all. Chaya stood before him, Dov cradled tenderly in one slender arm. Laughing, she pointed at the bright sky, then lowered her hand to reach for him. Joyfully, he moved into her embrace, bathed in the light and warmth of a thousand suns.

Klaus Brauer blinked and shook his head in an effort to clear it. Black spots drifted lazily before his eyes and, in the aftermath of the explosion, his ears buzzed annoyingly. For a moment he thought it was an air raid, then he saw the familiar cloud of black smoke spreading umbrella-like across the sky. It was not as big as the Breshkov explosion, but he had no doubts that it had accomplished its purpose.

Meintz's lab, of course. Fear awakened the ulcer in his stomach, and he nearly doubled over from the pain as he knelt by Kauffman's body. Quickly, he searched the dead man's clothing. There was nothing.

Around him his men stood frozen, staring at the sky. Brauer got to his feet.

"Spread out and search the grounds," he ordered. "Look for anything that might contain papers or documents."

Bitterly, he looked down at Isaac Kauffman, the cause of it all. He was not surprised to see that the dead man was smiling. Raising his right foot, Brauer brought the heel down on Kauffman's face, stomping repeatedly until the smile had been reduced to a gory hole. He wiped his boot on the grass and, as he did so, raised his eyes toward the Abbey.

At the top of the steps a gaggle of nuns stood huddled together, identical in their black habits. They were all pointing toward the mushroom cap of smoke fouling the sky. All but one.

At the edge of the group one nun, conspicuous in her aloneness, stared down at the scene in the garden. Though her face was only a shadow beneath the overhang of veil, and her body hidden by the bulk of her habit, Brauer received an impression of youth.

A nun in white appeared through the open doorway and hurriedly began ushering them back inside. The girl disappeared in anonymity among her sisters. The door closed behind them and, to Klaus Brauer, the sound was a death knell.

The formula was no more.

Kauffman was dead, and his knowledge with him. The only existing copy had now been reduced to atoms by the explosion at Meintz's lab. It was gone . . . and with it, his career. Standing in the ruin of the Abbey garden, Brauer felt all his ambitions and plans turn to ashes, soft and crumbling as the black dust drifting down from the skies.

No!

It was impossible. The scheming little Jew would have made a copy. The formula was Kauffman's creation, his legacy. Surely he would not let the fruit of his labors wither and die so easily. Brauer glared up at the Abbey, his eyes narrowing. The secret was there.

He knew it.

He could feel it.

Moving with determined strides he started for the doorway, at the same time motioning to two of his men.

"Come with me."

Mother Abbess closed the door, locked it, and leaned against it. For a moment she closed her eyes, trying to find that inner well of peace and center on it. Her heart was beating with machine-gun rapidity. Though she was uncertain of just what had transpired in the Abbey garden, she was sure that it meant trouble. Perhaps their luck had run out.

She opened her eyes and saw that the other sisters were staring at her, looking to her for guidance. They milled in the entry hall, speaking in excited whispers. Mother Abbess clapped her hands for silence.

"Sisters, I want you to go to your rooms and pray. Ask our Lord to—"

Behind her, a fierce pounding had begun on the door.

"Go quickly."

As the pounding increased, she ushered the frightened women toward the stairs. Young Margarethe was sobbing softly, and Mother Abbess put an arm around her, giving her shoulder a gentle squeeze.

"Courage, Margarethe. Remember, nothing was ever gained by tears, but prayer and faith can move mountains." She motioned to one of the older nuns. "Sister Ingrid?"

The Mistress of Novices took the girl's arm and urged her ahead of her up the stairs.

The pounding had become more furious, and Mother Abbess could hear the wooden door beginning to splinter under the blows. She waited until the last of her charges was out of sight, then opened the door.

Brauer glared down at the small woman in white who had calmly opened the door, then shoved her aside and swept past her into the entryway of the Abbey. He glanced around. There were no other nuns to be seen.

"May I help you, Herr Colonel?"

"Are you in charge here?"

"I am."

"A Jewish traitor was just shot on your grounds. I have reason to believe that, before he died, he was able to deliver classified documents to an accomplice within these walls."

"That is impossible, Colonel. Our sisters here are all loyal Germans." Her blue eyes met his guilelessly.

Brauer was used to getting what he wanted by intimidation. He found the woman's unshakable calm unsettling.

"Where are the others?"

"This is our quiet hour. Those who are not on duty at the hospital are in private prayer."

"Where? I must question them."

She took a step back, so that her body was blocking the staircase to the upper level.

"I'm afraid that would be impossible, Colonel. I—"

Brauer tried to shoulder her aside but she held her ground, surprisingly strong. He gave an impatient jerk of his head, and one of his men raised the butt of his rifle and struck her viciously on the side of her head.

A soft cry escaped her. She fell to her knees, her hands pressed to her left temple. Blood trickled between her fingers, running down her arm to stain the white sleeve of her habit. Brauer and his men pushed by her and started up the stairs.

Alone in her room, Margarethe pressed her ear to the wooden door. Downstairs, the pounding on the entrance door had suddenly ceased. It was followed by an eerie silence.

Slowly, she backed away from the door. Through the coarse wool of her skirt pocket, the corner of the envelope pricked against her thigh like a knife point. With shaking hands, she reached into her pocket and pulled it out. She let it drop on her desk top, and stared at it with the same mixture of fascination and loathing with which she would have regarded a snake.

What to do . . . ?

Her first impulse was to destroy it. It was the only thing that could link her with the dead man. With it gone, there would be nothing to condemn her. But she had sworn an oath to deliver it, and was therefore bound to do so. She'd made a promise to the dead man, and the very fact that he was dead seemed to make that promise all the more binding. No, she could not destroy it. The other alternative was to hide it somewhere where the Nazis would never find it.

Suddenly the sounds started again—heavy footsteps pounding up the main staircase. From the far end of the hall came the resounding booms of doors being flung wide. Then the first screaming began.

They were coming.

For a moment she froze, like a panicked deer caught in the headlamps of an automobile. Then her instinct for survival took over.

Frantically, she glanced around the room. Where to hide it? Where . . . ?

Her eyes fell on the letter. Next to it on the desk was a bottle of glue. The spine of her prayer book had come away from the binding, and she'd borrowed the glue to repair it. She'd fixed the book last evening, but had not yet returned the glue to Mother Abbess's office.

With the sounds of the search drawing ever nearer, she sat down at the desk and opened the prayer book to the back cover. There were several end papers following the last page of text. These matched the paper lining of the inside of the book's cover. Carefully, she centered the envelope against the paper lining and folded the last endpaper back over it. She glued the edges firmly in place, creating a false lining. After wiping away the excess glue, she studied her work with a critical eye. The change was not detectable.

The search had moved to the room next to hers. Quickly, she put the glue into the top drawer of her desk and knelt by her bed, opening her prayer book. Her hands were shaking, and soft hiccuping sobs of terror came from her throat.

Heavy footsteps sounded just outside her door. Suddenly the door flew open, and three men burst into the room. One she recognized as the man in the garden.

"Search her."

The two others pulled her to her feet. While one held her tightly, the other ripped off her veil and then hooked his fingers into the neck of her habit and ripped it off.

"Please . . ."

She looked up at the man in black, and any further entreaties died in her throat. His face was cold and hard, without a trace of feeling. She would find no mercy there.

"Nothing here, sir," said the one who'd searched her clothes.

"Search the room, then."

They threw her down on the floor. Whimpering, she scuttled into a corner, her prayer book clutched like a shield against her bare breasts. She huddled there while they tore the thin, lumpy mattress from her bed, slitting it open and scattering the stuffing about the room. After gutting the pillow in the same manner, they moved on to the desk. They searched the drawers, dumping the contents out on the floor. The glue bottle shattered, filling the small room with the reek of glue.

All the while the man in black stood over her. She could feel his eyes on her. It felt as if he were looking through her, into the darkest secrets of her heart.

He knows.

The two words were a mocking whisper in her mind. She nearly confessed right then and there, but those eyes, cold as ice, held her in terrified silence.

The men searched her closet and bureau, throwing her meager possessions into a heap in the center of the room. At last they straightened up and stood at attention.

"There is nothing here, sir."

"What is your name?" the man in black asked.

In her terror, it took a moment for Margarethe to realize that he was speaking to her. Fearfully, she raised her eyes.

"Margarethe . . ."

Without warning he bent and tore the prayer book from her arms. Holding it by the covers, he shook it. Only a worn book mark fell out from between the pages. With a snort of disgust, he hurled it against the wall.

Angrily, he reached down and, taking her by the upper arms, jerked her to her feet. His fingers digging painfully into her flesh, he shook her hard.

For a long moment his eyes locked with hers, searching her soul. Surely he must see the truth there. He would take her away. The Nazis' interrogation methods were well known. Her legs failed her. She dissolved into tears as she collapsed against him.

He let her fall to the floor. She looked up in time to see him brushing off his immaculate black uniform. He nodded to his men.

"Continue the search." She heard them move on to the room next door.

In the doorway, the man in black paused. "Pray, Fraulein. Pray that you have told the truth. If I find that you have lied to me I will be back, and any conception you have of the pangs of Hell will be as nothing compared to what I will do to you." He turned on his heel and was gone.

Margarethe crawled across the room and closed the shattered door. Drawing the torn remnants of her habit about her, she retrieved the prayer book and curled up in a corner. She huddled there all afternoon, as the sounds of the search continued. At last there was a clomp of heavy footfalls, returning down the hallway. They passed her room without pause and continued on down the main staircase. Moments later, she heard voices in the yard below. She crept to the window and peeked out in time to see the Mother Abbess being dragged across the yard between two guards. They hustled her into the back of the long shiny staff car. The man in black got into the front seat and they drove away.

Margarethe knelt by the empty frame of her bed. Guilt assailed her, and she burst into fresh tears of misery. That man was dead because of her, and now Mother Abbess . . . Once the Nazis took someone away, that person never returned.

"God forgive me," she whispered. "Dear Lord, please forgive me."

She tried to pray, seeking God's mercy, but the words would not come. She prayed the rosary, but the peace that usually flowed from it eluded her. Her prayers seemed to rise as high as the ceiling and then return to her. Empty words.

She tried to meditate, fixing the face of Christ in her mind. But the features seemed to melt and flow until it was not the face of Jesus, his gentle eyes looking into hers. The eyes were steel-blue, and cold. The face was that of the man in black, the man with the silver death's-head on his cap. It was a cruel face, a hard face, the face of an avenging angel. An Angel of Death.

Chapter Three

Harringdale, Pennsylvania
September, 1975

Gabrielle huddled in the sun-dappled shelter of her magic place, knees hugged to her body to form a terror-tight ball. Her light brown hair was stuck to her forehead in sweat-darkened ringlets, making a frame for the pale oval of her face. Her blue eyes stared ahead, unblinking. Around her, the blackberry thicket formed a thorny igloo. Sobs massed in her throat. Despite her efforts to choke them back they surged forward, eager to betray her. She bit her lips and clamped both hands over her mouth to hold them in.

She could hear *him* coming. He was crashing through the woods, snapping tender twigs, leaving a wake of crushed ferns and foliage. Her fearful mind formed an image from her picture books: Tyrannosaurus rex on the rampage, hungry and huge, with a mouth full of giant teeth. If only it were such a beast and not Daddy, looking to hurt, looking to kill . . . her.

The crashing moved closer, until it was very

near—right beside her. Suddenly it stopped. She could see the faded blue denim of his jeans through the screen of leaves. Inches separated her from him. In the stillness she could hear his breathing, panting and bestial. Her inside skin could feel the awful cold-heat coming off of him, and it made her heart shiver. It pounded loudly in her ears, loud as *The Lone Ranger*'s theme song that Daddy used to sing, as he galloped with her, piggy-back, round the backyard: *Pa-da-rump, pa-da-rump, pa-da-rump-thump-thump*. The sound was deafening, and she was certain he must hear it. Then his voice came, so close, just above her.

"It's no use. I'll find you, Brie. You can't hide in these woods forever. I'll find you, and we'll make an end of it. No more magic. No more hurting. Just sleep . . . sweet sleep, forever and ever. Wouldn't that be better, honey?" He paused. She heard him take a deep breath. "Come on, Brie. Come out."

The voice was calm, gentle. It was the same voice that had sung her nursery rhymes and read her stories of Triceratops and Brontosaurus. But Gabrielle wasn't fooled. This was the voice of Tyrannosaurus rex, insatiable, hungry for blood. She made no sound.

She could almost feel him listening. His breathing quieted, and the silence in the woods turned deadly. Seconds ticked by, became minutes. Brie held her breath. Beads of sweat broke out on her forehead and found their way into her eyes. Their saltiness made her eyes smart, but she didn't even dare to blink.

Fear grew in her, till she could barely stand it anymore. Part of her wanted to cry out, to end it, here and now. Some saner part kept her silent, whispered in her mind that six years old should be a beginning and not an end.

He moved on.

He was walking now, slowly, quietly. Still, his steps seemed like thunder to the child. She didn't relax, even when they had faded in the distance. She didn't trust the evidence of ears and eyes. Only when that inner sense felt the hot-chill of him vanish, only then did the little girl slowly uncurl, like a flower opening.

Flies found her. They lit on her hands, eager to feed on the blood there. She waved her fingers to shoo them away. There was blood drying on her legs, between her legs, too. Her thighs were sticky with it . . . and with something else.

Brie moved slowly. She hurt. Her face felt like a toothache all over. Her insides felt as if everything were loose and shifting. She squeezed her legs together tightly over the stickiness and tried to think magic thoughts, but she knew all the while that it was useless. The magic wouldn't work for her. It was a gift, meant only for others.

A gift. Mommy called it that. "It's a very special gift from God, Brie. It's better than gold or silver or diamonds. You're a very lucky little girl."

But she didn't feel lucky. Daddy didn't like the magic. He didn't even like *her* anymore. He called her "evil," a "jinx"—whatever that was. The magic made him angry. He seemed angry all the time now, and nothing she did was right. Out of the anger had come the hurting. At first he'd just hit her, for no reason. Sometimes it was with his hand, sometimes with his belt or the wooden spoon from the kitchen drawer. That had been bad. Today was worse.

Today she had come home from school as usual. She took the dishes out of the drainer and put them away, as he sat at the kitchen table and watched her. Her inside self could feel his eyes on her, could feel the terrible anger-chill growing in him. She finished her chore, anxious not to do anything that would bring the anger crashing down on her, like lightning from a blue sky. Then she went to her bedroom and took down her coloring book and crayons from the shelves. It was a book of dinosaurs, and she picked out Brontosaurus and began coloring him green. She had been very careful to stay inside the lines, just as Mommy had taught her.

Then he came into the room. She could feel the anger-chill coming from him, but it was different: strange and somehow more terrible. It was hot-cold, like boiling ice. The heat was in his body, as he moved toward her, and the cold in his eyes. He tore her dress. She backed away until her legs bumped against the bed. Then he was on top of her, pushing her down, forcing her legs apart. He hit her hard with his fist to stop her screaming. She remembered little after that, except for the terrible, ripping pain. Later, when he'd gotten off of her, she managed to slip away, out the back door, across the yard to the woods, to her magic place.

The snap of metal brought her head up. She'd been drifting, half from shock, half from exhaustion. A shrill shrieking cut the silence of the woods. It came from close by. Brie knew instantly what it was. Stiffly, whimpering with pain, she crept from the thicket. She was alone; she could feel no one near. Moving slowly, she made her way toward the sound.

She found the rabbit at the base of a tree. Its right rear leg was caught in the jaws of a trap. Blood covered the grass around it. As Brie approached, the little creature fell silent. Its eyes glazed over and it sat very still, except for its terrified trembling.

Brie searched among the fallen leaves until she found a flat rock. With the surety of long practice, she pushed it between the jaws of the trap, then slowly turned the rock on end, wedging the jaws apart. Taking the injured rabbit in her arms, she gingerly returned to her hiding place in the thicket.

She sat down slowly. Her own bleeding had stopped, and she didn't want to do anything to make it start up again. Cradling the frightened rabbit in her lap, she turned it over gently to examine the hurt leg. Her small fingers spread the bloody, matted fur, and she was dismayed to see white bone, sticking through the torn flesh.

"Poor thing," she whispered.

She closed her eyes and began stroking the rabbit's head. In the darkness of her mind, she let the magic thoughts begin to form. She thought of bones, white and long—and whole. She thought of soft fur, of rabbit skin, smooth and unscarred. The familiar tingling began at her shoulders, spread as a warmth down her arms, as a fire into her hands. But this was not a fire that burned. She thought of rabbits, hundreds of them, feasting, like Bugs Bunny, on an endless carrot patch. Beneath her hands the trembling of the little creature lessened, then stopped altogether.

Brie opened her eyes and looked at the leg again. A fine growth of new fur covered the place where the break had been. The injury was gone. There was no sign that it had ever happened. Silently, she drew the rabbit close and buried her face in the soft, warm fur of its neck.

"It's okay," she murmured soothingly, as much to reassure herself as to comfort the rabbit.

Her own pain throbbed dully through her body. She was helpless to relieve it. Weariness came over her, overshadowing the pain. Cuddling the rabbit to her, Brie curled on her side on the mossy ground. As the late afternoon shadows lengthened, child and rabbit slept.

Susan Prescott hurried up the hill, head bowed, her breath coming hard. The Indian summer heat caused her white nurse's uniform to cling to her, and she found herself huffing and puffing as the steepness of the incline began to drag at her legs. In spite of that, she didn't slow her pace. She was late.

Oh, it wasn't her fault. Just at change of shift, old Mr. Higgins had decided to pull the IV out of his arm. Susan had had to stay late to restart it. Finding a good vein in a ninety-three-year-old took precious time. She glanced anxiously at her watch and began walking even faster.

She didn't like to leave Brie alone with him, not even for the short interval between the time school let out and afternoon change of shift. She didn't like to leave Brie alone with Matthew at all anymore, but someone had to work. They had to eat.

In the two years since the steel mill had shut down, a change had come over Matthew. Without a job the sweet, gentle man she'd married had gone from bored, to bitter, to nasty. With the advent of the summer heat, he'd become dangerous.

The beatings had started in August. If supper was late or if she showed any lack of enthusiasm in their lovemaking, he would knock her around a bit. With nothing to do, he became totally self-centered and wanted her at his beck and call every moment. He resented anything that took her time and attention away from him: the housework, her job . . . and lately, Brie.

For several weeks now she'd suspected that he was beating their daughter, but she had no solid proof. There was only an occasional bruise to confirm her suspicions, and Brie always had some excuse.

"I fell," she would say. "I tripped and bumped my head on the radiator. I missed the bottom step."

Susan accepted the lies, even as she watched Brie shrink away from Matthew and become a shadow of the happy, outgoing little girl she'd once been. She let herself believe them, because she had nowhere to go, no one to turn to, and she simply didn't know what to do. She kept hoping that, if they could just hang on long enough, a job offer would come along, or they'd open the mill again, or something would happen to make everything all right.

Please, God, let everything be all right. She glanced at her watch. She should have been home over an hour ago.

Her path took her alongside the chain-link fence that bordered the mill. The blast furnaces were cold now. The great overhead cranes were turning to rust, and grass had sprung up to conceal the railroad tracks that ran beneath them. She looked at the empty, boarded-up buildings and felt a rush of resentment.

The mill had proved to be a betrayer, a mass of rusted lies. For years it had prospered, the blast furnaces working twenty-four hours a day, belching flame into the night skies. Generations of Harringdale men had made a good living here, and they had all believed it would go on forever. No one had foreseen the development of cheap, foreign-made steel, or the newer, smaller mills whose efficiency would turn the great complex into a dinosaur, doomed to extinction. Now Harringdale was a dead town, full of empty buildings, shattered windows, and equally shattered dreams.

Susan looked away, fixing her eyes on the cracked sidewalk. She thought of her marriage, of her dreams. Both seemed over. Matthew was sick, and whatever illness was festering in his mind seemed to be getting worse, not better. Lately it had begun to center around Brie and her gift. Matthew had once been as excited about their special little girl as she was. Now, needing something to blame his unhappiness on, he had fixed on the child.

Susan had found her daughter's talent for healing a bit unnerving at first, but she'd come to accept it. She and Matthew had kept the child's gift a secret between the two of them, unsure of what public reaction would be. Good always came of it, and Susan thought of it now as simply a natural extension of the complex bundle of love and wonder that was Brie. The child loved life, found joy in the simplest of things, so it seemed only right that she would want everything she touched to be whole and well.

Matt didn't see it that way anymore. He'd begun to call Brie a "witch," a "jinx." He blamed the child for the mill's closing down and for the increased tension in their marriage. If the truth were told, Brie was the only thing still holding them together, but Matt couldn't see that.

Maybe part of him could. Maybe, down underneath the meanness, some small remnant of the husband and father he'd once been could feel his family slipping away. Maybe that was why he couldn't seem to get enough of her anymore—her time, her attention, her body. Over the past few months his sexual appetite had become insatiable. It was as if, in keeping her physically close, he could somehow hold on to the rest. But it was driving a wedge between them. No matter how much she tried to give, he wanted more. When she came home exhausted after a day's work he was waiting for her, wanting, needing. If it weren't for Brie, she would have left long ago. Going off on her own was one thing; the responsibility of a child was quite another.

She reached the end of the dingy row of houses that included her own. Identical, two-story boxes, one attached to the other, they marched caterpillar-like up the hill. Each was fronted by a tiny wooden porch. Each had an identical oblong of brown grass stretching from the back door to the woods beyond. There was nothing pretty or inviting about them. Just seeing them used to be the worst part of coming home. Now that Matt was sick the sight was only one more sorrow, piled upon a mountain-sized heap.

The front door was unlocked. That was not unusual, in itself. What was strange was that Brie was not there to meet her. Heat and silence hung heavy in the still air.

"Matt?" she called. "Brie?" There was no answer.

She crossed the long, narrow living room to the kitchen. The dishes were put away. Brie's lunchbox stood on the counter by the sink. An empty coffee cup was on the table.

"Brie?" she called again. The shrillness in her voice betrayed her growing fear.

She hurried back into the living room and took the stairs to the second floor at a run. She paused at her own bedroom, and the bathroom, only long enough to see that they were empty. In Brie's room, she stopped and stared.

The white, ruffled bed coverlet had been pushed into a rumpled heap. Stains peeked from among the wrinkles. Susan reached out hesitantly and pulled at a corner of the cover, stretching it out taut, smooth. A pink ball of fabric rolled out from between the folds. Susan picked it up, stared at it dumbly. Slowly, the torn scrap of pink cloth that had been Brie's panties slipped from her fingers and dropped back onto the bed. The bed coverlet was an accusation. Blood was smeared on the white—Christmas-red in spots, already drying to rust in others. At the same time the familiar smell hit her and she backed from the room, shaking her head in mute denial.

She ran down the stairs, stumbling, clinging to the banister for support. If Brie had managed to get away from him, she'd be hiding. But where? Her mind frantically considered the alternatives and found only one answer.

The magic place! Besides Brie, she was the only one who knew about it. It was their secret. If Brie needed somewhere to hide, that was where she would go. Susan pushed open the back screen door and raced across the yard to the woods. As the trees and undergrowth thickened, she was forced to slow her pace. Prickers caught on her uniform, tearing the white fabric. Susan pushed on, heedless.

At last the thorn-studded, leafy dome of the blackberry thicket hunkered before her. She tried to call her daughter's name, but the sound would not come. Breathless, she dropped to her knees and carefully lifted the large branch that formed a natural entrance. She squinted into the dark, hollow square inside.

Without warning, the quiet afternoon burst into movement. Something exploded from the thicket in a flurry of dried leaves. Susan screamed and jumped backward, one arm thrown up to protect her face. Heart pounding, she turned in time to see a cottontail disappearing beneath a nearby pine.

Leaves rustled softly behind her . . . and there was Brie. The child stood silently. Her dress was stained and torn. One eye was nearly swollen shut, the cheek and flesh on that side of her face dark with bruises. Susan saw all this at a glance. And the blood. Wordlessly, she put her arms around the child and hugged her close. She buried her face in the tangle of dark curls. Brie smelled dirty. She smelled of blood, and there was a trace of that sharp, spicy scent that Susan had smelled in the child's room.

She'd smelled it often enough in the past months, as Matt's sexual appetite had become insatiable. It was the after-scent of lovemaking, but there had been no love involved in what had been done to her daughter. She hated Matt, then, and hated herself for her own blindness. It had never occurred to her that he would touch Brie.

She rocked the little girl against her and wept for both of them. "I'm sorry, Brie," she murmured into the damp tangle of hair. "Oh, baby, I'm so sorry." At last, she scooped the child into her arms. "We're going away, Brie. Where he can't hurt either of us anymore. I promise you, I will never let him hurt you again."

She began walking through the darkening woods, the child a silent weight in her arms. Where to go? The police were no answer. She'd gone to them when the beatings had started. They were sympathetic, but unwilling to get involved in a domestic quarrel. They'd sent her home. No. It had to be somewhere else.

And then she knew. There was one place where they might seek refuge, one place where Matthew might not look.

As the sun dipped toward the horizon, she turned off the path. Skirting along the edge of the woods, safe within their shelter, Susan passed behind the house that was no longer hers, behind the dead hulk of the mill, and headed for town. At her back, the darkness slowly gathered.

Gulliver's Tavern stood off by itself, a way station between the town proper and the rows of bleak hillside homes that housed the mill workers. It was a low, squat building of knotty pine, with an almost hokey rusticness. Across the street and slightly to the right the boundary of the mill began, while to its left Broad Street led the way into the heart of Harringdale.

Unlike many of the buildings in Harringdale,

Gulliver's looked clean and well kept. That was partly the doing of Peg Laurin, who owned Gulliver's, and partly a result of circumstance. As the only remaining bar in town, Gulliver's had patrons in good times or bad. Peg could well afford the upkeep. If anything, hard times made business better.

Peg Laurin reflected on this last fact as she drew a beer from the tap and made her way with it through the usual crowd of drinkers to the booth at the back. She didn't speak to the man who sat there but merely set the beer down, picked up the money that was waiting on the table, and quickly made change from her apron pocket. That done, she turned a stiff about-face and went back to her station behind the bar.

She set about scrubbing the slick, polished wood of the bar top, all the while keeping watch on the man in the booth from the corner of her eye. She didn't like Matthew Prescott. She didn't like his frequenting her place, but she knew that any effort to keep him out would only be inviting trouble. There was a meanness to the man, lying just below the surface, waiting to spill over.

He'd been drinking for over an hour now, drinking up money that should have gone to buy food and clothes for his wife and little girl. Peg knew their situation. They might be surviving on Sue Prescott's meager nursing salary, but not much more. There was certainly no extra money to support Matthew's drinking.

She'd said as much to him, once—but only once. She'd thought the comment had gone over his head, until it came to be closing time. He'd hung around, making sure that he was the last one to be shooed out the door. He'd put his arm around her shoulders then, all friendly-like, but his big fingers had closed on the nerve in her shoulder and squeezed—hard.

"Mind your own business, bitch," he'd whispered, softly enough so that only she could hear, and with a big smile on his face for the benefit of the others. Then he'd disappeared into the night, turning to wink at her and wave. She'd had a bruise on that shoulder for weeks.

She felt sorry for him, in a way. He hadn't always been a bad sort. When the mill was open he'd come in with his buddies, of a Friday night, have a few, then head home. With the loss of his job, that had changed. The TV preachers tell you that hardships bring out the best in people, but Peg had observed that in most cases the opposite was true. Adversity often made animals of people. It was destroying Matt Prescott. Now he drank late into the night, and he drank alone. Bitterness was in him like a poison; people could sense it and stayed clear.

It wasn't as if he ever caused trouble in the bar. He wasn't a brawler. If anything, when he drank he grew quieter, more sullen. He would brood, staring into space, becoming aware of his surroundings only when his glass was empty and needed a refill. From the bar Peg would watch the anger grow in him, until his eyes were gray as a thunderhead. Then he would stagger up from the booth and take the anger home.

"Hey, Peggy, how 'bout another round over here?"

Stan Kowalcyzk's booming voice roused her and she jumped guiltily. With a last glance in Matt Prescott's direction, she grabbed a tray and got down to business. She collected the empty glasses, trading jokes with the men all the while, then drew a fresh round from the tap. Returning to the bar, she rang up the sale and stowed the cash in the register drawer. When she looked at the booth in the back again, it was empty.

Matthew Prescott walked slowly up the hill toward home. He didn't hurry. There was nothing to hurry for anymore, no schedules to keep. Time spread before him like an endless road, with no destination in sight.

He walked hunched over, his large hands balled into fists at his sides. His six-foot-five frame was massive, but soft. The muscle built up by working in the mill had turned to fat. His dark, curly hair was too long, and he'd forgotten to comb it. His face was dark with two days' growth of beard. A crowd of teenagers was playing basketball by the light of a street lamp. One look at Matthew and they moved aside to let him pass.

He trudged along the chain-link fence that enclosed the mill, his fingers brushing the cold metal until he came to the gate. He stopped. Facing the mill, he locked his fingers through the wire of the gate and shook it. The gate sagged inward, straining against the padlock and stout chain that held it closed. Matthew pushed at it, pushed until his hands bled, but the lock held. He leaned his forehead against the cool metal of the gate and closed his eyes. Behind his eyes, there was only darkness.

"Brie."

The word was a whimper of pain. Tears rolled silently down his cheeks, as he thought of his daughter. He'd hurt her. If there was a Hell, he would surely burn in it.

Burning . . . It was in him all the time now. He craved Susan as much as food or air, but she was always working, or fussing over Brie, or just too tired. He couldn't recall at exactly what point his wanting had changed its focus from Susan to Brie. Thoughts had come into his head. Bad thoughts. For weeks he'd fought against the temptation, but this afternoon it had been too strong. Now any chance he'd had of saving his marriage was gone.

Witch.

The word whispered in his mind and he grasped at it, but it slipped away, like smoke. When he'd begun to look at Brie as something other than a daughter, that thought had been a justification. After all, she had powers that no normal human being should rightly have. He'd rationalized the wanting as a spell of some sort that she'd cast over him. Now he saw it for the lie it was.

There was no evil in his child, and there never had been. Any black magic had been conjured up by his own inner torment. Alone in the night, Matthew Prescott faced the truth of himself and beat his fists in despair against the unfeeling steel of the gate.

For a moment the darkness threatened to close in again. It spiraled in on his mind until it seemed to Matthew that he was looking down a dark tunnel, toward a single point of daylight. He strained toward the light and grasped it, but he knew that it would not last long. The periods of light were few and far between. The darkness would soon claim him for good.

He thought of Susan and Brie. He couldn't provide for them anymore, couldn't even be trusted to watch Brie while Susan was at work. Things were not going to get any better. When Susan found out what he'd done to Brie, she would take the child and leave. He couldn't live with them without causing them harm, but he couldn't live without them, either. The dim light that remained in his mind was enough to show him what he had to do.

Matthew Prescott turned his back on the mill and headed home.

Sister Margarethe paced the floor, wringing her hands in indecision. As she turned to face Susan Prescott, she tucked them inside the sleeves of her habit to hide their shaking. She tried to keep her voice stern.

"You can't leave her here. The child needs a doctor. Take her to the hospital where they can care for her properly."

"The hospital's the first place my husband would look. A doctor could examine her here." She looked directly into Margarethe's eyes; saw them waver. Quickly, she pressed home her advantage. "Please. We have nowhere else to go."

Clutching her prayer book to her breast, Margarethe turned away and walked to the convent window to stare at the brightly lit face of the hospital across the street. As Mistress of Novices, this decision should not have been hers to make, but Mother Superior was away on a week's retreat and Margarethe had been left in charge.

She looked at Susan Prescott and the little girl that the woman held protectively on her lap. The child was bruised and bloody. She hadn't made a sound since the two had entered Margarethe's office. Her eyes stared dully, dry with a hurt that surpassed tears. Margarethe shuddered at the thought of what had been done to her. Any man who could hurt a child in that way was little more than an animal; worse than an animal, since he possessed the power to reason. Margarethe sighed. She couldn't send the girl back to that, yet it was not up to her to give permission for the child to stay.

The mother must have sensed her indecision, for Margarethe saw her straighten up, saw the hope fill her brown eyes like starlight. She remembered other brown eyes, and how quickly the light of hope could die.

Isaac Kauffman: Remember the name, good Sister, for you have murdered me.

Oh, she remembered. It was the first conscious thought that jarred her awake each morning, and the last thing that crossed her mind before sleep took her each night. She'd come to America, to this terrible little town, to try to work away that memory, but it had stayed with her, a constant, unwelcome companion, for the past thirty-two years.

She glanced again at the mother and child and suddenly, like the blind man that Christ had healed, her eyes were opened. God, in His great mercy, was offering her a second chance. Here were two strangers in need of help. She had turned Isaac Kauffman away, but she would not make the same mistake again. She nodded to the mother.

"All right," she said. "You and the child may stay here until she is well enough to travel and until you can make further arrangements. I'll call Dr. Jeffries and ask him to see her here. He's very discreet."

"Thank you, Sister." Susan Prescott reached out and clasped the nun's hand. "I just knew you would help us. I knew God would take care of Brie. She's special. She—" Her voice broke and she buried her face in the child's hair, unable to continue.

Embarrassed, Margarethe pulled her hand from the woman's grasp. "Come, then. We'll get you settled."

Susan followed her down the dark hallway, past the chapel, to a small room at the end of the hall. Margarethe fumbled along the inner wall and the light came on to reveal a single bed, topped with a worn chenille spread. There was a nightstand, a scarred dresser, and a single straight-backed chair. A crucifix over the head of the bed was the only other furnishing.

"We use this room for visiting sisters. I'll have a cot brought in. Is there anything else you need? If not, I'll call Dr. Jeffries."

Susan eased Brie down onto the bed and began removing the child's shoes and socks. "Please go ahead and call the doctor. I'm going to have to leave Brie with you for a short time." As Margarethe started to protest, Susan held up a hand placatingly. "I have to go home. My purse is there, with my driver's license and all my identification, and I have a little money hidden away. Also, I'll need clothes for Brie and myself. If I go now, Matthew will be out drinking and I won't stand a chance of running into him." She looked up at Margarethe pleadingly. "Please, I'll be right back. Brie will be no trouble, I promise."

Margarethe looked from the mother to the silent child. The little girl was as white as the pillow on which she lay. The bruises on her face stood out starkly against her pale cheeks. She looked too weak to cause any problems, even if she had wanted to.

"Very well. Just stay a moment until I get one of the sisters to sit with her."

In her office, Margarethe telephoned the hospital and had Dr. William Jeffries paged. As she waited for the pediatrician to come to the phone, she opened her prayer book to the back cover and lightly pressed her fingertips against it, checking for the damning bulk of the letter, where it lay in its hiding place. The action was unconscious, performed so often each day that it had become a habit.

She had never mailed the letter—at first, for fear of the Nazis, and later out of a paranoid fear that it would somehow be traced back to her and her sin would be exposed. Over the years, the fear had grown into obsession. She never let the prayer book out of her sight, even sleeping with it under her pillow at night.

In some part of her mind, she knew she was sick. How she yearned for peace, that perfect peace beyond all understanding that Christ had promised His followers! But peace could be achieved only through confession, and the fulfillment of the promise she'd made to Isaac Kauffman. She could not bring herself to do either. Perhaps God understood that, and had sent her the child as a means for redemption.

Her grip tightened on the phone receiver until her knuckles went bone-white. Silent tears ran down her face.

"Please, let it be so," she prayed silently. "Please, dear Lord, let it be so."

* * *

Susan bent to kiss her daughter's forehead. "You rest, sweetheart. Mommy will be right back. I'll bring your dresses and your crayons . . . and your dolls. Would you like that?" She stroked the child's tangled curls, willing the little girl to speak. Brie stared, silent, unseeing. Susan gathered her into her arms and hugged her close. "You're going to be all right, Brie. We're going to make a new start. Everything's going to be just fine."

She eased the child back onto the pillows, tucking the blankets snugly about her daughter's small shoulders. By the time Sister Margarethe had returned with one of the younger sisters, Brie was asleep.

Susan looked down at her for a moment, loving the soft curves of her cheeks, the haphazard scattering of freckles over the tip of her nose, the stubborn point of her little chin. She gently brushed a stray curl back from the child's forehead. Brie frowned and stirred in her sleep. "It's going to be all right, baby," Susan whispered. "It's going to be just fine now. I promise." How she hoped it was a promise she could keep.

Susan found the house dark and silent. The front door was still unlocked, the way she'd left it. She slipped inside quickly and shut it behind her, slipping the deadbolt into place. If Matthew came home, at least she would hear him. It might give her time to get away.

She locked and bolted the back door, then quickly pulled the shades. Her purse was on the kitchen table. She snatched it up and took it with her as she climbed the stairs to the second floor, checking off in her mind the items she and Brie would need. She flicked on the light switch in her bedroom—and time stopped.

Matthew was sitting on the bedside chair, his shotgun resting lightly on his knees. He blinked at her dumbly in the bright glare from the overhead light. Susan could see that he had been crying.

"Matt . . . ?"

"I'm sorry. . . . What I did to you . . . to Brie. Oh God, Susan, believe me—I'm so sorry." His eyes met hers and it was her Matthew looking back at her, the Matthew she had loved and laughed with, not the stranger of the past two years. The gun tilted in his hands, the barrel coming up toward his chin. His eyes filled and the tears spilled over, making an irregular path through the beard stubble on his cheeks. He cocked the gun and the *click* made her jump. As he began to tilt his head back, Susan realized what he meant to do.

"No!"

She moved forward, wrenching the muzzle away from his head, grappling with him for possession of the gun.

"Matt, for God's sa—"

The shotgun went off.

Susan stared down in disbelief at the gaping black hole in the bodice of her uniform. As she watched, a red stain began to spread across the white, lightning-quick, like the crest of the flood when a dam was broken. Pain registered in her mind, but almost immediately began to fade. She looked up into Matthew's startled face. Then her knees buckled and she sagged against him. The pain dissolved. Life became a memory.

Matthew eased his wife's body onto their bed.

He stroked her hair with bloodied hands, begged, pleaded. At last he closed her brown eyes. He lay down beside her and put the end of the barrel in his mouth. Fate had been kind. Only one barrel had fired. If he leaned forward and strained, he could just reach the trigger.

When the darkness took him this time, it was complete.

Dr. William Jeffries stepped into the hallway and pulled the door closed softly behind him.

"How is she?"

He didn't answer Sister Margarethe, but put a finger to his lips and motioned her away from the door and into a small parlor farther down the hall. He opened his bag on an end table and, taking his stethoscope from around his neck, tucked it away inside. Anger formed his lips into a thin line.

He knew the Prescott family well. Brie had been his patient since birth, and the child was sweet and loving. At the hospital, he worked daily with Susan Prescott. He admired her, both as a nurse and as a woman making the best she could of a bad situation. He knew it had been hard for them the past two years. Until tonight, he'd had no idea just how hard.

He snapped the bag closed and jammed his hands into his pockets, balling them into fists. When he looked up at Sister Margarethe, his face was hard.

"You said her mother would be right back?"

"Yes."

"Good. I'll need her to sign consent forms for surgery. The child's got some vaginal tears that will never heal properly without stitching. Her bleeding's stopped and she's resting comfortably, so I think it can wait until morning. God knows, she's been through enough for today. I've put her on antibiotics and some mild sedation—Sister Rebecca knows what to do." He glanced at his watch. "I'm on call tonight, so just have me paged when Susan gets here. I have hair and sperm samples, so if she wants to prosecute this bastard ... Sorry, Sister. This type of case gets me so damn angry. Sorry ..." He picked up his bag and stepped into the hallway.

Suddenly a sound rose, high and shrill in the great, silent house. The door at the end of the hallway burst open, and Sister Rebecca motioned to them frantically.

"Dr. Jeffries! Come quickly!"

"Mommmmeeee! Mommmmmeeee!"

The child was sitting bolt upright in the bed, screaming. Her eyes were wide, the whites showing at the edges. She seemed to be looking through the far wall of the room, at something that she alone could see. Gradually, her eyes came into focus. Her small face took on a look of grim determination. She flung the covers aside and jumped to the floor, her bare feet making a dull thud on the polished wood. As she bolted for the door, Bill Jeffries caught her in his arms.

"Whoa there! Where do you think you're going?"

"Let me go! I need to get to my mommy! I need to make the magic for her! Let me go!" She struggled against him, her small fists pounding against his back with surprising strength.

Jeffries lifted her up and set her back on the bed. "Your mommy will be right back. You must lie still."

"Let me go! You don't understand—she needs

the magic! Please! Mommmmieeee!" She fought him, punching and kicking with a desperation far from childlike in its intensity. A blast of heat came from her. To Bill, it seemed as if he were suddenly standing at the open door to an oven. He frowned. In his examination, minutes ago, there had been no hint of fever.

"Hold her down."

It was all Sisters Rebecca and Margarethe could do to keep the small, wriggling body on the bed, as he drew a dose of sedative into a syringe. He gave the child the injection, then added his strength to theirs until she had quieted. Fever burned in her body until she almost seemed to glow. Finally, she lay still. Jeffries breathed a sigh of relief.

"Your mommy will be right back," he said. "Until she gets here you have to keep still and rest, or you'll hurt yourself. You don't want to do that."

Her blue eyes fixed on him, beginning to grow dull, but still full of accusation and hurt. "My mommy is dead. She won't be coming back . . . ever." Her eyes closed, as the sedative took effect.

Jeffries stood up and ran a hand through his curly hair. To his surprise, he was shaking. He took Sister Margarethe's arm and ushered her into the hallway.

"Where did Susan go?"

"To her house. She wanted to get some money and clothing." She glanced up at the face of the grandfather clock that stood against the far wall. "She should have been back by now."

"Call the police, and tell them to send a squad car to her house to fetch her."

"Surely you don't believe the child's ramblings?"

"Of course not, but right now that little girl needs to see her mother and know that she's okay."

"Very well."

As she moved off down the hallway, Bill Jeffries stepped back into the room. The child was asleep, breathing softly through her mouth. He laid a hand on her forehead. There was no trace of the strange fever now, and he wondered if he could have imagined it. He smiled wryly and shook his head, thinking of the little girl's ravings of a few minutes ago. Perhaps imagination was contagious. . . .

In the early, predawn hours, Brie crept from the narrow bed. Barefoot, she padded softly past Sister Rebecca, who sat sleeping in a chair by the bedside, and slipped down the dark hallway, until she came to the chapel. It was empty. With a quick backward glance, she stepped inside.

The long room flickered in the light of several banks of votive candles. Brie tiptoed down the aisle, past the rows of silent pews that smelled of lemon oil. At the front of the sanctuary, she came to a halt before a large statue of the Christ. His robe was parted over his chest, and one plaster finger was pointing to his exposed heart.

Brie knew that she should pray. She tried to begin the "Our Father," as Mommy had taught her, but the words wouldn't come. She looked up into the statue's face, searched it, found nothing. With soft puffs she blew out the candles that burned, row upon row, at his feet. Moving on to the tabernacle, she repeated the process.

The only candles left burning stood before a statue of the Blessed Virgin. Brie stared up at her. She was so beautiful. The painted face bore the faintest hint of a smile, and the arms stretched down toward her, as if in embrace. The child reached out hesitantly and touched the statue's bare feet. The plaster was cold. Brie whimpered softly.

Though they'd tried to be quiet, she'd heard them whispering frantically outside her sickroom door. She'd pretended to be asleep and had heard every terrible word. She knew what the police had found when they'd gone to her home.

Sobbing, she blew out the last of the candles. She sank to the floor and buried her face in her folded arms. In the dark, silent chapel, the little girl wept for all she had lost.

Chapter Four

Sister Ingrid searched among the blankets again, her gnarled, arthritic fingers poking clumsily between the folds. She felt under her pillow, then slipped her hands inside the case itself. Nothing.

"Gott in Himmel," she muttered.

They'd found her teeth and taken them again! With a snort of exasperation, she pushed back the blankets and began to inch her way toward the bottom of the bed. As she moved, her flannel nightgown hiked itself up her skinny white thighs and she stopped, every few inches, to tug it back into place.

The indignity of it all made her angry. At ninety-eight, her mind was still razor-sharp; only her aging body now betrayed her. She couldn't hold her water anymore, and her knees had developed an annoying habit of buckling at the most inopportune times. So here she was, rotting away in this tiled mausoleum that the diocese had the audacity to call a "Rest Home." She sniffed at the term. What with the nurses fussing over her, and most of the other patients in their dotage, she got precious little rest indeed.

She reached the bottom of the bed and maneuvered around the end of the metal side rail, stretching on tiptoe to reach the floor. If the nurses caught her, there'd be trouble. They'd scold her as if she were a naughty child, and probably tie her to the bed as well.

She hated to be tied down, but she hated even more to be without her teeth. Except on fast days, she always kept back a roll or a bit of cake from supper to eat at bedtime. It gave her stomach something to work on until morning; otherwise, hunger pains kept her awake half the night. She'd tried to explain this to the nurses, but they were unwilling to vary their routine. Every night, just after dinner, they'd rub her back, plump her pillows, and clean her teeth and put them in a jar in the bedside cabinet.

They'd forced her to be crafty. In the months since the order had sent her here, she'd become expert at hiding her dentures: tucking them up the sleeves of her nightgown or into the corner of the pillowcase. One time she'd forgotten them, and they'd gone through the laundry. You'd think that would have taught those nurses something, but no, they persisted. Still, Ingrid managed. She was adept at dawdling. It was simply a matter of slowing them down. She'd palm the teeth, then stall for time with one request after another: a laxative, a last drink of water, the head of the bed cranked down a turn or up just a hair, her rosary—there was always something she could think of. Most of the time they were in such a hurry that they gave up looking and moved on to the next patient, letting her have her way.

The nurse on duty this evening was new. The new ones were the worst: always trying to impress their superiors. Ingrid had nodded off—just for a moment—and Miss Efficiency had spirited the teeth right out of the pillowcase and into the cabinet. Well, she'd show her.

Ingrid bent and unfastened the catheter bag from the base of the bed, hooking it over one scrawny wrist like a grotesque handbag. Holding the side rail for support, she shuffled the length of the bed until she came to the nightstand. It was not difficult to see. The large nightlight, inset into the wall, bathed the room in a soft twilight. Ingrid preferred to sleep in total darkness, but that too was against the rules.

Her teeth were not in the nightstand drawer, and a check of the cabinet area below turned up nothing. Ingrid pursed her thin lips in annoyance. Mother of God, where could they be? She covered the short distance between the nightstand and the bureau, her frail body swaying like a ship in a high wind. The jar was in the topmost drawer.

She took it out and clutched it to her breast possessively. Just above the bureau, on the wall, was a large oval mirror. For a moment she paused and stared at the apparition there.

Little was left of the neat, tight bun the nurse had made of her hair earlier that evening. Her hair hung in long, white wisps, fanning outward from her face, giving her a wild, half-crazed appearance. She raised a hand and brushed it back. Her fingers lingered for a moment at the crepe-like flesh of her throat. She shook her head sadly.

"*Mein Gott*, I've seen better necks on a chicken," she said in disgust.

Did it bother everyone to grow old? She didn't know the answer, only that the matter of aging bothered her. The trouble was, she didn't feel old—not inside. The inner Ingrid was still young and vitally alive, and it always shocked her to look in the mirror and find an aged hag looking back. Somewhere, the years and the wrinkles had caught up with her. She was not certain when she'd become old; it had seemed to happen overnight, without warning.

By the dim illumination of the nightlight she caught a trace of movement in the mirror, just at the edge of her line of vision. That would be the nurse—and trouble. Ingrid set the jar on the bureau top with a soft sigh of regret. There would be no cake tonight. She turned to face the inevitable scolding.

But it was not the nurse. The dim light outlined the figure of a man. No, not a man, either. The face that peered back at her was a skull. The light glinted off the smooth crown and the gleaming rictus of white teeth that stretched in a crazy grin. The figure moved closer. Dressed in black, it seemed to blend with the darkness, and Ingrid wondered if her senses were playing tricks on her. Then he grabbed her wrist and twisted it. The pain was real enough.

"Don't scream," he hissed, his mouth close against her ear. "Not if you want to see daylight again." He pushed her back against the bed. She could feel the cold metal of the side rail at her back and, colder still, the tip of a knife against her throat.

"October 12, 1942, Sister. Mother of Mercy Abbey—you were assistant to the Abbess."

"Yes," she whispered.

"A man died that day in the Abbey garden. He was a Jew. Do you remember?"

"Yes."

"He told you something—gave you something— you or one of the other sisters. I need to know who. Who met him at the door that day? Who might he have spoken to just before he died?"

Sister Ingrid looked up at the pale face pressed close to hers and saw, not a man, but an instrument of retribution. Her fear began to subside, replaced by a sense of righteous exultation. She had always known that Margarethe had turned that poor man away. Oh, there was no proof to warrant an accusation. She had never spoken of her suspicions to anyone. But she was sure of it, just as she was sure that she was about to die. All these many years she'd kept silent, even as Sister Margarethe took her final vows, advanced in the order, and was sent to America to spearhead a convent there. A murderess: Her hand had not pulled the trigger, but it might just as well have. Ingrid would have forgiven her if she'd come forward and admitted her mistake. Everyone would have. But Margarethe had condemned herself by her own silence. God's justice might be slow in coming, but it could not be put off forever.

She told him what she knew ... what she suspected. She told him who had been on duty at the door that day. As the name left her lips, Sister Ingrid knew she had made a grave mistake. If ever she should have dawdled, it was now. She should have stalled for time, but it was too late.

As the knife did its work, her last thought was that when she saw God face-to-face, she would have a bone to pick with Him. After all these years of service, it was a cruel prank to let her die without her teeth in.

Rome, New York
May 28

"Fritzie. Fritzie, come. *Kommst du.*"

Hannah McGuire clapped her hands and peered into the darkness beyond her back door. Her tightly permed cap of white hair shone silver in the light of the outdoor floodlamp. Again she called, and was rewarded with the soft tap of claws on concrete. A small dachshund waddled into the pool of light.

"Well, it's about time. You naughty boy. You were making *Mutter* worried."

She stepped back to let Fritzie into the kitchen, then followed him inside, closing and locking the back door. She moved with a limp. They were predicting rain tomorrow—she'd heard the forecast on the evening news, but her hip had already begun warning of the storm at noon. She'd broken it, two winters past, in a fall on the ice, and now it pained her whenever the weather was changing.

Fritzie danced across the linoleum, his tail wagging expectantly. He knew this routine by heart. As Hannah opened the cupboard and took out a can of dog food he sat at her feet, his tail thumping against the floor. Hannah opened the can and spooned the foul-smelling mush into Fritzie's bowl. The dog's excitement had reached a fever-pitch by now. His whole body was atremble, and anyone watching might have thought that the bowl contained ambrosia rather than dog food.

Hannah turned to the little dog. "Well, do you want it?" Fritzie gave a short *gruff* of confirmation. "I can't hear you. Show *Mutter* how much you want it. Say your grace." The dog shifted from one paw to the other, his tail wagging frantically. He gave several short, sharp barks, then rose up on his hind legs and began to turn in tight circles, front paws crossed before him in an attitude of begging.

Hannah smiled. "*Gut* boy." Wincing at the pain in her hip, she bent and set the bowl beside his water dish. The dog quickly dropped to all fours and began to eat.

His mistress put the can in the trash bin and wiped down both can-opener and kitchen counter. She looked around the small, spotless kitchen in satisfaction, then made her slow way through the house to the living room.

Predictably, a baseball game blared from the television set. Ed lay on the sofa, a beer propped on his stomach, all his attention fixed on the game. He looked away from it long enough to give her a smile. "Fritzie all tucked in?" At her nod, he turned back to his game.

Baseball, football, basketball, wrestling. Hannah would never understand the American passion for sports. As the mantel clock chimed nine, she eased her bulk into her favorite chair and took out her knitting. The soft notes of the chimes were drowned by the roar of the crowd as a batter hit a home run. Hannah smiled.

This was the part of the day she liked most. When she and Edward were young, it had been their time together: a time to talk, to play a friendly game of canasta and catch up on the day's events. When the children were small, it was some-times the only moment alone together that they had in the whole day. A special time. Now that Ed was retired they had the whole day to share, and this was a time for companionship. She did not be-grudge him the sports he loved so. Being in the same room was enough. She was content. Her mind shut out the din of the game as her thoughts began to drift slowly backward.

Edward McGuire was a good man. Only the best of men could have lured her away from the beauty of convent life to this new life in America. They had met at the end of the war. A young novice, already in doubt of her vocation, she'd taken a leave of absence from Mother of Mercy Abbey and gone home to her parents' house. Ed was a young airman, part of the liberation forces. They'd met, fallen in love . . . and she'd never taken her final vows. When he returned to the United States, she'd come with him as his bride. An old story.

Life had been good to them. Four children and forty-seven years later, she had no regrets. He'd stayed with the Air Force and they'd traveled the country from base to base, before retiring here, near Griffiss Air Force Base in upstate New York. Her children were grown, successful, with families of their own. Hannah looked up at the pictures that filled an entire wall of the living room. Nine grand-children. How she loved them, though she never saw enough of them. Fritzie was her baby now. It amused Ed to see her fussing over the dog, but he understood. With the children gone, the mother-love in her needed an outlet, somewhere to go. Fritzie had helped to bridge the empty gap between her children's departure into adulthood and the arrival of the first grandchild.

Fritzie . . .

Hannah glanced up at the clock and frowned. Twenty minutes past nine. The dog always wolfed down his food and then came to sit at her feet. The ritual was invariable.

"Fritzie!" she called.

The noise from the television drowned the word. She wrapped the sweater sleeve that she was knitting around the needles and placed the bundle on the floor. Using the arms of the chair, she pushed herself to her feet. Her hip protested. She rubbed it absently as she limped toward the back of the house.

The kitchen was dark. Hannah couldn't remember having turned off the light, but then again she forgot a lot of things these days. She paused uneasily before the darkened doorway and listened.

"Fritzie . . . ?"

Through the background drone of the TV came the soft, steady drip of the kitchen faucet. The washer was wearing out, and if she didn't turn the spigot off *just so* the faucet would drip. Ed would fix it one of these days, but it was not high on his list of priorities. With a huff of annoyance, she reached to one side of the doorway and switched on the light.

Fritzie lay stretched on the white formica of the kitchen counter. His tail didn't wag a greeting, which was hardly surprising, considering the long, open slash in his throat. Blood poured from the wound, pooling beneath his head and making its way in a slow *drip, drip* to the yellow linoleum below. The dachshund's brown eyes, open in a permanent stare, reflected the light from the overhead fixture.

A man stood beside the dog's body. From the polished toes of his boots to the stocking cap which fitted tightly against his skull, he was dressed in black. His right hand clutched a revolver. Behind him, another man finished closing the back door and quickly pulled the shade down over the window.

For a moment, the trio all stared at each other. Then Hannah screamed. The man in black lunged for her. She felt his gloved fingers brush the back of her dress as she turned to run, heading for the living room.

"What the hell . . . ?"

Ed was sitting up, staring at her. His beer had tumbled onto the rug and was spreading out in a dark puddle which almost immediately soaked into the thick pile. At the sight of the intruder, he began to stand. From behind Hannah came a sharp spitting sound. Ed paused, halfway between standing and sitting. In the center of his forehead a small dark hole appeared. For a moment Hannah saw his eyes focus on her, confused, questioning. Then he toppled backward onto the couch. Blood began to seep from the hole, rolling down the slope of his nose to drip from its tip.

Panic was an anesthetic to the pain in her hip, as Hannah lunged for the front door. She would run into the street, scream for help. Surely someone would hear her. Her hands found the knob, fumbled with it. She tugged at the door but it held fast, and she realized, too late, that the deadbolt was in place. Just as her fingers closed on the bolt, rough hands caught her from behind, pulling her away from the door and any chance of escape.

She was too frightened to scream, as they pushed her back into the overstuffed chair she had left just a moment ago. The first man, the one with the gun, the one who had killed Ed, turned the head of her reading lamp around so that the light was shining into her eyes.

"Please," she whimpered. "Please. If it's money you want . . ." She slumped forward and began to weep softly.

"We are not interested in money, Hannah Muller. It is Hannah Muller, isn't it?" He cupped her chin in his hand and turned her face up to the light. "What we do want is information. I want you to think back to 1942, when you were a novice in the Mother of Mercy Convent, Berlin. The day the Jew was shot in the convent garden . . . I want you to tell me everything you can remember about that day."

He spoke in flawless German. It had been so many years since she'd heard her native tongue that Hannah stopped crying, and tried to peer beyond the blinding light at the face that went with the voice. From behind the light his breath wafted over her, sickly, foul with decay. She felt the cold metal of a knife come to rest against her cheek. The point pricked the soft puff of flesh just below her left eye.

"And if you remember well and cooperate, I will not hurt you."

Hannah closed her eyes. Her mouth set in a tight, stubborn line. She had seen their faces and could identify them. She knew they could not afford to let her live. Even disregarding that, she had raised four boys. If that experience had taught her anything at all, it was to recognize the sound of a lie when she heard it.

In the living room, the mantel clock chimed 2:00 A.M. Klaus Brauer's mind registered the small sound, cataloged it, filed it away. He stood before the sink in Hannah Muller McGuire's darkened kitchen. A full moon shone in through the window above the sink, and by its dim light he watched the water dance over the blade of his dagger.

It had taken the old woman a long time to give him the name, and an even longer time to die. If anyone had suggested that he'd enjoyed the details of her death he would have denied it, but there was a smile playing around the corners of his thin lips and he hummed an old folk tune as he watched the water spiral into the drain.

Close to half a century in a Russian prison camp had brought a stoop to his broad shoulders and whittled the padding from his frame. The stomach ulcers of his youth, left untreated, had turned cancerous. The cancer had spread throughout his body and was slowly eating him alive from the inside out.

The skin of his face, thin and yellow as parchment, was stretched tautly over his nose, brow, and cheekbones. His eyes were sunken deep into the shadows of their sockets, making his face all sharp angles and dark hollows. In the moonlight, it looked like a living skull. The resemblance was further heightened when he removed the black stocking cap to scratch his head. The mane of blond hair was gone. He was bald, his scalp so thin and tight that the plates of his skull made raised ridges in the smoothness.

As his partner entered the kitchen from the living room Brauer turned his head, and the moonlight caught his left side, bringing it into sharp relief. Where his left ear should have been only a stump of flesh remained. Its jagged edges puckered around the opening of the auditory canal, a grim reminder of the Russian methods of persuasion.

"Finished?" he asked.

Gunner Hahn nodded curtly. He was young, less than half Brauer's age.

"Get on with it then."

The younger man took a butane lighter from his pocket and returned to the living room. Hannah Muller sat propped in her armchair, the body of her dog slung across her fat knees. On the sofa, her husband's body had been arranged into a natural position, ankles crossed, pillow propped beneath his bloody head.

"This will not fool the police."

"No." Brauer smiled. "But it will give them something to think about. Let them earn their pay."

The young man averted his eyes from what was left of the old woman's face, as he knelt and lit the fuse of the small incendiary bomb that lay on the thick shag carpet at her feet. Brauer frowned at this sign of weakness.

Minutes later, as the house went up in flames, they were well on their way to Utica and the small motel where they had rented a room. A police car and a fire engine screamed by them, headed back toward Rome. Hahn watched their progress in the rearview mirror, until the red-and-blue flashing lights had disappeared into the distance. He caught a glimpse of Klaus Brauer's face, the teeth set in a grin of victory, and quickly fixed his attention on the road ahead.

In the backseat, Brauer turned his jaundiced eyes upward toward the roof of the car. The flicker of the passing headlights sent a scene dancing across his memory: the explosion of Meintz's lab, taking the secret of Brimstone with it.

In its aftermath he'd conducted an investigation, thorough, proper ... useless. The nuns, close-mouthed and eager to protect their own, had told him nothing. In the end it had come down to a simple matter of practicality. The nuns and their nursing skills were needed. A young colonel who'd failed his first major assignment was not. His reduction to the rank of corporal and his orders for the Russian front had arrived just two weeks later.

The words of the Brimstone report that Meintz had given to him were etched indelibly upon his mind. With his career in ashes he'd not sent the report on to Berlin, but had kept it among his personal things. His superiors need not know that the explosive had been a success. They were infatuated by Heisenberg's atomic bomb. If they had learned that they'd lost a weapon just as powerful, available for immediate use at a fraction of the cost, he would have found himself facing a firing squad instead of the Russians. Better to let Brimstone become a memory.

He'd watched his comrades die in the icy grip of the Russian winter. Promised food and medical supplies had failed to arrive. Starvation, disease, and exposure all took their toll, and when their numbers had been sufficiently reduced the Russians overwhelmed them. He could still see them pouring over the lip of the foxhole, like an unstoppable tide.

Then began the years of imprisonment. They had found the Brimstone report, of course. He'd been separated immediately from the rest of the men, put in solitary confinement, questioned daily. At first the treatment had been good, then, as he failed to cooperate, it had deteriorated rapidly. Yet torture and beatings had not broken him. At last he'd been locked away and forgotten.

Years passed. Summers brought flies, whose bites caused a pestilence of itching and whose eggs hatched in the rancid bowls of food, causing the slop to boil with maggots. In the winter there was the bone-numbing cold. And always there were the rats: thin, hungry, and mean. He'd become expert at killing rats and at eating them, when it had come down to a choice between that or starvation. He'd watched his youth slowly slipping away.

"Brimstone . . ."

Without realizing it, he whispered the word aloud. It had destroyed his career, his plans for the future; it had cost him everything he had. Yet, like a man infatuated with an unfaithful lover, he could not let it go. It was all he possessed. Over the years the words of the report had gone round and round in his head, until it had become an obsession.

Now, with the proliferation of atomic weapons, Brimstone's importance had faded. The Americans and the Russians had enough atomic bombs to blow up the earth several times over. Brimstone was a fossil, a myth. With death imminent, Brauer became more of a liability than an asset. Keeping an old, sick man in prison went against the new government policies. At last they'd released him. With the cancer far beyond the reach of any conventional therapies, it was only a matter of time. Still, the obsession remained. Even with death nipping at his heels, he'd begun his quest. He never expected it to be successful, yet it seemed he might succeed after all, for . . . he had a *name*.

Against all odds, he had a name. From the records of Mother of Mercy Abbey he had gleaned the names of all those who had been in residence in October, 1942. Over the last two years, he'd patiently traced them down. Most had been easy to find—their names were inscribed on stones in the Abbey cemetery. Fifty years had pruned their ranks down to only five. He had further pruned them, until now only one was left. All the other four, before their deaths, had given him the same name: the name of the young novice who had been on duty at the main door that afternoon. The miracle was that she was still living—and living *here*, in this country, less than a day's auto trip away.

His eyes narrowed. If the Brimstone formula still existed, its owner had kept it secret all these years. This Margarethe might not have it, but by the time he'd finished with her she would tell him where it was.

Revenge. It was the one thing that kept him going now. When he had the formula, he would wreak vengence on a world that had robbed him of his youth, his future, his life. Despite the new openness and friendliness between the superpowers, the world still teetered on the brink of destruction. A few well-placed bombs would shatter that fragile trust and bring on Armageddon. He would die secure in the knowledge that the rest of the world would soon follow him.

Brauer sighed deeply, feeling the first stirrings of pain in his cancer-ridden belly. Soon. The quest would be over soon, but it had to be carried out carefully. He could not let Brimstone slip through his fingers again, due to oversight or haste. No, he would move slowly and think each action through. Then Brimstone would be his, and neither man, nor God, nor the Devil himself would be able to stop him.

Chapter Five

Mother of Mercy Convent
Harringdale, Pennsylvania
June, 1992

"Enter."

The man whom Sister Marie ushered into the convent office was in his mid-thirties, tall, with the kind of blond, blue-eyed good looks that, in the outer world, must have made women's heads turn. But all that was lost on Mother Margarethe. She studied his face, trying to look beyond the surface handsomeness at the man beneath. Her heart was racing, skipping a beat here and there, in a pattern that she'd come to recognize as a warning. She nodded him toward a chair. He waited until they were alone before he spoke.

"Thank you for granting me this interview, Reverend Mother. I'll try not to take up too much of your time. My name is Saul Weiss. Over the past few years, at the request of my mother, I've begun to trace our family history. That research led me to you."

He spoke English with a thick German accent

and, though the smile on his face seemed genuine, something in his eyes filled her with unease. Margarethe fixed a look of polite interest on her face. She felt her heartbeat quicken its pace.

"How may I be of help to you, Mr. Weiss?"

"My uncle—my mother's brother—was named Isaac Kauffman. He was a scientist, working under the Nazis during the Second World War. He was also a Jew. On October 12, 1942, he and his family were murdered by the SS. He died on the grounds of Mother of Mercy Abbey in Berlin. According to the abbey records, you were in residence there at the time. Anything that you could tell me regarding his death or your memories of that day would be helpful."

At the mention of the name, Margarethe felt her heart give a lurch and begin to beat wildly. She clutched the arms of her chair, to hide the trembling that had suddenly crept into her hands. Mercifully, a knock sounded on the office door. Sister Marie entered carrying a small tray, containing two cups and a pot of tea. It gave Margarethe a moment to think. The truth . . . Now was the time to tell the truth.

She waited until Sister Marie had left, then poured tea for her guest and herself. Slow, careful breaths through her mouth failed to ease the pounding in her chest. When she spoke the words came too fast: false, unnatural. "Yes, I do remember. I was assigned to attend the main door. Unfortunately, your uncle never made it that far. The soldiers shot him in the garden, before he reached the house."

She paused to catch her breath. After so many years of telling it the lie had come, like a bad habit, almost against her will. Her heart skittered against her ribs; pain moved down her left arm and into her fingers. It took an effort to keep the pain out of her voice, as she continued. "Our sisterhood sheltered Jews throughout the war, and was responsible for saving many lives. I grieve with you that your uncle was not among them."

The young man nodded. "It is a sad thing; for our family, it was a double loss. My uncle had in his possession important family documents: wills, deeds, other records. No trace of them was ever found. I am sure that my uncle would have tried to save them, especially if he had realized he was about to die. Are you sure that nothing was found in the garden afterward: a briefcase, an envelope— anything?"

Margarethe heard the voice, as if from far away, but she could not answer. The pain was centered in her chest now, clamping down around her heart like a vise. It was a punishment from God for her lies. She had to tell him the truth, no matter what the cost. The nitroglycerin tablets were in her desk drawer. With trembling fingers, she pulled the drawer open and fumbled inside until she'd found the small brown bottle. The white plastic cap refused to come off.

"Here, let me help you."

Gratefully she surrendered the bottle, then watched as the young man's hands, sure and strong, removed the lid. The truth . . . She would tell him the truth, confess all, give him the letter. . . . Then she noticed that his hands had dropped into his lap, the opened bottle still in their grasp.

"The information, Reverend Mother?"

She realized what he was doing. Anger and fear

only made her heart beat faster. "Who are you?" she gasped.

He ignored the question and held out the bottle of pills, careful to keep it just out of her reach. The pain doubled her over, until her forehead came to rest on the polished surface of the desk top.

"Please," she whispered. "Please. He told me nothing. He gave me nothing."

"But I thought you did not speak with him, Mother?"

She closed her eyes, spoke a lie to match his own. "He died in the garden. He never made it to the house. Please . . . my heart . . ."

He set the bottle on the desk before her and she grabbed at it, knocking it over and spilling a shower of tiny white tablets across the desk top. Her thumb and forefinger closed on one. She managed to get it to her mouth. The tablet dissolved on her tongue, leaving a bitter aftertaste; slowly, the tight fist around her heart began to open. When he spoke, she was still too weak to raise her head. His voice floated above her.

"We hoped that you would cooperate, Mother. We know you have what we are looking for. I was kind today; next time I will not be so patient. Think about it. After all these years, what is so important that it is worth your life?"

She heard the door open and close softly. He was gone; but the question he'd put to her remained.

Gunner Hahn stepped into the motel room and quietly closed the door behind him. The drapes were pulled, leaving the room in semidarkness, despite the bright day outside. He didn't switch on the light.

He was just able to make out the outlines of the two double beds, and the figure lying on the one farthest from the door. He sat on the edge of the unoccupied bed.

"Well, what do you have to report?"

Brauer's voice was slurred with morphine. Gunner tensed at the sound. Apparently it'd been a bad day, and that meant the old man was in a foul mood. Gunner chose his words carefully.

"She either has the Brimstone formula or she knows where it is; I'm certain of it. I gave her the 'family history' story. When she heard the name 'Kauffman,' she immediately became agitated. I pressed her for information and she worked herself into an angina attack. She didn't break, but I'm sure that she will."

Brauer raised himself on one elbow. "I told you not to threaten her! She is our last link to the formula! What if she should call the police?" The sudden movement awakened the pain in his belly, like a knife twisting, twisting. He let himself down onto the bed again, closing his eyes wearily. Anger was useless.

"She won't go to the police. If she has kept her nasty little secret all these years, she will not reveal it now."

Brauer let his breath out in a long sigh. "What's done is done. We move tonight." He opened his eyes, fixed them coldly on the younger man. "But be warned, the next time you disobey my orders I will kill you. I have no use for free-thinkers. Obedience or death—the choice is yours. Do you understand?"

"Yes, sir."

"Get some rest, then. It will be a long night."

Gunner stripped off his coat, tie, and shoes. He lay down on his bed, his back to Brauer. He did not sleep. By the sound of the old man's breathing, he could tell that Brauer was still awake. A stand-off, then.

Brauer did not trust him. That didn't bother Gunner, as he suspected that Brauer was the sort of man who wouldn't trust his own mother. If he didn't trust Hahn, he at least tolerated him. Gunner Hahn was needed. After nearly half a century behind bars, Brauer had emerged into a world changed beyond his wildest imaginings. He had been an anachronism, barely able to function. Gunner was his guide in this new world.

Still, the old man did not trust him. True, Brauer had taken him into his confidence, told him about Brimstone and of his plan to recover the formula. But he kept bits and pieces of information to himself, and only let Hahn know so much. That plan, so far, had led only to the slow murder of four elderly women. Tonight, another would die.

Gunner closed his eyes, seeing the old nun's face, remembering the fear he'd seen there. Despite her religious beliefs, the fear of death was just as strong in her as in anyone else. Over the years he'd witnessed death in a hundred different forms, and fear was always the Grim Reaper's close companion.

Even Brauer, so quick to deal death to others, feared it mightily himself. The old man's body was wracked with constant pain. Still he clung to life like a leech, unwilling to give up even one wretched minute of existence.

Gunner smiled wearily. How very few saw death for what it really was: rest, peace, an end to sorrow, loneliness, and pain.

Tonight the old nun would know that rest, but not before her fear gave him the formula. Tonight. Let it end tonight.

Margarethe blessed herself and rose from her knees. She felt feather-light, filled with a peace such as she had never known in all her sixty-six years. She opened the door of the confessional and made her way down the aisle to kneel before the Blessed Sacrament. She prayed for guidance.

And there was an answer.

In the silent peace of her heart, she knew clearly what she had to do. The fear that had held her paralyzed for so long was gone, replaced by a fierce kind of joy.

After all these years, what is so important that it is worth your life? She'd had no answer this morning, but she did now. The important thing was what had led her to choose this life so very long ago: to serve God, to love Him, and with His help to love those He put in her path. Fear had caused her to stray from that purpose. Now, at last, fear had brought her back to it.

She had no doubt that the man would be back—and others with him. Whatever it was that Isaac Kauffman had given her, it was certainly not family papers. Her life was forfeit. Death was coming. She could feel its approach, like the winds that herald a storm. Still there was no fear in her now, just an eagerness to make things right. She had confessed everything and received absolution. There was only her penance left to do, one loose end to be neatly tied up.

She returned to her office and laid her old prayer book on her desk. The leather binding was cracked and faded, the corners worn smooth by the touch of her hand. She turned the book over and opened the back cover. Using the point of a letter opener, she pried the glued edge of the endpaper away. The envelope lay before her. Though the years had yellowed it somewhat, it was unwrinkled. She lifted it gingerly. The address was as clear as the day it had been written:

Samuel Kauffman
P.O. Box 270
Boston, Massachusetts,
USA

Clear, but incorrect. A year ago, when her heart condition had first made itself known, guilt had caused her to trace down Samuel Kauffman. It had been done carefully, discreetly . . . and cowardice had again overcome her good intention to contact him. She had kept his new address, however.

She pulled a small red address book from the top drawer of the desk and opened it to the section marked "K." There was only one entry: "Samuel Kauffman, 117 Oceanview Drive, Newport, Rhode Island, 02840."

She copied the address onto the lower right-hand corner of the envelope, then ripped the page from the address book, tore it into tiny pieces, and dropped these into the wastebasket. She laid the envelope squarely in the center of the desk top.

She would not mail it. After all these years, she wanted to do the right thing. It had to be delivered in person, so that she would know, once and for all, that it had been done. Then she could face death, in whatever form it might come, in peace.

Her health would not allow her to make the trip to Rhode Island herself, but there was one person she knew she could trust. Tonight . . . She would make the arrangements tonight.

On impulse, she walked to the window and flung it wide. The afternoon sun slanted through the leaves of the maple tree, dappling the convent lawn in green and gold. The air was full of the scent of roses. Margarethe took a deep breath, and laughed aloud at the joy there was in simply breathing. She felt like a child again, at her parents' home in the mountains. She closed her eyes and let the smell wash over her. Roses . . . and rain. There would be a storm tonight. Tomorrow the air would be cool and fresh—washed clean.

The Reverend Mother held out her hand. Gabrielle took it reluctantly between her own. She knew the question that was coming, and what her answer would be. But tonight, as her hands touched the old woman's, her blue eyes widened in surprise. Tonight, the answer would be different. From the twinkle in the old sister's eyes, Gabrielle realized that she knew it, too.

"What do you *feel*?"

The girl squeezed the hand sandwiched between hers. There was affection in the gesture. They sat facing each other on straight-backed chairs, in Mother Margarethe's office, almost knee-to-knee. Over the years it had been here, in this fashion, that Gabrielle had learned her lessons: English, French, mathematics, geography, history. Now, though school was behind her, she still felt as if she were being given some sort of test. She reached inside herself and analyzed the mixture of feelings emanating from the older woman, then shaped them into words.

"You are still ill—physically, Mother—but the terrible burden on your spirit has lifted."

Reverend Mother smiled and withdrew her hand from the girl's. "Correct, as always. It is that spiritual burden I wish to speak with you about."

Gabrielle frowned. She had lived here, in the care of the nuns, since she was six years old. All those sixteen years she'd sensed a deep darkness in Mother Margarethe's soul—not evil, but a profound sadness that never went away. Now it was gone. She licked her lips, then said, "Mother, if it's gone, isn't it best to let it be forgotten? The physical problem is something I can help you with, if only you would let me."

"No, child. That is my cross to bear; like St. Paul's thorn, it must remain. I do have a favor to ask of you, however."

"Anything, Mother. I—"

The Reverend Mother raised her hand and Gabrielle fell silent. She could see a tension in the older woman's face, growing, building. It was in her voice: a sharpness, a strident quality that Gabrielle had never heard before. "Agree to nothing, until you hear me out. What I am about to tell you may change your mind. Listen, now, and do not interrupt.

"My story begins many years ago, in Germany, during the Second World War. There was a young novice who, though she loved God and was anxious to serve Him, was also terrified of the Nazis. The order she belonged to was committed to saving Jews: hiding them and getting them safely out of the country. The girl was afraid that the Nazis would find out, afraid of what they would do."

The Reverend Mother's eyes seemed to pierce through Gabrielle. They burned with an intensity that made the girl quickly look away. Her eyes fell to the Reverend Mother's hands. They were grasping at the skirt of her habit, twisting the cloth in a desperate, wringing motion. Gabrielle closed her eyes, wishing she could close her ears as well. Reverend Mother's voice pressed in upon her, insistent.

"One day a man came to the convent, seeking refuge. In her fear, the girl turned him away. The Nazis killed him. Afterwards they searched the convent, looting and terrorizing. They took the Mother Abbess away with them, and she was never seen again.

"Because of this girl's sin two people died, and an untold number of her fellow sisters were brutalized.

"In the months—the years—that followed, the girl tried many times to tell her confessor what she had done, but fear always stopped her. At first it was a fear of the Nazis. Later it became fear of a different kind: a fear of shame and scandal, fear that if her superiors learned what she had done, they would make her leave the order, the only life she had ever known since the age of sixteen; a way of life she dearly loved."

Her voice broke and Gabrielle looked up, startled. Tears were running down the elderly nun's face. The Reverend Mother seemed unaware of them. Embarrassed, Gabrielle quickly looked away. Mother Margarethe took a deep breath, then continued.

"The girl did many acts of penance. She volunteered for the lowest and most menial chores, fasted until she was faint with hunger, and punished her body nightly with a whip of knotted cords.

"Her superiors mistook her actions for youthful enthusiasm. Though they forbade her to punish herself any further, they rewarded her supposed zeal by assigning her to a small mission team that was coming to America to found a hospital.

"In America she worked hard, trying with all her heart and strength to make reparation to God for her secret sin. Again her efforts backfired—instead of suffering, her hard work brought rewards. The years flew by and she rose in rank within the order: Mistress of Novices, Director of Nursing Services . . ." She paused. "Mother Superior.

"All this time the girl kept her secret, even from her confessors. She never told anyone . . . until today."

In the silence that followed, Gabrielle looked up. The Reverend Mother was watching her, waiting, expectant. Her aged face was lined with anguish. Gabrielle met her eyes.

"You were that girl," she said softly. The Reverend Mother nodded. "But why tell me, Mother? Surely this is a matter for you and your confessor?" She searched the older woman's face, trying to determine what was expected of her.

To her surprise, the Reverend Mother reached out and caressed her cheek, lightly. "Have you no words of condemnation for me, child? No rebukes?" She smiled, letting her hand drop back into her lap. Her hands were still now, peaceful. She seemed to be speaking to herself as much as to Gabrielle. "But of course. How could I have expected that of you? You do not have it in you. You never have and you never will, praise God."

"Mother? Are you all right?"

The question seemed to pull her back to herself. "Of course I'm all right. Better than I've been in a long time, if the truth be told. As to what this all has to do with you . . ."

She stood up and moved to stand behind her desk. "I spoke with my confessor this afternoon. The favor I must ask of you is part of my penance. You see, that man gave me something before he died: a letter, addressed to his brother, in the United States. He made me promise to deliver it, but after what I'd done, I couldn't bring myself to do it. I never kept that promise. I would like to fulfill it now. I wish you to deliver this for me." She picked up an envelope from the desk and handed it to Gabrielle.

Gabrielle took the envelope from her hand. It had a crisp feel to it, almost a brittleness. She handled it with reverence, studying the neat, careful printing on the front. The Reverend Mother leaned across the desk and pointed to the second address in the right-hand corner.

"The man's address has changed over the years. This is the current one. If you agree to this, you'll be on your way to Rhode Island tomorrow."

"Certainly, Mother. I'd be glad—"

"Not yet. You haven't heard it all. There is an element of risk in all this." She told Gabrielle of the stranger who had come to the convent just that morning.

"I believe he will come back," she concluded. "Whatever is in that letter, it is very important to him. He seems to want it very badly. So you see, by taking this on you may be exposing yourself to danger."

"But shouldn't you call the police and let them deal with it?"

The Reverend Mother shook her head. "Calling in the authorities could bring embarrassment upon the order. I don't want the Church to suffer from my mistake. Besides that, this man, whoever—whatever—he is, didn't seem afraid of the police. It was as though he were outside the law." She rubbed her forehead wearily. "I can't expect you to understand this, Gabrielle. You are of a different place, a different time. You can't know what it was like under Hitler. The SS were a law unto themselves, unanswerable to other authorities. There was a coldness to them, an absence of fear, of the normal restraint that is in each of us. That man this morning—he gave me the same feeling. The police would not be of any use against him. I feel the only way to be safe is to get that letter out of here, and as soon as possible."

Gabrielle looked down at the envelope in her hand. It all sounded so strange, so farfetched, like the plot of an old black-and-white movie. She searched within herself for fear, but found none. Still, it all seemed unreal. But if it was that important to the Reverend Mother, the decision was an easy one.

"I'll deliver it, Reverend Mother. The sooner the better."

"You're sure?"

"Yes."

"I hoped that was what you would say." Mother Margarethe bent and opened the top drawer of her desk. She removed a second envelope, smaller than the first, and much more modern-looking. She handed it to Gabrielle. "Here is money to cover your expenses on the trip. There's a bus leaving tomorrow morning at eight."

Gabrielle lifted the flap and thumbed through the stack of bills inside. She had never seen so much money before in her life. "But Mother, I—"

"No arguments, child. Stay in Newport a few days. See the sights." Her voice took on that no-nonsense tone that Gabrielle knew so well. "You've not seen much of the world beyond these walls. Maybe a few days on the outside will help you in making a decision about your future. There's—"

She was interrupted by a knock on the office door. It was Father Brennan.

"I hope I'm not intruding, Reverend Mother, but I was told I'd find Gabrielle here. We're overdue for our rounds."

"Forgive me, Father. She'll be right with you. It is my fault she was delayed." She motioned to Gabrielle. "Go ahead, child. The final instructions can wait until morning."

Gabrielle cast a guilty glance at the clock. Eleven-thirty, already. She quickly stuffed the two envelopes into the deep pocket of her dress and knelt for the Reverend Mother's blessing. The nun's hands were cool and gentle as they made the sign of the Cross on her forehead.

"God be with you."

"Thank you, Reverend Mother."

"I thank *you*, Gabrielle."

Margarethe stood in the doorway and watched as the two of them hurried down the hall. It was beginning to rain outside, and for a moment she nearly called after Gabrielle to remind her to take an umbrella. Then she caught herself.

The girl was not a child anymore. With an effort, she put aside her feelings and looked at Gabrielle as a stranger might see her. For the first time she realized how tall Gabrielle had grown—and how beautiful. With a mother's pride she admired the straight back and graceful walk; the thick, dark hair, gathered neatly into a knot at the back of the neck. The two stopped at the main door, and as Gabrielle shrugged on a rain parka Margarethe had a brief glimpse of her profile: the high forehead, the pert, upturned nose, the large blue eyes that had no need of makeup to catch your attention. Nothing remained of the frightened, awkward little tomboy she'd reluctantly taken in so many years ago. By some sleight of hand, Gabrielle suddenly had been transformed into a lovely young woman.

Father Brennan took up an umbrella and ushered the girl out of the door ahead of him. Margarethe waited until they were gone, then closed her door and returned to sit at the desk. She took out her ledger and recorded the five hundred dollars that she'd given to Gabrielle. Margarethe smiled. This was a night for accounting. For reckoning. She took out the month's checking account statement and began balancing it, but her thoughts kept turning back to Gabrielle.

She had first looked on the child as a burden, an imposition. After the murder-suicide of Gabrielle's parents, no relative had come forward to claim her. A sense of duty had caused Margarethe to take her in. She looked on that decision, now, as the single greatest achievement of her life—for the child was wonderful. Not merely for her gift, but for what she was. There was a sweet openness to her nature, and an innocence, that set her apart. The sisters had all fallen in love with her from the start, and the task of raising her had proved to be not a burden at all, but a joy.

Gabrielle's gift of healing had revealed itself so gradually and so naturally that the sisters almost came to take it for granted. Not Margarethe. She realized what a sensation the media would make of it, and was careful to keep the child's extraordinary talent a secret within the order. To that end she'd kept the child out of the public eye, tutoring her inside the convent walls, screening her from contact with outsiders. Father Brennan knew, of course. Over the years he'd helped to guide Gabrielle's upbringing, and to channel her gift where it would do the most good. Their visits to the hospital were always conducted discreetly, late at night, during change of shift, when they were least likely to be noticed.

Margarethe gave a sigh of satisfaction. What a fine nun the girl would be. Oh, not that she'd made a decision yet, but the Reverend Mother was sure that she would. If God had given her such a gift, He would surely call her to a vocation. She would make a wonderful addition to the order.

Thunder interrupted her thoughts. Its rumble was still distant, but the storm was moving this way. It brought back troubling memories of this morning's visitor. She'd had another purpose in having Gabrielle deliver the letter: It would get the girl away from here, to safety. Like the approaching storm, danger was coming, and soon. She could feel it. She did not know what form it would take, but she wanted Gabrielle far away when it happened.

Hopefully, by the time the child returned the threat would be past.

The desk lamp flickered briefly, then settled down to a soft, steady glow, as the Reverend Mother bent over her books. Outside, the rain became a slashing torrent. It struck the petals from the roses until the ground beneath the office window was crimson with them, like great drops of blood.

From the shelter of their car, parked half a block down the street in the darkness of an alleyway, Klaus Brauer and Gunner Hahn watched the priest and the young woman cross the street to the hospital. Brauer noted it and dismissed it. She was not the one he sought.

They waited fifteen minutes . . . half an hour . . . until the lights on the upper floors of the convent had winked out, one by one. At last only one light remained, on the ground floor.

"That is her office," Hahn said, matter-of-factly.

Brauer picked up a pair of wire cutters from the seat beside him. "Come, then. Let's get this over with."

Silently, the two men in black left the car and blended into the night.

Jessica Ortega lay very still, her body a small mound on the hospital bed. As she slept, her breathing came in short, shallow gasps. She was ten years old, but she looked half that, as if the leukemia that was ravaging her had snatched away some of her past as well as all of her future. Chemotherapy had left her bald and had failed to stop the progress of the disease. All the conventional therapies had been exhausted. The leukemia, in remission for the past four years, was now running wild through her system. Without a miracle, she would live no more than a few hours.

So Father Brennan had brought her a miracle . . . a miracle named Gabrielle.

He stood at the foot of the bed and simply watched as Gabrielle sat down beside the sleeping child. She reached over and switched on the bedside lamp, angling it so that only a soft glow fell upon the bed. For a moment she just looked at the little girl, and Father saw tears of pity well up in her blue eyes. One small arm had escaped the tangle of blankets. It was pathetically thin, branchlike against the stark white of the sheets. Gabrielle took the child's hand gently between her own. She bowed her head and closed her eyes.

Father Brennan swayed slightly and took hold of the bed for support. Sheepishly, he realized that he'd been holding his breath and was becoming light-headed. He consciously let the air out of his lungs in a silent sigh of wonder. He'd seen Gabrielle's gift at work a hundred times, but he was unable to take it for granted the way the sisters did. Each time was a miracle, fresh proof of God's existence and His boundless love.

He fixed his eyes on Gabrielle. The young woman was breathing softly through her mouth, her lovely face lined with tension, the fine line of her brows pulled into a frown of concentration. Beads of sweat stood out on her forehead. He knew that if he touched her now, she would be fever-hot. He and the sisters had conducted their own tests, and found that Gabrielle's body temperature reached a peak of one hundred and eight degrees Fahrenheit when her gift was operating. As he watched, her breathing increased until she was almost panting. Suddenly, her shoulders arched and her head slumped forward onto her chest. Her breathing gradually stilled and the tension left her. After a moment, she opened her eyes. Gabrielle smiled. Father Brennan followed her gaze.

The child had awakened. Even in the meager light of the lamp, Father Brennan could see that the color had come back into her pale cheeks. Where she had been bald moments before, a soft down of brown hair now lay close against her scalp. Her dark eyes shone as she raised a small hand to touch Gabrielle's face.

"Are you an angel?" she whispered.

"No." Gabrielle laughed. She stroked the girl's hair lovingly. "Just a friend. Go back to sleep now. You'll have a busy day ahead of you tomorrow."

The child's eyes closed. Gabrielle pulled the blankets up and tucked them firmly beneath Jessica's chin, then reached over and switched off the bedside lamp. As they left the room, Father Brennan paused a moment in the doorway and looked back at the sleeping child.

A busy day ahead, indeed. He knew from past experience that the doctors would study Jessica, poke and prod, conduct their tests. All that fuss was unnecessary, of course. He could tell them what they would find: a healthy child, with a ravenous appetite and not a trace of leukemia or any other malady. He shook his head to clear it, then lifted a silent prayer of thanksgiving as he followed Gabrielle down the corridor.

Mother Margarethe raised her head with a start. It was very dark, and she experienced a moment of disorientation, uncertain of where she was. A clap of thunder, even louder than the one that had awakened her, shook the glass of the window panes, and she realized that she was still in her office. She'd been dozing, her head resting on her desk atop the ledgers she'd been working on. With a frown, she felt along the desk for the gooseneck lamp and fumbled with the switch. Nothing happened. The power was out then, probably until morning.

With a huff of annoyance, she opened the bottom drawer of the desk and felt along the edge for the flashlight she kept there. She found it and switched it on, taking comfort from the small cone of yellow light it cast. She closed the ledgers and put them away, then started for the door. But even as the light of her flashlight touched the carved wood, the door began to open, swinging silently inward. The crack grew larger, and the light glinted off the tips of polished boots. She had begun to raise it higher when a flash of lightning lit up the room as bright as noontime. Her scream was lost in the roar of thunder that followed.

There were two of them. The second closed the door quietly behind him. It was the same man who had threatened her that morning, but it was the other man she feared. She backed away, watching his approach in the dance of the lightning, her eyes riveted upon his face. That face was older now, lined with the weight of years and a burden of evil, almost skull-like beneath the stocking cap he wore. Still, she recognized the cold blue eyes. Her imagination supplied another cap; another skull, silver and polished. The Angel of Vengeance had come for her at last.

The instinct for survival made her raise the flashlight to strike him, but he shrugged the blow aside. His hands caught her wrists, forcing her down into the chair at the desk. The younger man used tape to fasten her wrists to the arms of the chair, then took up a position by the door.

The Angel sat on the edge of the desk. He switched the flashlight on and balanced it on its end to enclose the two of them in a soft circle of light. When he spoke, his voice was as cold as the rain. "Well, Margarethe, we meet again. It is unfortunate that you chose not to cooperate with my associate. It would have saved a great deal of time and trouble."

As she watched, he took a pair of thin surgical gloves from his pocket and slipped them on. "I won't lie to you. You *will* die before this night is over. Death will come quickly and painlessly . . . or it will come very slowly, with great and needless suffering. It is up to you. Give me the formula, Reverend Mother. Tell me where it is, and it will go easily for you."

Margarethe's eyes narrowed. Formula? So, it was not a letter, after all. She was to die for a bunch of figures and symbols that had no meaning. Aloud she said, "I know of no formula."

His thin, colorless lips spread in a sorry smile. "I was afraid you would say that, Mother. It is a shame, really. At our age, death should be a peaceful thing." He bent over her and took her right hand in his. "Feel free to scream, Mother. On a night like this, no one will hear you."

As he began to break her fingers, one by one, Margarethe closed her eyes. She bit her lips tightly. She would not scream; she would not give him even that small satisfaction. Her heartbeat throbbed in her ears, the sound mixing with the wild patter of the rain. The heart condition that had manfested itself a few years ago had been gradually growing worse. She had always thought of it as God's punishment for her sin, and had forbidden Gabrielle to use her gift to heal it. Now, as the pain and fear sent her heart into a rapid arrhythmia, she was thankful. With God's grace, it would not last long. Aloud, she began to pray. She filled her mind with the prayer, attempting to block out the pain with the strength of the words:

"Pray for us sinners, now and at the hour of our death. . . ."

Chapter Six

Mother Margarethe slumped forward in the chair. Brauer took her by the shoulders and shook her, but she made no sound. Her head lolled on her shoulders, tipping back until her face pointed straight at the ceiling. Her face was barely recognizable. The nose was flattened, the flesh around her eyes puffed and dark with bruises. Blood streamed from her nose and mouth, running down her chin to splotch the white wimple below.

"Don't you die on me, old bitch. Not now. Not yet."

Brauer dealt her a tremendous backhanded blow across the face. It had no effect. Suddenly the desk lamp came on, as power was restored. The light reflected off the flat blue mirror of her eyes. They stared, sightless, uncaring. Brauer felt beneath the wimple, at the angle of her jaw. The pulse was still.

"*Verdammt!*" He sat on the edge of the desk, his knees suddenly gone weak.

She'd told him nothing. She'd died and taken the information with her. His stomach tightened with frustration, and the resulting pain nearly doubled him over. Aware that Hahn was watching him, he fought for control.

It could not end here. Not like this. He moved behind the desk and began searching the drawers. There were papers, account books, ledgers, and a small leather address book. He took the latter from the drawer and thumbed through it. It opened in his palm to where a page had been torn out.

Nothing.

Impatiently, he took the rest of the books from the drawer and opened them, one by one, to the last entries. The first was a journal of sorts, apparently a record of the daily life of the order. As his eyes scanned the page, his hope dimmed. Today's entry held nothing of importance. There was not even a mention of the Reverend Mother's meeting with Hahn. Impatiently, he slammed the book closed and took up the next. It was a ledger, a record of receipts and expenses. The final entry carried tomorrow's date and read simply: "To Gabrielle. Trip to RI (S. Kauffman)—$500."

The name seemed to leap off the page:

Kauffman.

The same last name as the dead Jew. And the address—RI, Rhode Island. The sister named Gabrielle was going there tomorrow. It could not be a coincidence.

Excitement made him forget the pain in his belly. The game was not over. Not yet. He joined Hahn by the door.

"We must question the others."

"But—"

Brauer cut him off. "Question each one. Establish her identity. The one named Gabrielle you will bring to me."

"And the others?"

Brauer took his gun from its holster, checked the silencer, slipped off the safety. He reached for the door.

"Eliminate them."

"How many is that you've healed now?" Father Brennan asked.

"God healed them," Gabrielle reminded him gently. She shrugged. "I really don't keep track of numbers, Father. That's your business."

They sat in the hospital lounge, each with a can of soda and a chocolate bar. Long ago they'd learned to avoid the stale, machine-brewed coffee that was the only other beverage the lounge had to offer. The other tables were deserted at this time of night. They sat alone and watched the lightning make giant rips in the fabric of the night sky.

Gabrielle swirled her drink in its can, listening to it fizzle against the metal. It had become traditional, over the years, for them to come to the lounge afterward for a snack and a talk. The work of healing drained her, especially since Father Brennan chose only those cases whose prognoses were hopeless unless Gabrielle were to intervene. The sugar helped bring her energy level back to normal.

When she was younger, she'd looked forward eagerly to the treat. Soda and candy were expensive, forbidden foods that the sisters seldom indulged in. Now, however, maturity had tempered her sweet tooth, and the talk detracted from her enjoyment. When Father Brennan cleared his throat, she did not look up.

"Well, have you made your decision?"

"No, not yet."

"But, Gabrielle, you can't put it off forever."

"I'm not ready to make that kind of commitment, Father."

"But what's holding you back? Tell me your reservations. We'll discuss them and work them out. You're special, Gabrielle. 'Many are called, but few are chosen.' Surely you can see that God has chosen you?"

"With all due respect, Father, I *can't*. I need time."

She got up from the table and tossed the can, still half-full, into the trash barrel. The candy bar was unopened. She tucked it into her pocket, next to the envelopes that Mother Margarethe had given her.

"I have to go back now. I have a lot to do tomorrow." Though she tried to keep her voice light, tension made the words come out stiff and formal.

Father Brennan came up behind her and laid a hand on her shoulder. "I'm sorry. I didn't mean to upset you. I certainly never meant to pressure you. It's just that your vocation is so obvious to everyone who knows you. We all want the best for you, Gabrielle. We're only thinking of your happiness."

She nodded, silently. Together, they took the elevator to the lobby. The rain was coming down hard, beating against the glass entrance doors. The street in front of the hospital ran ankle-deep with water. On the other side, the convent was shrouded in darkness.

Father Brennan rubbed a clear spot in the steamy fog that clouded the glass of the door and frowned. "It's a mess out there. I think we'd be better off taking the tunnel."

They boarded the elevator again and rode to the subbasement. The elevator doors opened onto a long, horizontal shaft. Lined with cement, it was clean and dry, with lights spaced every few yards along its ceiling. The tunnel ran beneath Main Street, connecting the hospital with the convent and rectory. It had been part of the original construction, built just for weather like this and for the long, snowy winters, to allow the sisters and priests to travel back and forth to their duties more conveniently. Halfway down its length the pair reached a second shaft, which branched off to the right. Here Father Brennan paused.

"Well, good night. Think about what I said, Gabrielle. You have so much to give."

"*Good night*, Father."

She lingered at the opening, listening to his footsteps retreat in the distance. They echoed strangely in the hollow space. Gabrielle shivered and hurried on. She'd never been one to be afraid of the dark or to jump at shadows. She'd often used the tunnel in the past and it had never held any fear for her, but tonight was different. She felt uneasy, and found herself looking over her shoulder every few seconds as she walked along. There was a chill around her and within her, which had nothing to do with the storm. By the time she'd reached the far end of the tunnel and the stairs leading up to the convent, she was almost running. She fumbled in her pocket for her key and finally found it, buried beneath the envelopes and the candy. Hurriedly she slipped it into the lock, almost expecting to hear footsteps on the stairs behind her. As the door swung open, she looked back. There was no one there.

She closed the door quickly and locked it behind her, leaning against it in relief. Still, the feeling of uneasiness did not go away. If anything, it intensified.

She chided herself for such foolishness. It was just nerves, of course. Over the last few weeks Father Brennan, Reverend Mother, and the other sisters—everyone—had been subtly pressuring her for a decision. Everyone seemed to know what was best for her . . . everyone but Gabrielle herself. Life seemed to be closing in around her, pushing her irresistibly onto a path she was not sure she wanted to take. Under those circumstances, who wouldn't be nervous?

It was dark in the hallway, but she didn't attempt to turn on the lights. She had roamed these halls since childhood and had no need of light to help her find her way. The light might awaken one of the sisters, and, in her present state of mind, Gabrielle did not want to talk to anyone. Sleep, too, was out of the question. Silently, she tiptoed down the hallway to the chapel.

By the light of the votive candles she made her way down the center aisle and genuflected before the tabernacle, before sliding into a pew. She slipped off her coat and laid it on the seat beside her. Making the sign of the Cross, she knelt and tried to pray. As always, the words seemed hollow, empty. There lay the crux of her problem.

God: The sisters all spoke of Him, of His love, of His grace, of His will. They spoke of answers to prayer, of His presence active in their lives. Gabrielle imitated them in their prayers and devotions, said the rosary, went to mass. She'd spent hours alone, listening, waiting for some small sign of what the others believed in so fervently.

But there was only silence and emptiness.

They told her God was calling her, but she felt no such call. They pointed to her healing gift, but even there she sensed no outside Presence. And they all expected her to enter the novitiate this fall.

How could she tell them that she could not spend the rest of her life serving Someone or Something that she was not even sure existed?

Gabrielle rested her head on her folded hands. She loved the Reverend Mother, the other sisters, and Father Brennan, too. Since the death of her parents they had been her only family, and she realized the debt she owed them. She wanted desperately to please them, only she couldn't live a lie.

She raised her head and looked up at the statue of Christ. "Please," she whispered. "Please, if You're real . . . if You care . . . help me."

Run.

The word burst suddenly within Gabrielle's mind. She'd been trying to pray, reaching down within herself, reaching out in search of Something . . . Someone . . . but she'd found only a void—endless questions without answers. Now the word inside her head made prayer impossible. She opened her eyes and looked around the small chapel. The pews were shrouded in darkness, the racks of votive candles standing out as oases of light. She licked her lips and tasted fear.

Without the benefit of sunlight, the stained glass windows were grayed and dull. The saints depicted on them seemed flat ... dead. A flash of lightning illuminated them for a moment. Like Lazarus, they came back to life. Their colors brightened, reached out to speckle the pews below in reds, blues, and greens, before the darkness swiftly descended once more. Through it all the word sounded an alarm in her mind, frantic, compelling. Uneasiness was like an itch beneath the surface of her skin.

Gabrielle shook her head in an effort to clear it. She was tired—that was all. Her eyes felt scratchy, and the sweet soda had left a stale taste in her mouth. The weariness was playing tricks with her nerves. It was time to get some rest.

As she rose from her knees, she heard voices in the hallway. The conversation was hushed, whispered, but even so she could tell that the voices were male. That in itself—at this hour, in this place—was an oddity, but the fact that they spoke in darkness, without turning on the lights, was stranger still. The sense of uneasiness that she'd felt all evening suddenly sharpened, focused. Evil: She could feel it in the air, thick as smoke.

Silently, she edged along the pew toward the side wall. Her inner sense sent cold chills of warning along her nerves, pumped adrenaline to her muscles, primed her sluggish body to run far and fast. The order was imperative. *Get away*.

Instead, she crept closer. Over the years, she'd learned to trust her instincts. Those instincts told her now that something fearful was in the hallway, but curiosity was stronger than instinct. It was a trait that had gotten her in trouble on more than one occasion, but she had to know. The sisters might be in danger. She couldn't just leave them and run away. A statue of St. Therese stood at the rear corner of the chapel. Gabrielle pressed herself against the wall, using the statue for cover, and listened.

"You didn't find her?"

"No, sir. One of them told me that her room was on the first floor. I did find a room at the end of the hall, but there was no one there and the bed has not been slept in."

"All the others are accounted for? You are certain you made no mistake?"

"No mistake. I made certain of their identities before I killed them."

Gabrielle put her hand to her mouth to stifle a scream and began to back away. She edged down the aisle, unable to think or act, except to put distance between herself and those terrible words. Her foot came up against something and she nearly tripped. When she looked down, the scream came and there was no stopping it.

Sister Mary Xavier lay in the aisle. There was a neat, round hole in the center of her forehead, just above her pretty brows. Her face was peaceful, if a bit puzzled-looking. Her rosary was still clutched in her hand. From beneath her head a dark stain spread lazily down the aisle, following the pull of gravity toward the front of the chapel.

Gabrielle looked up in time to see two men rush through the chapel doorway. Even in the dim light she could clearly see the guns they carried. As she backed away toward the altar they split up, one taking the center aisle, the other approaching along the side. There was nowhere for her to hide. Slowly, they began to close the distance.

*   *   *

When Brauer saw the girl, he felt a moment of confusion. By the faint glow of the candles he could see that she was far younger than the other nuns, and that she was wearing neither the long, cotton nightgown that the others had been clad in nor the traditional habit. Also, she seemed vaguely familiar. The familiarity nagged at him, until he remembered the girl he'd seen earlier that evening, walking across the street with the priest.

The entry in the ledger had read simply "Gabrielle"—not "*Sister* Gabrielle." Could it be?

"Gabrielle."

At the sound of her name, the girl froze. She was up against the altar now. She stood with her back against the marble top, like an animal gone to ground. Brauer moved closer.

"That is your name, isn't it? You have something we want, something the old sister gave to you. Give it to me, Gabrielle, and I promise no harm will come to you."

To illustrate the sincerity of his words, he holstered his gun, holding up his hands to show her they were empty. Hahn followed his lead and put away his gun, too. Slowly, Brauer held out a hand to her. She shrank from it. He continued to advance, watching her back away along the altar's edge. Hahn used the opportunity to rush her from behind.

Her name. The man knew her name. The Reverend Mother had told him, then, but she could not believe that Mother would betray her. Gabrielle's mind raced, seeking an explanation. She heard his words, and knew them instantly for the lies they were. Their putting the guns away did nothing to reassure her. She'd seen what they'd done to Sister Mary Xavier, and she knew, from eavesdropping on their conversation, that they'd killed the other sisters, too. They would never let her live. Whimpering, she backed away from his hand.

There was movement behind her. She sensed it and ducked beneath the altar, just as the second man tried to grab her. The altar was open, front and back, like a U turned upside down. She scuttled beneath it and out the other side, making for the door of the sacristy. If she could only make it to that small room, a second door opened to the outside. She would have a chance.

Suddenly, a hand caught her ankle. She went down. Hard. The fall knocked the wind out of her, sent pain spreading like ripples from the core of her body outward. Hazily, she realized that the second man had gone under the altar after her. She tried to kick her leg free, but he held on. She rolled onto her back, twisting, struggling, hoping to wriggle free of his grip. It was a mistake. The man yanked her toward him and got on top of her, using his weight to pin her to the floor.

Gabrielle could feel the length of his body pressed to hers, his hips grinding her down. His head was at the level of her belly. He raised it and began to inch forward, as she pummeled him with her fists. He ignored the blows and continued his advance. What little light there was came from behind him, and she saw only a silhouette, the face in shadows. Her mind and body recalled another time she'd been held like this . . . a time she'd almost forgotten. Her weary mind composed a face from the bits of shadow. Her father looked down at her, and she could smell the sweat on him and feel the raw vio-

lence flow hot-cold along his nerves, passing from
him into her. She felt pain and, in her terror, could
not tell if it was real or merely remembered. Panic
took her.

Hahn picked that moment to raise himself up on
hands and knees to get a better purchase on her.
Legs straddling her, his hands found her wrists.
When his weight came off her, Gabrielle wasted no
time. She kicked out, fighting for more than her
life. Her foot missed, but her knee connected solidly. For a moment, it seemed to have no effect.
The man hung above her. Then, abruptly, he released the grip on her wrists. His hands came up
to clutch himself and he tumbled off her, rolling
onto his side, whimpering softly. Gabrielle scrambled to her feet. She turned to sprint for the sacristy . . . and ran straight into the arms of the other
man.

His arms enfolded her in a bear hug and, for a
moment, his face was close to hers. His breath
reeked of decay, like something long dead. It came
in soft grunts—*uhn, uhn, uhn*—an eager sound that
filled the darkness and seemed to join in some obscene way with her own harsh, desperate breathing. He tried to pin her wrists to her sides, but she
wrenched one hand free and struck at his face. The
blow had little effect, except to knock off the black
stocking cap he was wearing.

A bolt of lightning lit the chapel for a brief second and Gabrielle had a clear view of his face. The
sight of him paralyzed her. He had no hair, and his
head was turned in such a way that the left side
was toward her. Where his ear should have been,
there was nothing but a hole. His face looked like
one of the Halloween masks that she'd seen chil-

dren wear for Trick or Treat. But she knew that this was no mask. This monster was real. His hideous face split in a grin and Gabrielle screamed.

Backing her against the altar, he wound his fingers into her hair, pulling until she thought it must come out by the roots. Slowly, he bent her head backward. She felt the cold point of a knife prick the flesh of her throat. She stopped struggling. The other man had gone silent. The only sound was the soft, terror-quickened cadence of her own breathing.

"Now," he said. "Now you will tell me where the papers are—the ones the Reverend Mother gave you."

His face was close to hers, his eyes gray and cold as ice. The stone top of the altar pressed painfully against Gabrielle's back. Her arm was bent behind her, resting on the cold marble. The altar . . .

As the knife pressed harder against her exposed throat, Gabrielle whimpered in pain and fear. Her free hand groped behind her, seeking.

"I hope you enjoy pain." He held the knife up before her eyes, turning it slowly, hypnotically, to catch the gleam of the candlelight. The point was red with blood.

Her blood.

"Just a small cut, but see how it bleeds." He laid the icy flat of the blade against her cheek. "Such a pretty face. It would be a shame to mar it. So tell me, Gabrielle. Tell me what I wish to know."

"The papers . . ." Her searching fingers brushed *something*. Lost it.

"Yes?"

Her hand closed on something hard. Gripped. Held.

"In the tabernacle. Over there." She inclined her

head slightly to the right. He followed the direction of her eyes.

As he turned the knife came down, away from her face. Gabrielle brought her left hand around, swinging the heavy, silver-plated crucifix that was the altar's only adornment with all her strength, knowing that she had one chance and one chance only. Her action caught him off-guard, momentarily pinning the hand with the knife between their struggling bodies.

Brauer saw the candlelight flash off of polished metal and tried to get out of the way without releasing the girl. He almost made it, but not quite. The crucifix came arcing down and caught him squarely across the face.

At first, his mind was overwhelmed by sensation. He heard bone break. The sound, coming as it did from inside his head, was strangely loud. He felt the blood spout from his nose and stream from his torn cheek in a warm tide. It ran down the back of his throat and into his mouth, nearly choking him. It left a thick, metallic taste on his tongue. Through it all, he managed to hold onto the girl. A moment passed. His stunned mind took all this in, processed it, analyzed it, sorted it, making room for other input from the torn and injured nerve endings.

Pain: It came suddenly, a fiery agony that seared across his broken nose and down his ruined cheek. His fingers lost their grip on the knife. The clatter, as it struck the marble floor of the sanctuary, reverberated inside his skull. He didn't remember letting go of the girl, but as he fell he was aware of footsteps retreating rapidly in the distance.

"Get her!" His voice was a hoarse screech. He didn't know if Hahn heard him, or if the man was even physically capable of carrying out the order. Vaguely, he thought he heard other footsteps, heavier, louder. Far off, a door slammed. Then there was only silence. The candlelight dimmed and faded to black.

Gabrielle ran out into the storm. The wind tore at her clothes. Rain stabbed cold needles into her skin. The darkened rectory loomed before her, while across the street the lights of the hospital beckoned. She hesitated at the steps of the rectory. Where to go? The rectory was closer, but the priests were all asleep by now. They might not hear her. Even if they did, they would meet the same fate as the sisters should the men follow her. She could not endanger them. The hospital, though farther away, boasted an armed security guard. It seemed the better refuge. But before she could act, fate took the decision out of her hands.

The sacristy door banged open. Heavy footsteps pounded across the wet ground behind her, coming fast. She crouched down among the rose bushes, beside the rectory stairs, hoping he hadn't seen her. The hope was in vain. At the level of her hip, one of the roses exploded in a shower of petals and something thudded dully into the wooden steps of the porch.

He was shooting at her! Even as Gabrielle realized what was happening, a second bullet pierced the folds of her skirt and grazed a path across her left thigh. She screamed with the fiery pain. Then she was up and running, weaving from side to side. The lights of the hospital were warm and inviting. She took a last look at them and turned away. The light would make it easy for him. He would pick her off before she'd even reached the other side of the street.

She ran away from the light, around the side of the rectory, across the black, shadowed lawn to the woods. Her leg throbbed painfully, but all the muscles seemed to work. As she reached the first line of trees she could hear him coming behind her, could feel the chill of him, worse than the cold of the rain. The bark of the nearest tree suddenly splintered away, leaving a white scar to mark a bullet's silent passage. She fled into the shelter of the trees.

Gunner Hahn ran, trying to ignore the sickening ache in his groin. At the corner of the building he stopped, took careful aim at the girl's fleeing shape, and fired off a shot, only to see his quarry disappear into the darkness of the woods.

He cursed softly. He must not kill her, not yet, not until she'd told him where the formula was.

He shoved a fresh clip of bullets into his weapon. As the black, wet trees closed around him, he gripped the gun more tightly and hurried after her.

Each step sent fiery pain searing along her thigh where the bullet had clipped away the flesh. Still, Gabrielle ran on. She knew every inch of these woods. They had been her playground in childhood, and a refuge during the moody teen years. Now that knowledge would be put to the ultimate test. Brambles tore at her dress as she fought her way through the underbrush. The path should be coming up soon. She tripped, went down on one hand, righted herself, and continued on. When she reached the path, she was running so fast that she nearly overshot it.

The path led uphill. It was a morass of mud and churning water, and for once she was thankful for the sturdy, sensible shoes that were standard attire at the convent. The rubber soles held on the rocks and slippery muck. She splashed her way up the hill. At the top she moved instinctively to the left, careful to stay away from the big tree root that grew up out of the ground on the right.

She ran-slid down the other side of the hill. He was close behind her. Too close. Her heart seemed to skip a beat. She was running as fast as she could, yet he'd already cut the distance between them in half. Lightning flashed—once, twice, three times in quick succession—and she dared to look back.

He was coming over the hill like a bull: eyes wide, nostrils flaring. Thanks to the lightning, he could see her clearly also. His eyes fixed on her. She saw the hand holding the gun come up. Time seemed to stop. She willed her feet to run, but they refused to move. The muzzle of the gun pointed down at her.

He was so intent on taking aim, he didn't see the tree root. The loop extending above ground caught his foot neatly. She had the satisfaction of seeing the look of surprise on his face before he fell. Above the howl of the storm, she heard him let out a string of curses. She didn't wait to hear or see any more.

Hahn went down.
Hard.
As he hit the ground the gun went off, the shot

going wild. The sound was lost amid the surrounding din of the thunder.

A flash of lightning revealed the girl, frozen in open-mouthed terror, staring up the hill toward him. The darkness descended again, leaving only a ghostly afterimage of her seared upon his retinas. Other lightning flashes lit the woods, showed her turning in a strange, jerky, strobelike motion and running away from him down the trail.

Anger filled him. She could not defeat his plans now, not when they were so close to completion. Cursing, he struggled to his knees. Mud, slick as grease, tried to pull his feet from under him as he stood up. Gingerly, he tested his weight on the injured ankle.

I hope he broke his ankle, she thought as she scrambled down the hill.

Instantly, her conscience chided her. Hadn't Reverend Mother taught her that the thought gives birth to the deed? In God's eyes, to think someone dead was nearly as bad as the act of murder itself. Murder. Reverend Mother and the sisters—gone. All gone. She brushed the back of her hand across her eyes, wiping away rain and tears.

I hope he broke his neck. This time the thought brought no guilt at all.

She glanced back over her shoulder. Incredibly, he was still coming. He hadn't broken anything, after all. She could hear him crashing through the trees, his long strides eating up the distance as he gained on her. Cold waves of rage preceded him, beating against her back. She was tiring rapidly. Her leg hurt, and there was the beginning of a stitch in her side. And he was coming.

Lightning flashed. She used the brief illumination to take her bearings. She recognized the huge oak, silhouetted against the night sky. Her magic place was not far away, but with him so close on her heels it held no refuge for her now. Besides, she was not a child any longer. Adults didn't hide from danger. They fought back. The odds were against her, that was true. She was injured and unarmed, and knew nothing about self-defense. He, on the other hand, had a gun and had no aversion to killing. Still, there had to be a way.

He was close now, so very close. She could hear the ragged *huff* of his breathing, feel his anger curl cold tendrils around her, as if to pull her down. Then his hand caught at her skirt, tugged hard. Gabrielle lost her balance. His hand closed around her ankle as she fell.

Hahn smiled as he held on to the girl. He was careful not to repeat his previous mistake, but clung tightly to her ankle, keeping well out of range of her kicking feet. He made no attempt to move closer. Using his body as a counterweight, he let her thrash and struggle, knowing she would soon tire herself out. It brought back memories of a trout he'd hooked when he was a boy. How the fish had fought the hook, how it had labored against the inexorable pull of the line! All to no avail. Just as had happened with the great trout, the girl's struggles were growing weaker. Careful to avoid her kicking feet, he brought the gun up. A bullet, strategically placed to wound, but not kill—he had learned much from Brauer. She would give him the information; before he was through with her, she would beg him to let her tell him. Sighting along the barrel of the gun, he took aim.

She was tired, so tired. She ached all over, and her knees were scraped raw. The temptation was to stop fighting, to give in to the weariness and the pain and to just let it be over. She opened her eyes. Lightning silhouetted him and she saw the gun pointed at her. His teeth made a white slash in the darkness. He was smiling.

Gabrielle suddenly felt afraid. It was not the fear of pain or of dying, though those fears were present as well. This was a different sort of fear, one she had never experienced before—a fear of the unknown. For the man felt *wrong*. It was not simply the evil she felt in him, or the anger whose chill waves still buffeted her. She had felt those a hundred times stronger in the other man and they had not affected her like this. This was something different, something alien and unidentifiable.

Stop the feeling, make it go away. That was her only thought as she picked up a handful of mud and flung it into his face. The gun went off. The bullet struck a rock just next to her head and went ricocheting off into the darkness. He dropped the gun, let go of her ankle, and reached up with both hands to claw at his eyes.

Gabrielle staggered to her feet and fled. Exhaustion slowed her steps, made her stumble. His anger had turned to rage. It was like a giant fist around her spirit, closing, closing, a noose ever-tightening. She heard him coming behind her, felt the strangeness of him grow nearer.

"Dear God," she whispered, babbling to herself in her terror. "Dear God, there has to be a way. . . ."

As swift and clear as the lightning, a memory came to her aid. There was one chance. It was a dangerous one. If she failed it would mean her death, but at the rate her strength was failing, he would overtake her soon anyway. She was certain that he would not let her escape again. Her luck was running out. She made her decision.

Beside the maple a smaller track led to the left, off the main path. The trail was narrow, almost invisible. It wound its way through the densest part of the woods to the brook. Few knew of its existence. This was a game trail, used by the deer and other woodland animals to get to the water. As a child, Gabrielle had come to know it well. She had played a game here, passing the lonely summer hours, sharpening her skills.

She turned onto the narrow trail and as she did so, Gabrielle closed her eyes. This was the tricky part. She hadn't attempted this since childhood, and even then never at a dead run, as now. The object of the game was to get to the brook without opening her eyes. She had to use her inner sight and trust to the accuracy of that extra sense. Gathering the last shreds of her courage and strength, she began to run.

Bushes pressed in on her from either side and came together overhead to make the path almost tunnel-like in spots. There were dangers to the trail: low-hanging branches, sudden twists and turns, thorn bushes, rocks, tree roots, and gullies. At this speed, a misstep would mean a bad fall and broken bones. Then the game would really be over. But if there were dangers for her, there were dangers for him as well. His eyes would be useless. He would have to feel his way.

There was a terrible temptation to open her eyes, but Gabrielle resisted it. Trust was essential for the inner sight to work. Doubt and fear blinded it. If she opened her eyes and tried to navigate the trail by normal vision, she would never make it. He would be upon her. Instead she let her inner sense guide her and ran full-out, eyes closed, her lungs pulling in great gulps of air.

Suddenly, images and feelings bombarded her mind, and her steps faltered. Blackness, darker than the night, pushed at her. Waves of pain, fear, and despair broke over her and threatened to drag her down. She saw red behind her eyes. Blood . . . blood, suffering, terror, pain and death. They hammered at her, beat against her senses . . . stronger . . . stronger.

Gabrielle waited until the terror was almost overwhelming, then covered her face with her hands, took in a last ragged breath of air, and jumped. The time she hung in the air was only the space of a heartbeat, but it seemed to last forever. If she was wrong . . . If she had miscalculated . . .

Her feet came down solidly on the path, the impact sending a bolt of pain through her injured thigh. A moment later, she reached the end of the thicket. She could hear the rush of the rain-swollen brook close ahead. Her strength was spent. Too exhausted to continue, she dropped to her knees at the edge of the path and waited. Slowly, she opened her eyes.

The thicket had indeed slowed him down. It was a full minute before she heard him coming, his feet a dull pulsing sound above the roar of the brook. He was moving slowly, hindered by the dark. She could hear the rasp of his breathing, the heavy thud of his footsteps on the sodden ground. Then she heard something else. *Click.* The blessed sound was extraordinarily loud, but the scream that the man let out a split-second later was much louder. Then there was only the sound of the wind in the trees and the mutter of the brook.

Gabrielle buried her face in her hands. Laughter welled up in her, and she was horrified by it. She tried to hold it back but it came, crazy, joyous. She staggered to her feet and set off along the edge of the brook at a limping run.

The woods around Harringdale were rich in game: foxes, deer, racoons, rabbits. Harringdale men had hunted here for generations. Gabrielle could abide the hunters. An arrow or a bullet was a small thing, and unless the man was a good shot the animal often got away. Death, if it came, was usually quick and sure. It was the trappers she hated. They set their traps on the animals' favorite trails and disguised them with dirt and leaves. Then they went home to their warm, comfortable houses and let the traps do their dirty work. There was no sport in it. Worst of all, a trap seldom killed the animal outright but simply mutilated it. The steel jaws would hold their suffering prey for hours, sometimes days, before death put an end to the pain.

As a child, Gabrielle had waged her own personal campaign against the trappers. A trap gave off a mental stench of suffering and death that was nearly overpowering. Her inner self could sense it, even when the trapper had taken great pains to conceal it. She'd become expert at locating and springing them. If she found an animal caught in one, she released it and made it well.

Now, for once, the tables were turned. The hunter had become a victim. The thought filled her with a righteous joy that she could not contain.

It was over. Thank God, it was over. Even the storm was moving off, the thunder now only a vague rumbling in the distance. The rain had stopped. As she walked through the dripping trees she began to tremble, and she realized that it was her taut nerves beginning to relax. The trembling increased, became a quaking that rattled her teeth and shook her to the very bones. It was more than cold, more than nerves. Deep down, some wiser, more practical part of herself knew that it was really not over at all. Not for her.

She'd won a battle, a brief skirmish. But her enemies were not dead and though she'd hurt them, she sensed they would not give up. They knew who she was. They would be back.

The war had just begun. It would not end except in death—theirs ... or hers. Cold closed around her, and it was not due to her wet clothes, the bite of the wind, or shock from her injury. It was the icy touch of Death on her soul, and it stayed with her, an unwelcome companion, as she made her way through the dark trees toward the distant lights of the highway.

Chapter Seven

Shaking. The earth was shaking. Klaus Brauer put out a hand to steady himself. There was a roaring in his ears. Soon there would be light ... white, searing the eyes like a thousand suns. The sound and the shaking changed to pain. It filtered into the dark recesses of his mind, pulling it from unconsciousness to merciless clarity. Brauer opened his eyes, or, more accurately, his left eye. The right was pasted shut. Confusion filled him. There was no light, as he had expected. Only darkness and pain.

Gunner Hahn's voice came from the dark. "Hurry. We must get out of here." He shook Brauer again and reality reasserted itself. This was not the Berlin of 1942. He was lying in a chapel, in a convent full of dead nuns, and the danger of discovery was becoming greater with every passing minute. Impatiently, he shoved Hahn away.

Hurry was impossible. He sat up carefully, cradling his ruined face in his hands. The pain made him groan aloud. With trembling fingers, he explored the damage. Beneath his hands ran an unfamiliar landscape. Where the jut of a cheekbone should have been, a great hollow now existed. The smooth slope of his nose had become a slalom of bloody flesh and cartilage. His hands came away sticky with gore.

Slowly, awareness reached beyond the pain. How long had he been unconscious? The chapel was quiet . . . too quiet. The rain had stopped. In spite of the pain, he turned his head and tried to look around. By the candlelight he made out Hahn, looking winded and weary, leaning on the altar for support. There was no sign of the girl.

Sensing the unspoken question, Hahn answered, "She got away."

"You let her escape? You—"

Brauer broke off. The words were thick, garbled. His mouth was full of blood. He spit it out, along with several broken teeth. However, it was not that that made him silent. He had lived out his life unhindered by rules, except for one. He had always insisted on personal honesty. He might lie, cheat, steal, or murder to accomplish his goals, but he would never lie to himself.

You. You let her get away. Not Hahn. The fault is yours. Now she is gone . . . and Brimstone with her.

Moving with infinite care, he shifted onto his hands and knees and reached out to the altar for support. It took an effort of will just to hold his head up. The right side of his face was beginning to swell, and it felt like a hundred-pound weight. Using the edge of the altar, he began to pull himself up. Hahn caught him under the arms and hauled him to his feet. Brauer noticed that the younger man's face was scratched and bloody, and that Hahn seemed to be favoring one leg.

"Report," he said.

"She led me on a chase through the woods, straight into a rabbit trap. I think my ankle's broken."

"We must go after her."

Hahn shook his head. "We'd never find her in those woods. At this very moment she's probably on her way back here with the police. I can barely walk, and you're not going to be able to keep on your feet much longer. We both need a doctor. Face it, Colonel. It's over. We've lost."

"No."

Brauer shook his head in denial. The resulting pain nearly caused him to black out. He rested the uninjured side of his face on the cool marble top of the altar and fought for control. Hahn was right. They could not go after her tonight. And probably not tomorrow, or even the day after. The mending would take time. But he was very wrong about one thing. It was not over. They might not have the girl, but he was fairly sure of where she had gone. Rhode Island was the smallest of the states. Somehow . . . some way . . . he would find her.

Leaning on each other, welded together by the darkness so as to resemble some shambling, two-headed, many-limbed monstrosity, the two made their way back to the car. Hahn drove, working the gas and brake with his good foot, his teeth gritted against the pain.

Brauer lay on the backseat. Every bump and turn of the road sent ripples of agony through the shattered bones of his face. As if that were not enough, the tumor in his belly suddenly flared to life, like a furnace kicking on. Consciousness dimmed to a single red ember. Then, blessedly, even that small flame gutted out.

* * *

Jake Morgan sat in the corner booth of Kreppner's All-Nite Diner, his face toward the window, his back to the rest of the clientele. Even at this time of night, the diner was crowded. It had a reputation for good food, and was a favorite stopping point for most of the long-distance truckers, like himself.

Jake ate mechanically, a human steam shovel, the eating utensils looking like a child's doll's toys in his great hands. One forkful of beef stew after another found its way into his huge maw. He mopped up the gravy with Kreppner's famous buttermilk biscuits and washed the whole mess down with a tall glass of Coke. When the waitress came to clear the dishes away, he ordered coffee and a helping of apple pie. The girl was nervous. The dishes clattered in her hands as she stacked them, and a fork skittered from the untidy pile to fall with a loud *ping* onto the gray linoleum floor. Jake bent and retrieved it for her. Avoiding his eyes, she scuttled away without so much as a "thank you."

Jake sighed and steepled his hands, gazing out through the broad pane-glass window at the night. The rain had stopped. That was not part of his plan, but it would not interfere. The road was still wet. That was enough. It would have to be. His thoughts were interrupted as the waitress returned with his pie and coffee.

She set them before him, and her eyes met his reflection in the window. The coffee sloshed out of the cup, filling the saucer and spilling over to form a small brown puddle on the Formica tabletop.

"I'm sorry. I'll get you another cup." She began to mop at the spill with a paper napkin.

"It's all right. Just bring the check, please."

He paid the check, adding a generous tip. He was used to awkward service, and he didn't want to be remembered as a bad tipper. The girl retreated at last, leaving him alone with his coffee, his dessert, and his thoughts.

He added cream and sugar to the coffee and then, cupping the mug in his hands, stared down into the muddy liquid. Faces seemed to form there. Gwen, Jeremy, and the baby. The thought of his granddaughter's toothless grin brought a lump to Jake's throat. He took a swallow of the coffee and quickly forced his train of thought to chug on by to Ellen. A lawyer in the family—who would ever have thought it—but by next year she'd have her degree in hand. He had no doubt about that. Ellen went after whatever she wanted, and she always got it. Heaven help the poor attorney who went up against her. His daughters made him feel proud. Both had found their happiness. They would be just fine when he—

Abruptly, Gracie's face appeared. It bore a disapproving frown, so out of character with her usual sunny disposition. Her voice chided him.

"Jacob Morgan, whatever can you be thinking of? It's a sin against God and against everything we had together. I'll not have it!"

The camera of his mind moved back, from a closeup to a long shot, and he saw her stamp her foot in emphasis.

"I miss you, Gracie. I've tried to get on with it, just like I promised, but it's not working. I can't go home to that empty house anymore. Try to understand."

But she wouldn't understand, of course. Gracie

had never been one to abide a coward. The figure wavered, then faded. He saw only coffee once more.

Jake stabbed angrily at the pie. Anger was not a good thing in a man of his size. It was an emotion he seldom allowed himself to indulge in, but the unfairness of life made him seethe. Gracie had been the best part of that life. More than a wife, she'd been his best friend. She'd given him two wonderful daughters, and years of happiness, and not a night had gone by that he hadn't gotten down on his knees and thanked God for the gift of her. Then, without the slightest warning, God had taken that gift back.

The stroke had been massive and quick. She was in the kitchen, fixing their dinner, when he heard her crash to the floor. By the time he'd reached her, she was gone. All the joy in his life had gone with her.

Jake finished the pie and sipped at his cooling coffee, remembering the "What If" talk. They'd had it one sleety afternoon, when the sky had been cold and gray and the talk had turned morbid: the old "If-You-Go-First-And-I'm-Left-I-Promise-To-Carry-On" Talk. He'd promised and she'd promised, never suspecting that the bluff would be called so soon. He'd tried. God knows, he'd tried for six long months, and that was too long. The plan was simple. It would put an end to his pain and tie up all the loose ends of his life, all at once.

Just outside of Harringdale, over the next rise, was a stretch known as Three Mile Hill. Its name pretty much described it. The highway curved its way down the mountain, the grade so steep that it made your ears pop by the time you reached the bottom. The hill ended in a sharp left-hand curve. Here the shoulder of the road dropped away, seventy-five feet of sheer rock face, with more rock below. The state police made their presence felt on the hill, in an effort to slow people down. When winter storms made the going slick they closed the hill altogether, detouring traffic onto a safer route. At all times, trucks were required to use low gear.

Still, several times each year some hapless trucker or motorist failed to make the curve and hurtled through the flimsy guardrail to smash on the rocks below. To date, no one had survived. Jake did not intend to break that record.

Oh, there would be an investigation. That was sure as death and taxes. But it was a moonless night, and the road was wet. The insurance company would pay in the end. Gwen and Jeremy would have a down payment for the house they'd always wanted, and Ellen would have more than enough to finish her schooling. They'd be just fine, all taken care of . . . and so would he.

There'd never be another like Gracie: someone who could overlook so much and still love him, just as he was. Other men might be able to find someone else, but not he. She'd been one-of-a-kind. He couldn't go home to that house, so empty yet so full of memories. No. It would be better this way. Better for everyone. Jake Morgan took a last swallow of his coffee and stared out into the lonely night.

The lights of the diner looked warm and inviting to Gabrielle. Trucks filled the parking lot—great eighteen-wheeled rigs, lined up in hulking rows. She limped from the woods into the dark corridor between two of them and peered around the back corner of one to stare longingly at the diner.

How she needed that warmth and light. Still, she hesitated. People meant questions. Questions required answers ... answers she couldn't give. They would call the police. She didn't want that. The police would be drawn into it soon enough. Tomorrow, Father Brennan would come to the chapel for nine o'clock mass and discover what had happened. Before then, Gabrielle wanted to be far away.

Mother Margarethe hadn't trusted the Harringdale police to save her. Gabrielle had even less reason to put faith in them. Memories of her childhood filled her mind, still fresh, as if they had happened yesterday, instead of fifteen years past: *Her father coming home late at night in a drunken rage and beating her mother—not just the usual black eye or swollen lip—but backing her into a corner of the kitchen, up against the wall where she couldn't escape him, and then hitting her over and over again. Awakening to the dull, persistent thud of the blows and her mother's screams. ... Creeping silently down the hall to the phone in her parents' bedroom and calling the police.*

Gabrielle frowned. They came quickly enough ... and took both her parents away; her mother to the emergency room and her father to a warm cell to "cool off." Gabrielle had spent the night with a neighbor. The next day, her parents came home. Her father was hung over and sullen. Her mother moved around the house like a silent ghost. Gabrielle had used her gift to heal the cuts and bruises, but she could do nothing to erase the fear from her mother's eyes. After the police left, things had gone back to normal. That afternoon, while her mother was at work, Matthew Prescott took out his anger on Gabrielle. She hadn't bothered to call the police that time. Two months later, a shotgun blast had ended it all.

She closed her eyes and leaned against the cold, solid bulk of the truck. If she went to the police, they might protect her for a time. They would investigate the murders, make their reports ... but it would come to nothing. They would not find the men. She knew that, just as she knew that her two attackers were not dead. Eventually the police would give up, and the men in black would return and finish what they'd started. She had to get away.

Reluctantly, she turned away from the diner. She had to get to Rhode Island and rid herself of the envelope in her pocket. That was what they wanted—not her. With that gone, they might leave her alone.

She'd been walking slowly behind the row of trucks, feeling safe in their giant shadow. Suddenly, a hand shot out of the dark recess between two of them and caught her wrist. She was yanked roughly into the darkness, and before she had time to scream Gabrielle found herself trapped against the side of one of the trucks. Strong arms held her from behind in a great bear hug and a hand was clamped tightly over her mouth. She couldn't move.

"Well, what have we here?" said the one whose hand was over her mouth.

"I don't know, but it sure looks nice." This came from over her shoulder. He laughed. At the same time Gabrielle felt a hand close on her left breast and squeeze. "Feels nice, too."

"What you doin' out here at this time of night, pretty lady? Looking for a good time?"

Gabrielle's eyes were becoming accustomed to the dark. In her initial terror she'd thought that the men in black had found her, but now she saw that she was wrong. There were two of them. She knew nothing of the one behind her, except that he was big and very strong. Her arms felt as if they were in a vise. The man before her she could make out all too clearly.

He was half a head taller than she and smelled of onions and old sweat. His hair was long and uncombed. A greasy, tangled shock of it hung down over the center of his forehead, like a horse's mane. The front of his shirt was unbuttoned halfway to the waist and dark curls of hair, thick as moss, showed through the vee. A toothpick jutted from the corner of his mouth. It jerked nervously up and down as he played with it with the tip of his tongue. It danced spasmodically when he ran greedy eyes down the length of her.

"Oh my, but I had a feeling this morning that today was my lucky day." With his free hand he reached up and took the toothpick from his mouth, flinging it away into the darkness. " 'Come into my parlor, said the spider to the fly.' But you're no fly, baby. More like a honeybee."

He reached out and pulled the few remaining pins from her hair, watching the thick, heavy weight of it fall about her shoulders. "What do you say, sweetheart? You got some honey for me?"

His hand locked in her hair, forcing her head forward. His other hand came off her mouth. Then he was kissing her, his mouth grinding brutally into hers. In desperation, she bit his lip and managed to wrench her head away. She tried to scream, but the sound was cut short as his hand clamped across her mouth once more.

He licked blood from his lip, rolling his tongue across the wound slowly, lazily, watching her eyes follow the movement. He grinned. "Get her into the truck."

They half carried, half dragged her toward the cab of the nearest rig. She knew what they meant to do. She could feel the waves of heat that came from them, and the hard urgency of the one who held her as he pressed himself against her back. She fought them with all her strength, kicking and struggling.

One kick must have hit home, for the smaller one let out a muffled grunt. He released his hold on her legs. Gabrielle saw one hairy hand rub at his shin, then tighten into a fist. He hit her hard across the side of her head. Pain exploded like a supernova inside her skull, as brain and bone collided. Then she was falling down . . . down . . . to a place where the pain and terror could not follow. She knew no more.

Chuckie Carson—C.C., to the few friends he had—climbed into the cab and pulled the door closed behind him, leaving Stan Pitoniak to keep watch outside. Stan would have his turn, but only after C.C. was through. C.C. liked his meat fresh. If Stan had no imagination and was content with leftovers, that was his problem, but C.C. always had first dibs. That was understood.

C.C. was lucky. Even those who hated his guts had to admit that. Today had been no exception. He was supposed to have spent this morning in court on a rape charge, but the victim, one Susan J. Warner, age fourteen, had suddenly decided to drop the charges. When she'd apprised her lawyer of this she failed to mention that she'd been getting obscene and threatening phone calls for a week, and that just yesterday the family cat, Muffin, had been found hanging from the apple tree in the backyard with his eyes cut out. Yes, C.C.'s luck had held, and he'd spent the day at The Blue Moon pool hall instead. He and Stan had dropped into Kreppner's for a cheese steak and were just about to cruise the town, in search of a little action, when they'd spotted the girl coming out of the woods. With C.C.'s usual luck, the action had come to him.

Luck: C.C. had it, and there was no denying it. Even finding this particular truck unlocked was part of it. The cab was new, plush and padded, with a sleeping compartment in the rear. For the most part C.C. was used to taking his pleasure where he found it: in the backseat of a car, or under the bleachers at the high school stadium. Tonight, it would be first-class all the way.

He licked his swollen lip, tasting onions and the sweet, overlying flavor of the girl. She lay huddled in the curtained-off sleeping compartment, where Stan had dumped her. She was conscious, but just barely. Her eyes were glazed. Her breathing was coming fast and shallow and she was trembling all over, like a palsy victim. C.C. had seen the look before. It disappointed him. He liked it when they fought. He knew just how to take the fight out of them, and he enjoyed doing it. But there would be no more fight from this one. She was far away, in another world—another universe, even.

Sitting behind the wheel, C.C. unbuckled his

belt. He unbuttoned the bulging fly of his jeans and, arching his back, pushed them and his shorts down around his knees. The rain-cooled air touched the heat of him and he moaned softly in anticipation. He moved onto the edge of the cot and began to pull the curtain in place behind him. It would be a disappointment to Stan, for Stan liked to watch. But the luck belonged to C.C. and not Stan. It was a shame, in a way, for tonight C.C. was feeling good, and it would have been a hell of a good show. He hooked his fingers into the neckline of her dress, taking his time. The truckers who pulled into Kreppner's were tired and hungry and, though the food was excellent, the service was notoriously slow. C.C. had all the time in the world.

Behind him the latch of the door clicked, and cool air brushed across his bare buttocks as the curtain billowed inward. He began to turn, angry at the interruption. He would give Stan a tongue-lashing the dumb Polack would never forget. The words froze on his lips.

The hulking frame that filled the doorway did not belong to Stan Pitoniak. For a moment C.C. was not even sure it was human at all. Irrational images of bears and apes filled his mind as ham-sized fists closed on his ankles and jerked him from the cab. His head struck the door frame on the way out.

The hands released him. Dazed, he scrambled to his knees. He looked up. His assailant towered over him, a monstrous shadow. A stray beam of light from the café glittered off the tire iron in his hand. Behind him C.C. could make out the dark silhouette of Stan Pitoniak, sprawled prone on the asphalt.

"Get out of here." The voice was a low growl. "Take that other piece of ratshit with you and get gone, or I'll fix you both so you never want a woman again."

"You got no right to order me around," C.C. squeaked. "I'll call the police."

"You've got no right to what's in there." The tire iron tapped the window of the truck lightly. "This is my rig. Now you get your skinny ass moving, or I'll call the police and we'll just see whose story they listen to."

C.C. didn't argue anymore. He lurched to his feet, nearly tripping in his haste, as his pants tangled about his ankles. He yanked them up and, holding them in one hand, turned to run. Stan was all on his own. Before he could take a step, however, a giant hand had caught him by the waist of his jeans and lifted him clear off the ground.

"I said take him with you."

The hand released him and he nearly fell on top of Stan, who was awake now and making a strange keening sound, like a puppy taken too soon from its mother. C.C. got him under the arms and hauled him to his feet. Together, they staggered across the parking lot to the highway, C.C. battling to hold up both his jeans and Stan. Just at the edge of the lot, beneath Kreppner's flashing neon sign, Stan's feet hit a patch of mud and the battle was lost. He went down, taking C.C. with him. A passing motorist was treated to a twin moonrise as C.C.'s pants went south while the rest of him went north.

As he landed full-length in a puddle, C.C. was forced to the realization that perhaps his luck was changing for the worse . . . or maybe had run out altogether.

*   *   *

Jake Morgan peered through the driver's window of his rig, apprehensive at what he would find. The creep hadn't been in there long enough to really do anything to the girl. He knew that. But the truck was too still, too silent. Softly, he opened the door.

The sleeping compartment was cloaked in shadow. Jake gingerly pulled the curtain aside. The young woman was huddled in the far corner. She didn't react when Jake leaned toward her. In the red light from Kreppner's sign, her eyes were glassy and staring. One side of her face was beginning to swell slightly. For one fearful moment, Jake thought she was dead. Then he picked up the soft, desperate sound of her breathing.

Shock. He'd been on the road enough years to have seen more accidents than most state troopers, and he knew the look. He'd seen it on the face of a young father, whose minivan had rear-ended an oil truck and burned, along with his wife and three children. The unfortunate man had been thrown clear. He'd seen the look on his own face too many mornings lately, when he looked in the mirror. Blinking rapidly, he reached out, took the girl's hand, and began chafing it gently.

"Hey. Hey there, Miss. It's okay now. They're gone. Nobody's going to hurt you. It's all right."

The girl continued to stare. As Jake's eyes grew accustomed to the darkness inside the cab, he noticed something strange. Her clothes were muddy and torn. Her skirt was hiked up high, almost to her left hip, and there was a long, angry-looking weal on the flesh of her outer thigh. Jake knew a bullet graze when he saw one. Both curious and embarrassed, he reached out and pulled the hem of her skirt down and into place. There were two telltale holes in the gray cloth, where the bullet had come and gone. Jake frowned.

He'd seen the two creeps through the window of the diner and known immediately that they were up to no good. Remembering that he'd neglected to lock the truck, he'd followed them. Sure enough, they'd worked their way down the line of rigs, testing the doors until they found that his were open. But instead of trying to jump-start the truck, they'd gone around the back. Curious, he'd crept up on them, staying low, waiting for an opportunity to get at the tire iron that he kept for just such an occasion, mounted in a custom-built set of brackets above the coupling on the exterior of the cab.

He'd seen them grab the girl. He'd had to wait until they were both up front, on the driver's side, busy getting her into the truck. Then he'd edged around the passenger side and gotten the iron. At any rate, in those moments between when he'd left the diner and when he'd ambushed the big one, who was too busy gawking through the window to keep guard, he hadn't seen any sign of a gun. To be sure, if they'd had a gun, he'd be dead meat right now. So where had the bullet wound come from?

He edged along the cot and pulled the girl's limp form into a sitting position. He didn't want to leave her alone, but if she didn't respond soon he'd have to do just that, and run into Kreppner's to call an ambulance. He decided to give it one more try.

"Miss, everything's all right now. Please wake up. Miss . . . ?"

Gabrielle heard the voice, as if from a great distance. It filtered down through layers of graduating darkness to the silence where she lay. Warmth came with it. It touched her, like sunlight on her skin, comforting, healing. She reached for the warmth ... and saw, not sunlight, but more darkness.

Her eyes took in the night-shrouded cab of the truck and the silhouette of the man, hunched beside her. With remembering, came terror.

"No!"

She struck out at him with her fists, but he caught her arms easily and held her at bay. He was talking, but the words did not penetrate beyond her fear. At last, it was the warmth that got through. She realized that it was coming from him: compassion, concern. This was not one of the men who had attacked her. She felt only good things from this man. As she relaxed, he quickly released her wrists and retreated to the driver's seat.

"I'm sorry. Those men ... I thought you were one of them."

"It's okay. They're gone. Do you want me to call the police? Or I could take you to the hospital; I saw your leg's hurt."

"No. No police. No doctors." Gabrielle paused, aware that the words had come too quickly. She edged from the shelter of the sleeping compartment and sat down in the passenger seat. "Please. I just need a minute to think."

Her hand came to rest on her thigh, and she quickly drew it away as pain burned along the wound there. Taking care not to touch it again, she smoothed the folds of her skirt, playing for time. She tried to decide what to do.

She couldn't go back ... or to the police ... or to a hospital. The men who'd murdered the sisters would find her. She had to go on and fulfill her promise to Mother Margarethe. That was the only path to possible safety. She was hurt, hungry, and tired, nearly at the end of her strength. There was no one she could turn to for help, no one but ... Brushing her hair back from her eyes, combing the tangled mass with her fingers, she surreptitiously studied her rescuer.

He sat in shadow behind the wheel, a great mountain of a man. If his size was intimidating, the warmth that emanated from him reassured her. She sensed only kindness here, goodness, and a fathoms-deep sorrow. There was no harm in him, and right now he was all that she had.

"Where are you going?" she asked.

"North—Maine. Then on into Canada."

"Are you going anywhere near Rhode Island?"

"I could be." He hesitated, staring off across the parking lot. He didn't look at her when he spoke. "Look, I don't know what kind of trouble you're in, but I do know that that's a bullet wound on your leg. You don't want to go to the police. You don't want me to call a doctor. What am I supposed to think? Except for a speed limit or two, I've never broken the law in my life. I don't want to start now."

Gabrielle took a deep breath. "I'll tell you what I can. There are two men after me—evil men. They want this." She took the envelope from her pocket and held it out to him. "I don't know what's in it and frankly, I don't want to. It was entrusted to me by someone I love, for me to deliver to Rhode Island. She died because of it. A dozen people have died tonight, and I may be next. I only want to get it to the person it belongs to. Then, I believe I'll be safe. I haven't done anything illegal, unless defending yourself is a crime."

"Then why don't you go to the police?"

"I don't think the police can protect me from these men. If you had met them, you'd understand. Look, maybe it's unfair of me to ask you for help. I won't blame you if you just tell me to get out, and you go your way. There's a real chance that you could get yourself killed. I promise you one thing, though: By helping me, you might be putting yourself in great danger, but you won't be breaking the law."

She bit her lips. There was nothing more to say. If he refused to help her, she didn't know what to do. He sat hunched over the wheel for a long time, a dark, stony silhouette. He turned the envelope over and over in his hands. It crackled, the sound dry and brittle, as if from a thing long dead.

Jake stared at the envelope, shook it, squeezed it, but did not open it. He thought of the girl's warnings of danger and almost laughed aloud. He wondered if she would be so anxious to ride with him if she had any suspicion of what he'd been contemplating in the diner, just moments ago. Dying didn't worry him at all. Living was the hard thing.

There was something about her ... something that made him believe her cockeyed story. The earnestness in her voice engendered trust. As to his other plans ... Well, he'd be back this way again in a week or two. The hill and the curve would still be there.

Abruptly, he handed the envelope back to her, then leaned forward and turned the ignition key. The great diesel engine roared to life.

"Where in Rhode Island am I taking you?"

"Newport ... Oh, thank you! Thank you so much!" Gabrielle felt tears prick at her eyes and forced them back. If she let herself cry now, she would not be able to stop.

He turned toward her to glance at the side mirror, then the huge rig began to back slowly out of the lot. As the truck swung around, the light from Kreppner's sign illuminated his face. Gabrielle gasped. The whole left side was an angry, mottled red. The discoloration extended across his cheek, past the angle of his jaw, and down the side of his neck. Its upper limits spread around his left eye and then moved in a ragged line across his forehead to disappear into his thick shock of gray hair. His face looked seared or horribly scalded.

He jammed on the brakes and put one hand to his cheek to cover the deformity, quickly facing forward again so that his good side was toward her. There was something defensive in the gesture. He turned toward her slightly and peered at her out of his right eye.

"I'm sorry. I should have warned you. In all the excitement, I forgot. It's a birthmark—the doctors call it a 'port-wine stain.' It's not catching or anything. I didn't mean to scare you."

"It's okay. I was surprised, that's all." Gabrielle, who was starting to recover from her fright, now felt embarrassed both for him and for herself. She sought to ease the awkwardness of the situation. "We never really introduced ourselves. Do you have a name?"

He smiled. Slowly he turned his head until he was facing her, and she sensed the immense courage the movement had required of him. The birthmark didn't seem so frightening now that she was prepared for it. He held out a huge hand. "Name's Jake Morgan. What's yours?"

She shook his hand with a seriousness that turned his smile to a laugh.

"Brie," she said, after a moment's thought. "My name is Brie."

Chapter Eight

Newport, R.I.
4:15 A.M.

David Kauffman tossed and turned, unable to find
a comfortable position on the large double bed. The
night was hot, despite the breeze off the ocean. The
sheets lay in a sweat-soaked tangle at the foot of
the bed. He tried to lie still, to synchronize his
heart rate and breathing with the slow, steady ticking of the grandfather clock in the hall. Even that
didn't work. His mind was still racing at light
speed.

At last, he gave in to the inevitable. He knew
from past experience that there would be no more
sleep for him tonight. Wearily he sat up, running
a hand through his black, curly hair. He stood up
and stretched. Tension had formed a knot in the
hollow between his shoulder blades. Pulling on
jeans and a T-shirt, he padded barefoot down the
hallway, past the closed door of his father's bedroom, and tiptoed downstairs to the kitchen.

Working quietly, he brewed a pot of coffee in the
coffee maker. He fished about in the cabinet above

the refrigerator until he'd found a pack of cigarettes. When the coffee was ready, he lit up. As
the smoke filled his lungs, he let himself think
about the manuscript.

The book was driving him crazy. Oh, he would
get it back on track—four novels on the bestseller
list in as many years attested to that. Still, the
process didn't get any easier. Like a runner in a
long-distance marathon, he always hit the wall just
past the midpoint of each book. The action that had
been going along so nicely suddenly would die, the
characters seem hopelessly lifeless and boring. There
was nothing to do but tough it out, keep battering at
the book, trying one approach after another until his
subconscious coughed up the right one.

When he hit the wall it started him smoking
again, a habit he'd formed in Vietnam. He always
managed to give it up once the book kicked back
into gear. He hated the habit, but rationalized that
it was better than the steady diet of alcohol that
had seen him through the first two books. He had
not become an alcoholic, but the potential was
there. He drank only rarely these days, and never
when he felt he needed to, as now.

He finished his first cup of coffee. Before pouring
another, he tiptoed to the den and took a fistful of
pencils and a folder of manuscript pages and blank
paper from the top drawer of his desk. Returning
to the kitchen, he fixed another cup, lit a second
cigarette, and began to mark the manuscript, adding here, deleting there. Later, when the sun rose,
he barely noticed.

David dumped the cold remnants of his cup of
coffee into the sink as footsteps sounded on the

stairs. When they entered the dining room and approached the kitchen, he quickly stubbed out his cigarette and stashed the ashtray full of butts on the kitchen windowsill, behind the frilly Cape Cod curtains. Both actions were to no avail. His father bustled into the kitchen, sniffed the air, surveyed the empty cup with a frown.

"So, you're breakfasting on tar, nicotine, and caffeine once again. Things are still not going well."

David shrugged. "Jacob had an angel to wrestle with. I have this damn book."

"So, look on the bright side. Angels are tough characters, and still Jacob won. You'll win, too. You have before." Samuel Kauffman swept the curtain aside, emptied the ashtray into the garbage pail. "That is, if the coffee and cigarettes don't kill you first." He shooed David toward the kitchen table. "You clean up that mess and I'll fix you some breakfast. You're too skinny. When you turn sideways, you look like a toothpick. Soon there'll be nothing left of you. Then who will support me in my old age?"

"You're already in your old age, and you're doing just fine without any help from me."

"Bite your tongue."

Smiling to himself, David began gathering up the sheaf of papers that was now scattered across the kitchen table. Balls of crumpled paper littered the linoleum floor, mute testimony to last night's wrestling match. His father's voice droned on. David dropped into a chair with an attitude of bemused resignation. He knew what was coming next, line for line, like a movie script they'd rehearsed over and over.

"I shouldn't be doing this, you know," Samuel

chided, as he cracked eggs into the skillet. "You should have a wife to cook your breakfast, and your children should be running around the table, making fingerprints on the windows and walls. Your walls are entirely too clean."

"You're right, Dad. You shouldn't be doing this. I'm thirty-six years old. If I want breakfast, I'm perfectly capable of cooking it myself."

The older man ignored him, dropping slices of bread into the toaster. "You sit all hours of the day and night in front of that computer thing, and—"

"Word processor, Dad."

"You sit there with no companionship, getting thinner and older every—"

"I don't need companionship. I need to be alone in order to write."

"Soon you'll be so thin and so old that the women won't even look at you."

"I don't need women to look at me. I'm perfectly happy just the way I am. I'm fine, really. Anyway, I don't see you rushing out to marry again. All these years you've done just fine."

"Some women are irreplaceable. Your mother, God rest her soul, was one of them. I could not find another like her in a thousand years, and I will not settle for less. But my situation is not your situation. Look at your Marsha. She didn't waste any time finding another man after the divorce. She has a family now. So should you."

"Maybe Marsha was irreplaceable," David countered.

"Marsha was a mistake, and you know it. She wasn't right for you. You find the one that's right for you, settle down with her, raise a family. Then you'll find out what happiness is. At this rate, I'll

be in my grave before you give me some grand-
children."

"Are you going out to the plant today?" David
asked, trying to change the subject.

"Maybe, maybe not. I'll see how I feel. The research department is all bright young college kids
now, full of energy and new ideas. They don't need
any old schlepp like me hanging around there."

"If they don't need you, why are you still assigned a lab?"

"They just don't want me to feel like I've been
put out to pasture, that's why. And while we're
talking about 'whys,' why are you so anxious for
me to go to the plant? First you nag me until I sell
my house and come to live with you, then you can't
wait to get me out. Tell me the truth, David. Is the
old man beginning to get on your nerves just a bit?"

"You know that's not true. I just think you'd be
happier if you went to work. When it comes to
research, you can dance rings around those young
college kids you're always harping about. The doctors said you could go back to all your normal activities. There was no need for you to retire."

"So what do the doctors know? I had a full physical just three months before my heart attack. They
tell me I'm sound as a dollar, and three months
later I'm in intensive care."

David held up his hands, placatingly. "Look, I'm
sorry. You do whatever you want. I'll stop nagging
about you going back to work, on one condition."

"Excuse me, now there are conditions. So what
is this big condition?"

"A truce. No more talk of marriage and grand-
children. In return, I won't nag you to go to the

plant. You can sit in a chair until cobwebs form on you and I won't say a word. Okay?"

The old man started to say something, thought better of it. "Okay, you win. Truce. Now eat your eggs. They're getting cold." He poured oat bran into a bowl, added skim milk. "If you want me, I'll be in the living room. I'm missing the *Today* show."

David watched him shuffle from the kitchen. He was worried about his father. Until last year, Samuel Kauffman had been a sprightly man who looked far younger than his seventy-odd years. That same youthfulness marked his work as Director of Research at Hampton Chemicals. At home, he'd led an active and varied social life. The heart attack had changed all that.

It had happened while he was home alone, in the small house in Boston where David had grown up. Samuel had barely managed to get to the phone and call for an ambulance before he'd collapsed.

The doctors had been optimistic. They'd prescribed a low-cholesterol diet and regular exercise, but other than that had encouraged Samuel to resume his normal routine. The prognosis for a long and happy life was excellent. Samuel would have none of it. Though the damage to his heart was minimal, the effects of the heart attack on his independent spirit were devastating.

Fear: David had seen it in the older man's eyes on the day they'd discharged him from the hospital—fear of pain, fear of dying, fear of being alone. He'd invited his father to come to Newport and live with him. Samuel had readily accepted, moving into one of the spare bedrooms and quickly making it his own.

Over David's protests, he'd handed in his resig-

nation at Hampton. The company had accepted it
with reluctance, at last persuading him to stay on
as a consultant, with a lab at his disposal. He did
go to the lab occasionally, when curiosity and boredom overcame the fear, but for the most part he
stayed at home, trying to help David out with the
cooking and cleaning, trying to stay out from un-
derfoot, and lately, trying his best to marry David
off.

David sighed, picking halfheartedly at the rapidly cooling eggs. The banter about grandchildren
was an old joke between them, a form of good-
natured teasing that had been going on for the past
twelve years, since his divorce from Marsha. Since
the heart attack, however, the teasing had taken
on an underlying earnestness. Faced with his own
mortality, Samuel was anxious for the reassurance
that a small bit of himself would go on into the
future. David understood, but after his painful and
short-lived marriage to Marsha he was reluctant to
become seriously involved again.

He didn't resent his father's sudden reentry into
his life. For the most part, they got along well. David's mother had died at his birth, and Samuel had
raised him alone. He'd been a devoted parent, more
than adequately filling the roles of both mother and
father. As David grew up, their relationship had
matured into a deep friendship.

David stood up and carried his plate to the sink.
He rinsed it and put it into the dishwasher, then
stopped for a moment to stare out the kitchen window. The backyard was a vast, green-gold expanse,
spreading down to the tall chain-link fence. Beyond
that, the deep blue of sea and sky began.

He pushed open the old wooden screen door and

set off barefoot across the lawn. At the far left corner of the property a gate was set into the fence,
held closed with a rusting chain and padlock.
David fished a key from the pocket of his jeans and
opened the lock. Once on the other side he fastened
it again, then scrambled down a short embankment
to a path that ran parallel with the shoreline.

This was Newport's famed Cliff Walk. It offered
a breathtaking view of the ocean on one side and a
behind-the-scenes peek at Newport's mansions on
the other. David glanced back at the house. Though
large, the old Victorian could hardly be called a
mansion. It was dwarfed by the huge estates on
either side of it. Still, David wouldn't have traded
it for all the mansions in the world.

The house had been the summer home of a
wealthy clothing manufacturer. It had come up for
sale just after David had gotten his advance for
Dark Morning. One look and David had fallen in
love with the place. The house was old and run-
down, badly in need of a face-lift and a new coat
of paint. Despite its appearance an inspection had
showed that its heart was sound, free of termites
or rot. David had paid the exorbitant price they
were asking and never once regretted it.

He turned off the path and clambered over the
rocks, cautious with his bare feet, until at last he
was standing on a huge boulder just above the surf.
He sat down and rolled up the legs of his jeans so
the spray could touch his bare skin. Content, he
sat and watched a flock of gulls that had come to
rest on the calmer water beyond the breakers.

This was the reason he'd invited his father to
come to live here. He found that the ocean had a
healing effect. There was peace in the rhythm of

the waves, in the sunlight's sparkle on the water. No matter how badly a book was going, no matter what he read in the headlines, when he came out here things seemed to fall into place and there was a fundamental rightness to the world. He had wanted to share that with his father, had felt sure the healing would touch him as well, but so far it hadn't happened.

Samuel's life had lost its meaning. Day after day he sat in front of the television set, his brilliant mind wasted on the endless drivel of soap operas and game shows. He needed a focus, something that would capture his imagination and draw him back into the mainstream of life. Still, knowing what was needed and finding it were two different things.

David stayed by the water long enough to take the edge off his worry, then started home. There was work to be done. A month ago he'd begun the facelift on the old house. Doing a little each day, he'd patiently scraped away the layers of cracked, peeling paint and then added fresh coats of pristine white.

The gingerbread trim was rotted in spots, so he'd taken down the damaged portions and, using compass and jigsaw, faithfully reproduced their lacy designs in his workshop. Last night he'd given the finished products their final coat of paint. Today they were ready for rehanging. Then the worst of it would be done.

As he stood in the center of the backyard and gazed up at the gleaming white expanse of the house, a feeling of frustration cooled the warmth of his accomplishment. The job had taken months of work, had torn the skin from his knuckles and put aches in muscles he hadn't known he had. Still, how he wished that he could rebuild his father's life so easily.

"Gracie was something. All those years I was on the road, she kept the family going . . . never complained. I'd be gone for days, sometimes weeks at a time, but she always sensed when I was coming home. I'd raise her on the CB, and by the time I pulled into the driveway she'd have a full meal waiting, dessert and all. She was a great cook, but it was her I came home to. The food didn't matter. I always fussed over her cooking 'cause it seemed to make her happy, but I should have fussed more over her. There was so much I wish I'd told her."

Jake took a deep breath. He couldn't stop talking. From the time they'd left Harringdale he'd been running off at the mouth, and he just couldn't stop. The thing was, Brie listened, *really* listened. It seemed to have nothing to do with politeness. Clearly she was interested, and genuinely cared.

"What would you have told her?"

"Well . . . how proud I was of her. I was gone so much she practically raised our girls by herself, and she did a good job of it. They're fine. Real fine. Then when the girls grew up and went off to college, she came along with me on the road. She learned to drive the rig. It's not easy. This thing's sixty-seven feet long and thirteen and a half feet high. It's no picnic to handle, but she managed it. She could drive as well as any man I know, and better than some.

"I think . . . mostly I'd tell her how much I loved her. And I'd tell her how much her love meant to me." He glanced at Brie. "I know it's hard to believe that a woman could love this ugly mug of mine, but she did. Lord, she loved me. It was the one sure thing in my life." His voice broke, and he looked quickly back at the road.

"I don't find it hard to believe at all, Jake. You're kind and good. I've only known you for a few hours, but I can tell you that when your Gracie looked at you she saw a beautiful man. Your face has nothing to do with it." She reached out and laid a hand on his arm. "And I think Gracie knew all those things, without you having to tell her. She was a lucky woman, and she knew it."

Silence fell between them, but it was a comfortable thing. Brie leaned back against the seat and closed her eyes. Her thoughts strayed for a moment—to Mother Margarethe and the other sisters. Tears threatened. She hastily pulled her mind back to the present and concentrated on Jake Morgan.

This gentle man would never know what he had done for her. As the night passed and he talked about himself, she clung to his words like a lifeline. His memories of his wife and family: small, everyday, normal things; they helped her to hold on to her sanity in a world that seemed mad and full of dangers. The very fact that people like Jake Morgan existed in that world—good people, kind people—replenished her hope.

It had been over twenty-four hours since she'd slept. The soft, steady hum of the tires and the gentle motion of the truck acted as a hypnotic. Somewhere in Connecticut sleep took her, deep and dreamless.

It was close to noon when Jake woke her. They were in Rhode Island, about to cross the Newport Bridge.

"Sleep well?"

"Yes, thank you. I feel much better."

Brie stared in awe at the blue expanse of water flowing beneath them. Born and raised in the mountains, she had never seen so much water in her life. She looked ahead to where the town squatted at the base of the bridge, and fear twitched at her mind. She felt safe with Jake Morgan. Soon she would have to leave his reassuring presence and go on alone. The unknown frightened her. Suddenly, the water looked very cold and deep. The thought of Jonah swallowed alive by the whale came to her mind. Brie shivered.

Much too soon for her liking, Jake pulled the truck into the parking lot of a small shopping center. He maneuvered it into a loading zone, set the brake, then turned to face her.

"Well, this is it. You can still change your mind, you know. There's lots of places you could hide out until you've had time to think on things." He hesitated, then added, "You're welcome to stay at my place for a spell. Lord knows, there're plenty of empty rooms."

Brie shook her head. "The offer's tempting, but I made a promise and I intend to keep it. I've put you to too much trouble already."

"It was no trouble."

He dug in his hip pocket, came up with two ragged twenties and some ones, and held them out to her. "Here. It's not much, but it'll get you a room for the night and a decent meal."

"That's not necessary. I have money." Brie pushed his hand away gently. She ran a hand through the tangled mass of her hair. "I could really use a comb, though."

Jake fumbled in his pocket again and pulled out a battered black pocket comb. Brie took it gratefully and began to work the knots out of her hair. Her eyes darted around the cab, in search of a mirror. Jake pointed to her right.

"Roll the window down, and tilt one of those until you can see yourself. I'll readjust it when you're through."

There were three mirrors mounted on the outside of the cab. Brie tugged at the large center one and it moved obligingly toward her. She frowned at her reflection. Her face was pale, her eyes redrimmed with exhaustion, her hair flaring out every which way. She did her best to smooth it down, then offered the comb to Jake.

"Keep it."

Brie tucked the comb in her pocket. "Thank you for everything."

They sat for a moment and simply looked at each other, then Brie leaned forward and took the trucker's grizzled face in her hands. Pulling him toward her, she kissed the disfigured left cheek. She let her hand linger there for a moment.

"God bless you, Jake Morgan. You'll never know how much your kindness has meant to me."

Jake swallowed hard. "Goodbye, Brie. Stay safe."

She opened the door and stepped down to the sidewalk. The summer heat closed around her. She didn't say good-bye.

Jake put one hand up to his cheek. Where she had kissed him, his face felt all warm and tingly. "Sentimental fool," he chided himself. Behind him, a horn honked impatiently.

"Okay, keep your shirt on. I'm movin'."

He stood up and leaned across the passenger seat to readjust the wing mirror. As he did so, he caught a glimpse of himself in its silvered surface.

He froze.

Reaching out with trembling hands, he jerked the mirror until he could face it head-on. His knees had gone all soft and rubbery. Unable to think or move, he sank down into the passenger seat, as the chorus of horns outside reached a furious crescendo.

Jake was oblivious to it. He stared into the mirror, watching tears weave a path through the two-days' growth of beard stubble on his face—an ordinary, everyday face, lined with sorrow and the years, but otherwise unmarked.

The hideous birthmark was gone.

Through a blur of tears he looked for her, but there was no sign of the plain gray dress among the throngs of brightly clad tourists crowding the sidewalks. Whoever she was . . . whatever she was . . . she was gone. Perhaps that was best. You just didn't question a miracle.

Jake fixed the mirror and moved back to the driver's seat. If he drove right on through, he could reach home by suppertime. Gwen wouldn't mind if he dropped in to visit with his granddaughter. Suddenly, he wanted to hold the baby real bad. It was important to hold her and tell her what a really beautiful world she'd been born into.

Chapter Nine

Gunner Hahn lay on the bed, his injured ankle wrapped in a towel. It wasn't broken, he'd determined that much. The trap had cut the skin and badly chewed into the surrounding muscle. It hurt like hell, but the bones seemed intact. From the adjacent bed, an intermittent moaning assured him that Brauer was still alive. Daylight had come. The grimy Venetian blinds on the windows did not keep out the bright sunlight, any more than they had kept out the red flashes of the "Vacancy" sign last night.

The motel was small and shabby, too far from any of the Poconos' main attractions to be a success. Hahn had roused the owner from sleep at 3:00 A.M., and the old man had needed their money too badly to be angered by the interruption. Hahn left the semiconscious Brauer in the car while he paid for their room. Despite the proximity of the flashing sign, Gunner had chosen the unit on the far end, close to the road, in case a quick getaway was needed. It was also far away from the office area and prying eyes. The owner had cared only for the money and asked no questions. Once he had the cash in hand, he'd given Hahn the key and quickly returned to the comfort of his bed. With the darkness as cover, Hahn had carried Brauer inside. He'd emerged from the room only once after that, to use the pay phone mounted in a lighted booth outside the motel office.

The crunch of tires on the gravel outside made him tense. A car door slammed. Taking his gun from its holster, he limped silently to the window and parted the blinds a finger's width. An old green station wagon was parked out front. Gunner edged to the door just as a knock sounded.

"Who is it?"

"Doctor Hutchinson. You called me."

Hahn slipped the chain lock from the door and edged it open just enough to allow entry. When Hutchinson was inside, he quickly locked the door once more. He pressed the gun to Hutchinson's rib cage and carefully patted him down, then rummaged through the small black bag the doctor carried, not putting away his weapon until he was certain the doctor was unarmed. Hutchinson tolerated the search with an air of boredom.

"All right," he said, when Hahn had finished. "You've seen what I don't have. Now you show me what you've got."

Hahn took a wallet from his back pocket, extracted five one-hundred-dollar bills, and handed them over.

Hutchinson pocketed them. He watched Hahn limp back to the bed. "Are you the patient?" he asked, coolly.

"Just give me something for the pain and leave some bandages on the bed. I'll take care of it." Gunner motioned toward Brauer. "Your patient's there."

"Suit yourself." Hutchinson opened his bag and extracted a bottle of tablets and a package of gauze bandage. He tossed them to Hahn. "Take two every four hours for pain."

Gunner swallowed the tablets dry, wincing at the bitter taste. He lay back against the pillows and studied Dr. Hutchinson. He had wondered what sort of doctor would respond to the emergency number that Brauer had given him. He doubted any reputable physician would be linked to the Neo-Nazis. The man was the sort he had expected, dressed in a shabby suit that sagged at the knees, his breath reeking of old beer. As the doctor reached to open the blinds, Gunner shook his head.

"Leave that alone. Use the lamp."

Hutchinson obliged, angling the shade of the small table lamp so that the light fell across Brauer's face. He took a pack of cigarettes from his bag, offered one to Hahn. Gunner refused. The pills were beginning to take effect. Already, the throbbing in his ankle had begun to ease. He closed his eyes, feeling strangely detached from the pain, from this place, this time. Sleep came, and he hadn't the strength to fight it off.

Dr. Randolph Hutchinson looked down at the ruin of a man that lay on the bed. He curled his lip in disgust. His cigarette was balanced precariously on the edge of the bedside table. The tip had burned down, and was beginning to blacken the light pine of the tabletop. As Hutchinson picked it up deftly between thumb and forefinger, a gray shower of ash fell onto the worn blue rug. He ground it into the pile with the toe of his shoe, took a last drag on the cigarette, then stubbed it out against the metal frame of the bed. He turned his attention back to his patient.

Using gauze pads and a liberal amount of disinfectant, he cleaned the blood away from what was left of the face. The flesh was laid open all the way from the right cheekbone, across the smashed bridge of the nose, down the left cheek to the corner of the chin. The left side of the upper lip was split wide. Yellowed teeth showed through the gap in the flesh. Examination showed that the left ear was gone, but that was an old wound.

Plastic surgery was needed, and that was not his field. He could stitch the torn flesh back together, give antibiotics to prevent infection, but the cosmetic repairs that were necessary went far beyond his skills. He shuddered inwardly at the thought of what his crude repair job would look like when it healed. Still, the poor bastard would not have to live with the result for very long.

Cancer.

He had recognized the look immediately. The old man was a walking corpse, undoubtedly in constant pain. He had weeks—perhaps a month or two—left, at best.

The doc took a packet of sutures from his bag and opened them on the nightstand, careful to maintain their sterility. No matter what the world thought of him, Randolph Hutchinson still had his standards. He took out a package of disposable gloves. Best to get this over with while the poor sonofabitch was still unconscious.

"What are you doing?"

The voice was surprisingly strong, though thick from the torn tissues. Like the other man, he had a heavy accent. German? Hutchinson saw dark eyes peering at him through the swollen slits of the lids. He removed the outer paper from the pack of gloves.

"I'm going to stitch up your face."

"Who are you?"

"I could ask you the same, though I doubt you'd give me a straight answer." Hutchinson took a syringe from his bag, and a small vial of local anesthetic. "I'm a doctor. Your friend contacted the people I work for, and here I am. That's all you need to know." He drew several cc's of medication into the syringe.

"Some doctor. You smell like a beer hall." The slitted eyes flickered toward the syringe. "What's that?"

Hutchinson was growing tired of the questions. "It's anesthetic. . . . Or would you like me to stitch you without it? It's going to be a long job."

The man laid a scrawny hand on the doctor's wrist and pushed the hand with the syringe away. "That won't be necessary. I have my own anesthetic." His jaundiced eyes swept the room, finally coming to rest on the bureau that stood against the far wall. "There. Bring my kit."

Hutchinson hesitated, then he shrugged, capped the syringe, and returned it to his bag. He plucked the small leather overnight kit from the bureau and deposited it on the bed. The old man gestured impatiently.

"You handle it, *Herr Doktor*. You'll find everything you need there. Two hundred milligrams should be sufficient."

Hutchinson opened the bag and raised an eyebrow in surprise. Inside, all carefully swathed in cotton batting to protect them from breakage, were vials of morphine sulfate, arranged in neat rows. Beside them was a sheaf of paper-wrapped disposable syringes, bound together with a rubber tourniquet. "The dose . . ." he protested.

The ruined lips moved in an attempt at a smile, that quickly became a grimace. "A lot. Yes, I know. It would kill you, but not me. I am quite used to it." The slitted eyes narrowed further. "Damn it, stop wasting time and give it to me."

Hutchinson drew up the required dose. He rolled up the sleeve over one of the old man's skinny arms; a trail of needle marks traced the path of a vein. He applied a tourniquet and administered the drug, then waited and watched as the man's breathing slowed and the pupils of the yellowed eyes constricted. The eyes closed.

"Get it over with, then. I must be up and gone."

"You won't be on your feet for at least a week."

The injured head turned from side to side in negation. "Tomorrow . . ." He ran a tongue over his ruined lips.

Hutchinson didn't argue any further, but pulled on the pair of gloves. "Hold still."

The admonition was hardly necessary. The job took less time than he had anticipated, and before he'd pulled the last stitch tight the old man was snoring loudly. Hutchinson stood back and surveyed his handiwork for a moment, then took a roll of bandage from his bag. He quickly swathed the man's wounded face with the gauze.

He made a last turn with the bandage and used adhesive tape to secure the end of the roll. Wearily he stripped off the gloves, noting with clinical interest that his hands were steady. Either the sudden phone call, jolting him from his bed, had sobered him, or he had developed such a tolerance to the alcohol that his nerves were immune to its effects. He didn't consider either point too long. Indeed, when he wasn't drinking he didn't think about much of anything these days, except how he would pay for his next drink. When he was drinking he didn't think about anything at all, but simply let his mind ride along on the sweet wave of oblivion.

He didn't like working for the Nazis, or the Mob, or the Klan, or all the other clandestine groups that supplied him with patients. He publicly and privately abhorred what they stood for. Still, he owed them. And it was a debt, he felt sure, that they would never count fully repaid. No matter how many dirty jobs like this he handled for them, the account would never be closed. They would never allow him to forget . . . as if he could.

He turned and began putting his instruments back in his small black bag. The leather was cool and smooth beneath his hands. He closed his eyes and saw the girl's dark flesh, felt the clammy coolness of shock on her dusky skin. In his mind, the screaming began. How long had she screamed that night? He couldn't remember. He could only see his hands, shaking uncontrollably, unable to keep their grip on a scalpel. He'd put off the needed cesarean, hoping he'd sober up and the shaking would stop, hoping Mitch Komitzky would make it back from the ski trip in time . . . hoping . . . hoping . . .

But Shamara Trexler had died, of course, and the twins she was carrying had died with her. Happy endings happen only in fairy tales. Most times the cavalry doesn't come over the hill in the nick of time. Shamara had been black, a runaway, unwed, and a heroin addict. All the family she had were in Alabama, and when, three months later, they decided to file suit against Randolph Hutchinson and the hospital, the Klan had taken it upon themselves to come to his aid. They had burned a cross on the Trexlers' front lawn, and the family had settled out of court for a sum substantially less than a jury probably would have awarded them.

Faced with the choice of expulsion from the hospital or early retirement, the doc chose the latter. Though he no longer officially practiced medicine, he'd held onto his license and still had pharmacy privileges. He drank openly now, and supplemented his Social Security checks with jobs like this one. Bullet and stab wounds, the occasional abortion, kept him in a steady supply of beer and cheap whiskey. If his mortality rate was high, his patients were not in any position to complain.

He raised his right hand and held it up before his eyes. The tremor was there, barely perceptible . . . but it would soon get worse. Hutchinson glanced at his watch. Eight o'clock. Two more hours and Brennan's Liquor Store would be open for business. He replaced the old man's kit on the bureau, took up his own bag, then hesitated a moment. The young man who had let him in, deep in his drugged sleep, did not stir as the doctor added a second bottle of painkillers and one of antibiotics to the pile on the bed. At the door, he pulled back the chain and stepped out into the sunlight. He reached around inside and pushed in the lock button on the door, then pulled it closed behind him.

Anesthesia. That's what it was all about. Everybody had their own brand. In two hours he'd be feeling no pain. No pain at all.

When Gunner Hahn woke, it was nearly noon. He glanced at Brauer. The old man was sleeping soundly, each breath a loud, rumbling snore through his broken nose. His face was wrapped in bandages. The doctor was gone.

He sat up, rubbing at his forehead, trying to wipe the drug-induced cobwebs from his mind. The painkiller had left him with a dull, throbbing headache. The pain in his ankle was back now, stronger than ever. At that realization his head cleared, and he could feel his heart begin to pound with excitement.

There should have been no pain. By now, there should have been nothing but shiny scar tissue to mark where the cut had been. By tomorrow, even that would be gone. He bent and, with shaking hands, carefully unwrapped the folds of the towel.

The wound was still there, the ragged edges seeping blood, the flesh around it puffy and discolored. Gunner touched the blood, rubbing its stickiness between thumb and forefinger. His mouth had gone dry.

Could it be happening? Were all these years of waiting coming to an end at last?

He was tempted to hobble to the bathroom and look in the mirror, but feared to see the same strong, blue-eyed features looking back at him.

No. He'd wait a bit. Wait and see.

He lay back on the bed again and closed his eyes, reveling in the pain.

Brie trudged slowly down the tree-lined street. Despite the shade, she was hot and sticky. The dark gray of the dress absorbed the heat. The cloth was plastered to the hollow between her shoulder blades, and the edges of the collar chafed her neck. The bullet graze on her thigh stung painfully with each step, as salty sweat pricked at the wound. Trying to save money, she had walked from the shopping district, following directions given her by one of the shopkeepers.

At any other time she would have enjoyed the walk. A stroll down Bellevue Avenue was like stepping into another world. Huge mansions flanked both sides of the street, each with its own distinctive name: The Elms, Chateau-Sur-Mer, Rosecliff, Beechwood, Belcourt Castle . . . Brie read the signs, but the sign she was looking for eluded her. She stopped and leaned against the coolness of a stone wall, wearily brushing damp tendrils of hair back from her forehead.

She had not taken into account how far the walk might be or how very tired she was. Her stomach rumbled in empty protest. The chocolate bar had melted to a shapeless lump in her pocket, and she couldn't bring herself to eat it. She was exhausted, hungry, and nearly at the end of her strength when she looked across the street and saw a small sign, white letters on blue: OCEANVIEW DRIVE.

Quickly, she crossed the avenue and turned onto the shady side street. It was cooler here; that, and the nearness of her destination, refreshed her. Brie quickened her pace. On either side long driveways peeled off of the main street, cutting a swath through broad, manicured lawns, each ending at the doors of an imposing mansion.

Brie's steps slowed. She had pictured a small house, a normal, everyday house. She had never imagined a street like this. When she came to the neat, hand-lettered sign that read TRADEWINDS and beneath that 117 OCEANVIEW DRIVE there was no sign of a house at all, just a narrow driveway of crushed shells disappearing into the trees.

Brie swallowed hard, gathered her courage, then resolutely set off up the drive. As she rounded a bend, the trees opened up and a house came into view. It was large, but not nearly as huge or intimidating as the other expensive homes she'd passed. It was a three-story Victorian, painted white. Wildflowers made a colorful hem for the broad expanse of porch that stretched across the front of the house.

Brie stopped where she was and looked down at her soiled, sweat-soaked dress. She tugged at the skirt, vainly trying to smooth away the wrinkles, then gave up and pulled Jake Morgan's old comb from her pocket, using it to pull her hair back from her face. It was the best she could do. She took the envelope from her pocket. Despite all she'd been through the vellum still looked crisp and clean—a darn sight better than she did, she mused. Offering up a silent prayer, she set off across the lawn to the front door.

From his position under the eaves of the porch roof, David watched the figure approach up the drive. She stopped for a moment and stared at the house, obviously uncertain. She didn't see him in the shadows of the porch. To his amusement, she straightened her dress, ran a comb through her hair. Her graceful back straightened, and her shoulders set, in the manner of a soldier heading into battle. She started toward the porch.

When she'd reached the steps he saw that she was not only graceful, but lovely: a beautiful young woman clad in one of the ugliest dresses he'd ever laid eyes on.

"Hello there!" he called out, stepping down from the ladder. "May I help you?"

The voice, so near and so unexpected, startled her. A man emerged from the shadows at the corner of the porch. As her eyes adjusted to the dimness she made out a ladder, and she realized that he'd been working when she came upon him.

"I'm sorry. I didn't mean to frighten you."

He was tall, more than six feet if she estimated correctly, with black hair that curled over his forehead and the tips of his ears. He looked to be in his mid-thirties. His eyes were a deep brown, almost black. A painter's hat was jammed onto his head, but it had not kept his hair and face from becoming speckled with white. He held out his hand.

Before she could respond, he noticed the mixture of wet paint and grime on his outstretched palm and quickly withdrew it.

"Sorry about that," he said, wiping his hand on the leg of his jeans. "I'm David Kauffman. Is there something I can do for you?"

His smile was warm. Brie returned it hesitantly.

"I'm looking for Mr. Samuel Kauffman. I have a letter I must deliver to him."

"That would be my father." He wiped his hands on his jeans a second time and opened the screen door. "Why don't you come inside out of this heat? I'll get him." He ushered her ahead of him into a spacious living room. "Please have a seat, Miss . . . ?"

"Prescott, Brie Prescott. The name wouldn't mean anything to him, though."

She perched on the edge of a sofa, nervously turning the letter in her hands. The living room was bright and airy. The furnishings were simple and uncluttered, but not stark. An oriental rug set off the polished, wide-board floor. At the far end of the room, a flagstone fireplace took up almost the entire wall.

David returned with an older man. Even before they were introduced, Brie knew that this must be Samuel Kauffman. Though the father was considerably shorter than the son, the facial resemblance between the two was remarkable. She stood and held out her hand.

"Mr. Kauffman, my name is Gabrielle Prescott. I have a letter that I've been instructed to deliver to you."

He took her hand, clasped it firmly, then motioned her back to her seat. He sat down in a large, overstuffed wing chair across from her. David excused himself and left the room. To her surprise, Brie felt a twinge of disappointment.

"And who might this letter be from?"

She hesitated. "This may come as a bit of a shock to you, Mr. Kauffman." She held the envelope out to him. "It's from your brother."

He frowned. "That's impossible. My only brother

is dead. He was killed in Germany, in 1942. I know that for a fact." He took the envelope from her, turning it over in his hands to study the address.

Brie nodded. "Yes, sir. This was written before he died. It was left with a sister of the Mother of Mercy Abbey, with instructions to see that it was delivered to you."

They were interrupted by David. He was carrying a tray with a pitcher of iced lemonade and three glasses. He sat down on the couch next to Brie and poured lemonade for each of them.

"Is this a private discussion, or can anyone listen in?"

"David, you might want to stay and hear this out. Miss Prescott has just given me a letter, purportedly from your Uncle Isaac."

David looked at her, a frown replacing his smile. "If this is some sort of joke, it's not very funny. My uncle died almost fifty years ago. He was murdered by the Nazis."

"It's no joke." She looked from one to the other. "Please believe me."

"I believe you, Miss Prescott." The elder Kauffman tapped the letter on his knee. "If this is a joke, someone went to a great deal of trouble to pull it off." He handed the envelope to David. "That's Isaac's writing. I'd recognize it anywhere. His script was like chicken scratch, so he took all his notes in block print. It forced him to slow down, and made it more legible for anyone else who had to read it. I'd swear on my life that Isaac wrote this."

He leaned back in his chair and folded his hands on his stomach. His eyes moved over Brie. She could feel him studying and weighing the muddy shoes, the soiled dress, the unkempt hair.

"My intuition tells me there's more to this than you're telling me, Miss Prescott. My intuition is seldom wrong. Before I open this, suppose you start at the beginning and tell me the whole story."

Brie took a long swallow of the lemonade. She shook her head wearily. "So much has happened in the last twenty-four hours that I can barely sort it out and keep it straight, but I'll try. Please bear with me."

She told what she knew of Isaac Kauffman's death, of Mother Margarethe's involvement in it, and of how shame had kept the nun from delivering the letter all these years. She told them of the man who'd come to Mother Margarethe looking for the letter, and of Mother's fear of him. At last she related the events of last night: the murder of the sisters and her escape with the letter.

"Those men are out there somewhere. I don't know what's in that envelope, but whatever it is they want it very badly. They'll stop at nothing to get it." She looked from one to the other, saw the shock and disbelief on their faces. "You seem like good people. I'm sorry to bring danger into your lives, but I didn't know what to do. Maybe I shouldn't have delivered this letter at all."

The two men were silent for a moment, then Samuel cleared his throat. "You did the right thing. That story is too wild for you to have made up. I believe you, Miss Prescott . . . and I think it's high time we had a look at this."

Wordlessly, David handed the envelope to his father. The older man took his key ring from his pocket and ran the tip of a key under the flap.

Inside was a stack of paper, folded in thirds. He opened it on his lap, smoothing out the crisp folds until it lay flat.

He motioned for the others to join him, and when Gabrielle hesitated he said, "Come on, young lady. You certainly have as much of a stake in this as we do."

The writing was the same neat block print as that on the envelope. It was not English. Samuel paged through the stack. The first sheet was obviously a letter, but those after it appeared to be filled with numbers and symbols, interspersed with short paragraphs of print.

"It's German," he said, his voice tight. "Let me try to translate." Slowly, haltingly, he read:

My Dearest Samuel,

If you receive this letter, you may assume that Chaya, Dov, and I are dead. Things worsen here every day. I am beginning to fear that this accursed Brimstone Project may prove to be a knife in my back and not the salvation that I hoped for.

The Nazis are seeking a super-explosive, but that is only the smallest part of what Brimstone is. Fortunately, they are so shortsighted that they have no real interest in anything beyond that. If they did, if they put all their efforts behind making this project a success, all would be lost. The more I work on this, the more I feel that it is a thing best left alone. But it is too late for that.

I have enclosed the formula in the belief that the only true defense against it is for both sides to possess the knowledge. Use it wisely, Samuel. It may prove to be the greatest achievement of my life, or my gravest mistake.

May God grant us all His peace. Farewell.

Your loving brother,
Isaac

When he had finished, they sat in silence. Samuel shook his head sadly.

"Poor Isaac. I tried to convince him to leave Germany with me while it was still possible. He refused. He was so wrapped up in his work, so sure his knowledge would protect him. It was his undoing."

"So this is the formula to a bomb?" Brie asked.

"Apparently," David said. "If I recall from my history books, Werner Heisenberg was working on an atomic bomb for the Germans at the same time that Enrico Fermi was doing the same for our side. Could it be that Uncle Isaac was also working on nuclear fission, and had actually built a working model for a bomb?"

Samuel was scanning the papers containing the formula. He shook his head. "No—not an *atomic* bomb, at any rate. These are chemical formulae. There's no mention of uranium, hydrogen, or anything else we would commonly associate with an atom bomb. At the same time there are references here that can only apply to sound: megahertz, decibels . . ."

He stood up. His face was alight with enthusiasm. "I'd like to go over these figures and check out Isaac's equations."

"Don't you think we ought to call the police?" David asked.

The older man's face sobered. "That would be prudent. I'd be interested to know why Miss Prescott didn't do that in the first place."

"I was afraid. I ran. The only thing I could think of at the time was to get as far away as possible, and to get that letter out of my possession. Mother Margarethe didn't trust the police to protect her and, frankly, I don't trust them either. I have nothing to hide, Mr. Kauffman, but I do want to live."

David picked up his glass of lemonade. His thumbs made swirling patterns on its frosted surface. "Supppose I could arrange for you to give your information to the police in confidence? I have several friends on the force here. If you'd allow them to ask you some questions, I think we'd all feel a bit more comfortable about this whole affair."

"If you can arrange for a confidential interview, I'd be willing to talk to the police. I can't give them much to go on, but I can give them a good description of the two men who killed the sisters. Would that satisfy you?"

David nodded.

"Please don't tell them about the letter," Samuel cautioned. "This is a family matter, and I'd like to keep it as such for now. I'm not going to have them snatch this out from under my nose before I have a chance to figure out what it is." He refolded the papers and tucked them back into the envelope. "If you want me, I'll be in the study."

He started for the doorway, then paused. "And David . . . if you're as smart as I think you are, you'll invite the young lady to stay for dinner." He winked at Brie.

"Don't let the pallor and the skinniness scare you—he's a damn good cook."

Chapter Ten

Brie felt a warm flush of embarrassment creep up her neck and across her face. She stood up quickly.

"I've troubled you enough. If you'll just call the police and arrange for me to speak to them, I'll be going."

"Nonsense," David said. "The police station is clear on the other side of town. You're going to walk there? You're so tired you look like you're going to collapse, and I'll bet your stomach's running on empty, too." He looked her up and down. "If I had to guess further, I'd say you have no place to go and not even a change of clothes to your name."

Brie's blush deepened. "I have some money," she stammered. "I can find a room for the night. I can buy some more clothes in the morning." Her chin set stubbornly. "I'll manage."

"It's a shame to waste your money on a hotel when we have a perfectly good guest room upstairs that you can have for nothing. And another thing: I'll admit my father can be irritating and a bit pushy at times, but he's right about one thing: I am a great cook. You'd really be missing something if you left before dinner."

Brie hesitated. In the past twenty-four hours, her only thought had been to deliver the letter. Now that that task was accomplished, she had no idea where to go or what to do. His assessment of her condition was all too accurate. She was exhausted and hungry. And if she was honest with herself, she had to admit that she liked David Kauffman. He emanated strength and warmth, and she sensed that he was a person to be trusted.

"I'll stay on one condition: that you stop calling me 'Miss Prescott.' My name is Gabrielle. Friends call me Brie."

"Brie it is, then." He glanced at his watch. "Suppose I show you where your room is, so you can get cleaned up a bit? I'll ring the police station and set up an appointment."

"That would be fine." She glanced down at her dress. "I'm a real mess."

He held up his paint-stained hands. "Uniform of the day. No non-messes allowed. Come on, messy lady, I'll show you to your room."

Brie woke to a soft rapping. She sat up quickly and looked about her, feeling a start of alarm. The shadows in the room had lengthened. She had taken a shower and then lain down on the bed for a moment to rest. She had never intended to fall asleep. The digital display on her watch read 4:30. She was clad in a terry robe that David had given her, and her hair was still damp, wrapped in a towel. She pulled the belt on the robe snug and opened the door.

David held out her clothes to her. "Kauffman's laundry, at your service. Here are your things, madam, all fresh from the dryer." His expression became more serious. "Are you feeling any better?"

"Much better, thank you. I must have dozed off."

"I called the police station. They wanted me to bring you right over, but I convinced them that you'd be able to answer their questions better on a full stomach. I set up an appointment for seven tonight. Is that okay?"

"Fine."

They fell silent. Brie was stunned by the change in him. He was wearing a white shirt, open at the neck, and a loose-fitting pair of tan slacks. He'd combed his hair back, but one lock fell stubbornly forward to curl at the center of his forehead. Without the silly hat, he was strikingly handsome. She took her clothes from him, feeling suddenly awkward, acutely conscious of her wet hair and the too-large robe.

"I really should be getting dressed."

He nodded, shoved his hands deep into his pockets. "Dinner will be in half an hour. Come on down to the kitchen when you're ready."

"Thank you. Thank you for everything."

She closed the door and hurriedly set about dressing. The clean clothes felt good against her skin. She toweled her hair to get out all the excess moisture, then used Jake's old comb to smooth out the tangles. She had no pins to put it up. It fell about her shoulders in soft brown waves. Ten minutes short of the half hour, she was on her way down the great curved stairway.

She followed her nose to the kitchen. The house was full of a wonderful smell she could not identify. She found David bent over the stove, energetically stirring a colorful mixture of vegetables in a large bowl-shaped pan. He smiled when he saw her.

"Just in time. Take that bowl of rice there and follow me."

The table was set outdoors on a large flagstone patio. David's father joined them, holding the chair for her as she sat down.

"It's been a long time since a beautiful woman has graced our table."

"You're a flatterer, Mr. Kauffman."

"Please, cut the 'Mr. Kauffman' business. It makes me feel as old as I am. Call me Sam."

Neither of the men had exaggerated David's skill as a cook. The stir-fry of shrimp and vegetables over rice was delightful, followed by a simple dessert of fresh strawberries and cream. There was a comfortableness around the table, and Brie found herself relaxing and even joining in the exchange of light banter that passed between father and son. All too soon, Samuel pushed back from the table and stood up.

"Well, if you young people will excuse me, I'll be getting back to those papers."

"Have you learned anything yet?" David asked.

"Nothing that makes any sense. Your Uncle Isaac's ideas are pretty farfetched." He looked sadly at Brie. "I'm afraid my brother and your friends may have died for nothing."

"I can't accept that. I have to believe that their deaths had meaning." She looked to David. "Can we go talk to the police now? Maybe if they catch these men they'll be able to make some sense of all this."

"Certainly," he said. "But don't get your hopes

up. It's been my experience that life holds far more questions than answers."

David sat across the table from Brie, listening while Lt. Ron DeRobbio interviewed her. The office was small but private, Ron doing his best to fulfill his promise to keep the interview as confidential as possible. David trusted him. Ron had helped him with some research on police procedures for *Dark Morning* and the two had become good friends. However, David didn't like the direction his current line of questioning was taking.

"Miss Prescott, you must understand our position. You have no driver's license, no Social Security card, no form of identification whatsoever. Since this afternoon, I've been on the phone with the Harringdale police. They have a birth certificate for Gabrielle Marie Prescott, but after that nothing—not so much as a school report card or a high school diploma. As a police officer involved in a multiple homicide, I need to know that you are who you say you are."

"I never learned to drive, so I have no license. To my knowledge, the sisters never registered me for Social Security. After my parents died, they just took me in. They tutored me themselves, so there are no school records. Mother Margarethe wasn't one to deal with red tape. I'm sitting here, Lieutenant. I don't know how else to prove to you that I truly do exist."

DeRobbio cleared his throat. He turned his pencil nervously end over end and there was a note of apology in his voice. "I gleaned some facts from the Harringdale police about Gabrielle Prescott. If you could answer a few questions, I'd believe you."

"Go ahead."

"How old were you when your parents died?"

"Six. My birthday is April 23rd."

"How did your parents die?"

It was Brie's turn to hesitate. She folded her hands, and David saw the knuckles go white with tension. "It was a murder-suicide." When DeRobbio remained silent she looked up at him, a flash of anger in her blue eyes. "My father shot my mother through the heart with one barrel of his shotgun and used the other to blow his own head off. I'm sorry, Lieutenant, but I was only six years old and they didn't allow me to see their bodies, so I can't give you a clearer description than that."

"Was that really necessary?" David demanded of DeRobbio, covering Brie's hands with his own to steady her. She gave him a weary smile.

"I've got a job to do. We're talking a *dozen* murders here, and nobody from Harringdale even has a photo of what this girl looks like. I'm sorry, Miss Prescott—I accept that you *are* Gabrielle Prescott. If you could just tell me what happened last night, we can get this over with."

"It was around midnight. I was returning from the hospital with Father Brennan when—"

"What were you doing at the hospital so late at night?"

She licked her lips nervously. "It's a Catholic hospital. Father Brennan and I often go there late at night to pray with some of the more seriously ill patients. When you're sick and in pain and can't sleep, the nights can be very long. It was part of the ministry I was being prepared for. It was planned that I would enter the novitiate this coming fall."

Listening to her, David heard something in her voice, a hesitation, as if she were picking and choosing her words very carefully. Not lying, but perhaps not telling the whole truth either.

She went on to tell about going into the chapel to pray and hearing men's voices in the hallway.

"They both spoke with an accent—German, I think. At least the older man's was. Mother Margarethe, our Mother Superior, is—was—German. His accent was identical to hers. I'm not certain about the other man."

She continued on, repeating essentially the same story that she had told David that afternoon, but omitting any mention of the letter she'd been asked to deliver.

DeRobbio leaned back and stuck his pen behind his right ear. "And what made you choose to come to Newport?"

She hesitated, her eyes meeting David's across the table in mute pleading. He smoothly came to her rescue, improvising as he went along.

"The Mother Superior had been an acquaintance of my late Uncle Isaac in Germany. She'd promised him she'd look us up. She and Gabrielle had been planning a trip here for some time. When Gabrielle had no one to turn to, she remembered us. I called you as soon as she told me what had happened."

DeRobbio looked from one to the other, and David could see that he wasn't buying it. However, the lieutenant closed his notebook and tucked his pen into his shirt pocket. He stood up.

"That's all I have to ask you, for now. Before you go, I'd like you to spend some time with our artist and try to come up with some sketches of the two men you saw."

"Of course."

Brie stood up and DeRobbio led her from the room. When David moved to follow he put a restraining hand against his chest and pushed him back down into the chair. "I am *not* finished with *you* yet. I'll be right back."

When he returned, he sat down across from David. He took out his pen and began toying with it nervously. "So, is there something else you'd like to tell me?"

"I don't think so. I think Miss Prescott told you everything."

"Then why do I get the feeling there's something missing here—some big secret that the two of you aren't letting me in on?"

"I don't know, Ron." David shrugged. "Maybe you're just getting paranoid."

"Yeah ... Well, I know you too well to believe you'd have anything to do with murder, or harbor someone who did, so I guess I'm going to have to let the two of you go. But I don't like it, David. There are gaps here—just little inconsequential things like motive, for instance. I have a feeling that you and the lovely Miss Prescott could fill in some of those gaps if you chose to." When David remained silent, DeRobbio sighed. "I need to know where to get hold of Miss Prescott, in case I have further questions."

"She's staying at my place." David stood up and moved toward the door.

"Curiouser and curiouser. Somehow, after Marsha, I thought you'd sworn off women for good."

"Curiosity killed the cat."

"So they say." He leaned forward, tapping the end of the pen lightly against David's chest. "Just make sure that whatever this is that you're not telling me doesn't kill you."

Brie was silent on the way home. In the kitchen, David poured her a tall glass of iced tea, then took a beer for himself. He sat down at the kitchen table.

"You don't lie very well," he said, taking a long swig of the beer. "I mean that as a compliment."

She was standing in the doorway to the backyard, staring out at the night. David could hear the low rumble of the breakers in the distance. She brushed a long strand of hair back from her face, the movement nervous, too quick.

"I was brought up to be truthful—both by the sisters and my parents. It's not an easy habit to break."

"I'm sorry about your parents. Ron shouldn't have pushed you like that."

She turned around, setting the half-full glass on the counter. "It's all right. He had a job to do. It happened a long time ago, and it doesn't hurt anymore. I don't like to be reminded of it, because that's not how I remember them. My mother was a sweet, giving person, and my father was a good man until he lost his job. I loved them both very much. I try to remember the good times, when we were still a family—before his mind snapped, before . . ."

Her voice trailed off. David tried to think of some way to change the subject, but she beat him to it.

"You *do* lie well. Somehow, you don't come across that way—don't strike me as a liar, I mean."

"He's the worst kind, a professional liar." Samuel bustled into the kitchen, opened the refrigerator, and poured skim milk into a glass. "He lies for a living, and gets paid well for it."

David smiled at the look of confusion on her face. "I'm a writer," he explained. "All fiction is really nothing but a pack of lies set down on paper. The only difference between a good writer and a bad writer is that the good writer is a better liar. It's not something they teach you at college, but it's true."

"David has lied himself into a pretty nice tax bracket. Last four books in a row made the *Times* Bestseller List."

"Dad . . ."

"Well, if you're not going to try to impress her, I certainly am. Would you like to see some of his books?"

"Yes. Please."

Samuel bustled from the room before David could stop him. He looked at Brie apologetically. "You don't have to do this."

"But I want to. What sort of things do you write?"

"Murder, mayhem, world-threatening conspiracies."

Samuel returned with an armload of books and set the stack in the center of the kitchen table. He grasped his glass of skim milk and held it up in mock salute. "Now that you two have something to talk about, I'll be getting back to my studies."

"We were doing just fine without you, Dad. . . ."

"Then you should do even better when you're alone." He began to leave, then paused in the doorway as if he'd forgotten something. To Brie he said, "And I have it on good authority from his first wife that he's a terrific kisser—even better than his cooking."

"Goodbye, Dad."

"Don't blame me, David. You've been out of practice so long, you need all the help you can get." To David's vast relief, this time he really left.

Brie was laughing. "Is he always like that?"

"Only when there's a beautiful woman present."

She dropped her eyes at the compliment and made a big show of looking through the pile of books on the table, picking up each one and studying the colorful dust jackets.

"May I read them?"

"Sure." It was David's turn to be embarrassed. It usually didn't matter to him one way or the other, if his friends read his books or not. Suddenly he realized that it mattered to him very much that Brie read his books . . . and like them. The realization startled him.

He picked up *Dark Morning* from the pile and held it out to her. "This one's my personal favorite."

She took it from him, holding it with the appreciative reverence of a true book lover. "I really enjoy reading," she said. "Mother Margarethe never allowed me to watch television—she thought it was a waste of the mind—but she put no restrictions on books." She put a hand to her lips. "Oh—I forgot. I should have told the lieutenant. I have a library card. I guess that proves I'm a real person." She shook her head in wonderment. "How strange that no one exists nowadays unless they're documented in a file somewhere."

David nodded. His expression turned thoughtful. "I understand Ron's problem, though. Sometimes *I* can hardly believe you're real."

She looked up at him, and he found the words tumbling out before he could stop them.

"You drop into my life—out of the nowhere into the here—with a story wilder than anything I could invent. And there's something about you ... something scary and wonderful, all at the same time. You're sweet, innocent, and open, yet I feel secrets in you—not lies, but maybe truths left unsaid."

The words kept coming. "Brie, you seem like a little wild bird that may startle and fly away any minute. And I don't want that to happen. I want to be your friend, Brie ... and if it grows into something more than that, I want that, too."

She turned away from him, her arms hugging herself as if she were suddenly cold. "But you hardly know me," she said.

"Then give me time to get to know you. Promise me you won't wave your magic wand or wiggle your nose and disappear—that I won't wake up tomorrow morning and find you gone as suddenly as you came."

She turned back to him and gave a wan smile. "I don't plan on going anywhere, and if I do you'll be the first to know."

He returned her smile. "No magic? No tricks?"

"There is no such thing as magic," she whispered. "No such thing."

In the study, Samuel Kauffman worked by the light of a single gooseneck lamp. His fingers flew over the keys of his pocket calculator, as he covered the sheets of a yellow legal pad with neat columns of penciled figures. At last he switched the calculator off and sat back in his chair. He rubbed thoughtfully at the slight stubble of beard on his chin. His dark eyes sparkled with excitement.

The figures checked. He'd gone over them five times, and the answers were identical to Isaac's calculations.

"Isaac, Isaac," he whispered. "Were you a genius or a madman?"

There was only one way to tell. Tomorrow he would go to the lab. Following Isaac's instructions, he would try to produce a test quantity of the Brimstone substance. After that . . .

The hypothesis that followed from those computations was preposterous . . . and yet . . . and yet, the figures checked.

Gunner Hahn rose in the darkness of night. He'd fallen asleep while watching the evening news. "The Convent Murders," as the media had dubbed them, had been featured on all the channels, but there'd been no mention of him or Brauer—or the girl. The station was off the air now, the screen a silent flicker of electronic snow. Hahn used its light to guide him as he limped his way to the small bathroom. Brauer was still snoring loudly. From the room next door music blared, barely muffled by the wafer-thin motel walls. Hahn frowned. Night was meant to be silent. He would never become accustomed to the constant din that others took for granted. Television, radio, traffic, rock 'n' roll—the noise never ceased. Even in the middle of the night brakes squealed, sirens screamed. Silence was one of the things he missed most in this country, that precious, natural silence broken only by bird song or the liquid riffle of rushing water. Only a memory now.

Closing the bathroom door quietly, he switched on the overhead light. He leaned forward and studied his face in the mirrored surface of the medicine cabinet that was mounted on the wall above the sink. Crow's-feet had begun to etch the skin at the outer corners of his eyes. He leaned closer, lightly running his fingers over his nose and forehead. His skin had begun to lose its elasticity. The flesh was becoming large-pored and coarse. He hadn't shaved in days, and the stubbly growth on his face was liberally peppered with gray.

Next door, the music changed to a deep rhythmic throbbing that made the door to the medicine cabinet vibrate and seemed to pulsate into the bones of his skull. He turned and hobbled back to the bedroom, noticing for the first time the smeared trail of bloody footprints that marked his passage. The sight had no effect on him.

Gingerly, he lowered himself to the bed. His joints felt brittle. The ache seemed to have spread upward from his ankle to encompass all his muscles and bones.

The music next door was suddenly switched off. In the silence that followed, the pulsing in his head became like the ticking of some giant clock. He became conscious of the echo of his heartbeat, thundering through his body.

Of seconds passing. Passing.

Brie closed the bedroom door and leaned against it, listening until she'd heard David's footsteps retreating down the hallway. Despite her shower earlier, and the nap, she felt weary and dirty. Lying did not sit well with her conscience, and the truth that she had withheld from David nagged at her.

The room had its own private bath. She ran hot water into the tub and undressed. As she waited for the bath to fill, she washed out her bra and panties and hung them over the shower curtain rod overhead to dry. When the tub was full, she lowered herself slowly into its warm depths. The bullet graze on her thigh stung as the hot water touched it, and she had to bite her lip to keep from crying out at the pain. After a moment, it passed. With soap and a washcloth she scrubbed at her body with a vengeance, as if in washing away the dirt she could wash away the realities of the past few days as well.

When she'd finished, she dried herself and slipped on a large T-shirt that David had given her to sleep in. The word *Newport* was emblazoned across the front of it, along with a screen print of sailing ships. The hem fell halfway to her knees.

She sat cross-legged on the bed and picked up the book that David had given her. She read the dust jacket, then turned it over and stared at the black-and-white photo on the back. The face was serious and unsmiling, and it was hard to reconcile it with the man she was beginning to know.

She should have told him about her gift, but his talk of magic had chilled her.

Witch.

Jinx.

What if he didn't understand? She looked at his photo, studied the eyes, remembering the terrible look in her father's eyes: half fear, half loathing. The picture in her mind became a kaleidoscope of changing faces, one melting into the next: her mother, her father, Sister Mary Xavier with a bullet hole in her smooth white brow, and the jaundiced eyes and masklike face of the murderer. Her own eyes filled with tears, and though she tried to stop them they overflowed and ran in a torrent down her cheeks.

Sobs began to shake her. She tried to make them stop, but the sobbing only came harder. She gave in to it at last, burying her face in the pillows to muffle the sound, weeping until she had emptied herself of the grief. Gradually, she quieted. Calm flowed over her like a tide, bearing a flotsam and jetsam of memories.

Mother Margarethe was there, stern yet gentle. And the other sisters, too: old Sister Irene, whose gnarled, patient hands had guided Brie's first clumsy attempts at sewing; Sister Marie, that lover of Bach, Mozart, and the Beatles, who had taught her to play piano; Sister Ellen, Sister Janice, Sister Anne ... their beloved faces passed through her mind one by one, and there was no sorrow accompanying that passage, only a strange sense of peace and, yes—joy. Somehow she knew that they were at peace, knew that whatever it was they had searched for together in that small house of prayer, they had found it at last.

She fell asleep with their presence all about her, yet it was the face of David Kauffman that filled her dreams.

Chapter Eleven

"I can't let you do this," Brie said. "It's too much."

"Nonsense. What's the good of having all this money if I can't spend it? I'm enjoying myself. You wouldn't want to spoil my good time, would you?"

"But I can't repay you."

"Who said anything about repaying?" David saw the doubt in her face. He drew her away from the checkout counter for a moment, away from the amused appraisal of the sales clerk and the curious ears of other customers. He took her hands, chafing them gently, and lowered his voice so that only she could hear. "There're no strings attached to this, Brie. I just want to help out."

"But I really don't need all this."

They'd been shopping for over two hours. It was soon obvious to David that the price of clothing simply overwhelmed Brie. She'd chosen a simple skirt and blouse, a change of underwear, a package of panty hose, and a pair of low-heeled pumps, then watched in alarm as the total mounted. Though she wouldn't admit it, he suspected that the money in her pocket was all she had. He watched patiently as she put everything back and tried again . . . and again . . . with the same results.

Then David had taken things in hand. Over her objections he'd selected dresses, skirts, blouses, slacks, a robe, and nightgown, even a bathing suit that she protested she would never have the courage to wear. As fast as she put an item back David would choose another, usually more expensive than the first. A heap of clothing now covered the checkout counter, some of it overflowing onto the floor.

David glanced at the waiting clerk. "Look, suppose we compromise? We'll put *some* of the things back. That way I'll be buying you a lot less than I'd like to, and you'll still have more than you think you need. We'll both lose. What do you say?"

Brie laughed. "You make it sound so simple."

"It is simple. For each thing I pick for you to keep, you can pick an item to put back. That's fair, isn't it?"

"How can I argue with that, especially since you're paying?"

Together they went through the stack of clothing on the counter, choosing some items, rejecting some, haggling over others. At last everything was boxed, bagged, and paid for, including the bathing suit, which David had retrieved from Brie's pile of rejected items when her back was turned.

The day had grown uncomfortably hot. As they left the air-conditioned store the heat closed in around them, heavy, almost suffocating. Their arms laden with packages, the two hurried to the car.

David stowed their purchases in the trunk. He took a handkerchief from his pocket and mopped the sweat from his face. Brie looked just as uncomfortable as he felt. The thought of getting back into the hot car was not an appealing one.

"There's a Newport Creamery just across the

street. I could go for some ice cream right now. How about you?"

Brie nodded. "That would taste wonderful."

"Oh, no," he corrected. "In this heat, we're not going to waste it by eating it. We're going to rub it all over our bodies and smear it in our hair and let it melt slowly and run down our necks. We'll pile whipped cream on top of that. With a cherry on your nose, you'll be beautiful."

She was trying to keep a straight face. "We'd better hurry then."

"Your hand, m'lady."

Arm-in-arm, he maneuvered her through the crowds of shoppers who were eyeing the window displays. The pair halted at the curb. Traffic on Bellevue Avenue was brisk, and despite the fact that they were standing in a crosswalk the drivers refused to stop. They had to wait while a long line of cars streamed past. A young boy wobbled by on a bicycle. His front wheel grazed the curb as he passed them, nearly dumping him onto the side-walk at their feet. David caught him by the shoulders, righted him, and sent him on his way. He frowned after the child in concern. The boy seemed much too young to be riding on such a busy street.

"Be careful!" he called after him.

The boy waved a hand and pedaled on. There was a break in the traffic. David and Brie were about to step down from the curb when someone screamed.

To their right, brakes squealed. David turned his head and saw the child with the bike. But the boy was not close to the curb any longer. He had veered out into the traffic, straight into the path of a small delivery van. The driver's efforts to stop were in vain. As they watched in horror the van struck the small two-wheeler, tossing it into the air. The child's body arced up over the hood and hit the windshield, his head leaving a great starburst crack in the glass. The impact threw him sideways and back. He landed on the sidewalk, not five feet from where they were standing.

"Oh, my God!"

David drew Brie to him, quickly turning her face away from the sight of the blood spouting from the child's shattered skull. He had seen enough in Vietnam to know that there was nothing to be done. There was no way the child would live with an injury like that. His only thought was to get Brie away. He started to pull her back toward the car.

To his surprise, she fought him.

"David, let me go! I've got to help!"

"He's dying. He's probably already dead. There's nothing you can do."

"I can help!"

She wrenched free of his arms and ran to kneel by the child's side. The little boy's legs were kicking slightly, spasming in a strange dance of death. The skin of his forehead was peeled back, revealing white, shattered bone. Blood spouted from the gaping wound, coloring the surrounding pavement a bright crimson.

Brie ignored the blood and slipped her hands gently beneath the child's ruined head. She cradled him on her lap. Heedless of the crowd of onlookers that was beginning to gather, she placed her hands over the wound and closed her eyes.

David knelt beside her. Her face was pale. She was obviously in shock. Gently, he tried to pull her hands away. Blood bubbled up between her fingers.

She seemed unaware of it. With a grimace of annoyance, she shook him off.

"Brie," he pleaded. "Give it up. There's nothing you can do."

"Leave . . . me . . . alone . . ." The words were forced. It seemed to him as if they came from far away, over some vast distance that he could neither see nor understand.

Then, to his surprise, the child stirred. It was not the mindless, spasm-like kicking of moments before. The boy moaned softly, shifting his weight to a more comfortable position.

He opened his eyes.

As David watched in astonishment, the boy brushed Brie's hands aside and sat up. The child put his hand up to his head, pushed back his hair, and stared in puzzlement at the blood that reddened his fingers. He looked from Brie, to David, to the crowd that had gathered around him, then back at the blood. His eyes strayed to the mangled bike that lay in the gutter.

"Boy, am I ever in trouble now," he said. "My mom's gonna kill me."

Some part of David's mind heard the murmur of the crowd, the scream of approaching sirens. But it was all background noise. Faraway. Unreal. His attention was riveted on the boy's face, on his forehead, blood-smeared but otherwise whole. When Brie touched his arm, he startled.

"Please get me out of here, David."

She was milk-white, obviously shaken. David realized that she was on the verge of collapse. Taking her bloodied hands, he pulled her to her feet. The crowd pressed in around them. The smell of blood made the air seem thick, almost solid. The heat was stifling. She swayed against him.

"Get back. Give her air."

He shoved his way through the crowd, propelling Brie along with him. They'd nearly made it to the car when he heard the sound of footsteps, running close behind them.

"Wait a minute! What's going on here? What did she do?"

A hand caught his arm, spun him about. David recognized the face of one of the reporters from the local newspaper. A photographer was close on his heels.

"Your story's back there. Leave us alone." He opened Brie's door, pushed her into the seat.

"At least give us her name."

David ignored him. He got behind the wheel, put the car in gear. As he pulled away, the glare of a flashbulb seared his eyes. As he drove red spots continued to swim across his field of vision, red as the blood that covered Brie's hands and soaked the gray cloth of her dress. Blood from a wound that—incredibly, impossibly, indisputably—no longer existed.

Samuel Kauffman put down the papers he was reading and rubbed at his eyes. The neat block printing had begun to blur, and he felt as if hot needles were being driven into his corneas. He resisted the temptation to put his head down on the desk. Instead he poured a fresh cup of coffee from the tall, stainless-steel thermos that he'd brought with him from home. By doctor's orders the stuff was decaffeinated, and theoretically would do nothing to help his alertness, but the simple act of drinking the hot liquid revived him somewhat. He looked up, letting his eyes rove the length of the lab and hoping that looking into the distance would relax them.

The left side of the room was bare, except for a large industrial barrel filled with water. A long counter stretched along the right side. On its gleaming surface was assembled an elaborate array of equipment and machinery. Close to him, an area had been cleared of its usual contents and now was cluttered with a jumble of wires and tools and an electronic keyboard. He'd purchased the items this morning at Radio Shack.

The keyboard looked like an animal that had been killed and gutted. It lay opened, its insides dismantled. Samuel smiled at it, fingering the small, cigarette pack-sized transmission device in his right pants pocket. The keyboard had been designed for the amateur musician, and normally it played three octaves. But the transmitter he'd made from its innards was designed to play notes that were not in any musician's repertoire.

Samuel stretched, pushing away from the desk and leaning back against the wall. He felt the cramped muscles in his shoulders and neck relax with the change of position. He was proud of this room. The Hampton Chemicals plant had many labs, but this particular one was his alone, custombuilt to his specifications. Many of Hampton's most successful products had had their beginnings here. But none so promising as this.

In the center of his desk was a football-sized mass of the compound that Isaac Kauffman had christened "Brimstone." He had followed Isaac's directions to the letter, and this was the result. It was gray and doughy in consistency, like a child's modeling clay. Samuel broke off a hunk of it and rolled it between his hands. Pinching it here, molding it there, he formed the crude figure of a man. He stared at it thoughtfully.

Protocol demanded that he wait for the final test, take the proper safeguards, get official sanction. But that would mean bringing others into his confidence: the cost-and-effect people, bureaucratic pencil-pushers who had no respect for the scientific method but cared only for the almighty dollar. There had been a time when his own authority had been unquestionable, when he'd had to answer only to John Feldman, the chairman of Hampton. But those days were past. Now all work was subject to the approval of these glorified accountants and the stockholders they represented. There were checks and doublechecks to slow down each step of a product's development, with the FDA, EPA, and other government agencies getting into the act.

No. If Brimstone worked, they would have to be brought into it eventually. But not now. Not when they could stop the experiment before it had a chance to prove itself. He would test a small amount, a mere speck, for if Isaac's notes could be believed a speck would be more than enough. He squeezed the figure he'd been toying with until it was just an anonymous gray ball once again, then molded it back into the larger mass of compound.

He took a sheet of white paper from the drawer of the desk. Using a bit of wire, he scraped a crumb from the lump of compound and deposited it in the center of the paper. He placed the rest of the Brimstone compound in a plastic bag, sealed it tightly, then carried the package across the room and submerged it in the barrel of water.

After washing and drying his hands, he returned to the desk and carefully folded the sheet of paper over and over, so there was no chance of the particle of compound falling out. He carried this compact packet to the far end of the lab. Here, the clean white plastered walls gave way to a layer of firebrick over solid steel. A protective screen separated this portion of the room from the rest. It was four feet thick, made of cement blocks. This morning, Samuel had further reinforced the outside with a layer of sandbags. In the past he had pioneered the development of rocket fuels and had even toyed, for a time, with a cheap synthetic substitute for gunpowder. The screen was a necessary safety precaution. There had never been an accident, so it had not been put to the test, but he was confident of its design.

Behind the screen was a small, square table, its surface pitted and scarred by past experiments. He placed the paper in the center of the table, then returned to the other end of the lab.

He donned goggles and ear protectors. Theoretically, the screen and the emergency blowout vents in the ceiling would take care of much of the force of the concussion, but in this enclosed area the sound would be deafening.

He took the transmitter from his pocket and placed it on his desk. There were two toggle switches mounted side-by-side on its black plastic surface. Above them was a light indicator. He flipped the first toggle switch to the "on" position. The small light glowed yellow. For a moment he hesitated, glancing at the barrel of water containing the bulk of the Brimstone compound. According to Isaac's notes the water would disperse the sound, alter the frequency, and render it harmless. The sound was the catalyst. Without it, Brimstone was perfectly safe. It could be dropped, torn into pieces, molded, shaped, burned. Nothing would happen. . . .

Samuel took a deep breath and crouched down behind the desk. Keeping his head down, he reached up with one hand and flipped the second switch on. The light changed from yellow to green. There was no sound—the frequency was far beyond the range of the human ear—but there was a feeling, a strange tingling along the nerves.

The feeling built.

Samuel waited.

Nothing happened.

Either he'd made an error, or Isaac's creation was a failure. With a sigh of frustration, Samuel stood up.

At that precise moment, the far end of the lab erupted in light and sound. Even through the goggles, the light seared his eyes. He fell backward onto the floor and scrambled blindly under the desk as the sound boxed his ears, effortlessly penetrating the thick padding of the protective headphones he wore. He could feel the pressure beginning to crush his skull. Then the white specks of light that had dazzled his eyes went out.

Brie sat huddled on a corner of the couch, her feet tucked under her, the white terry bathrobe wrapped about her like a shield. A cup of tea sat untouched on the end table at her side.

The police had come and gone. She had answered

their questions as best she could, without revealing the existence of her gift. The reaction of the crowd, of the reporters, and especially of David, had alarmed her. Through all the questioning, David had remained silent and remote.

The phone rang. David answered it and almost immediately slammed the receiver down, then took it off the hook. Another reporter, Brie guessed. At David's request, the police had evicted the television news crew that had set up their cameras on the front lawn and had stationed a cruiser at the entrance to the driveway. He'd gone about the house, closing drapes and pulling down shades. The old Victorian had taken on the look of a fortress under siege. Now silence lay like a vast desert between them, and Brie could feel his eyes on her and the terrible weight of questions they held.

"Please stop looking at me as if I'm some sort of rare bug."

David quickly looked away. She knew he didn't mean to stare, and she could only imagine what he must be thinking. She held out a hand to him.

"Please come sit down. . . . Please."

He sat beside her on the couch. When she touched his hand, he flinched away.

"I'm sorry, Brie. . . . It's just that . . . well . . . I *know* what I saw back there. I know that what you told the police is a lie and—"

"I told them the boy was all right. He is. That's not a lie."

"But he wasn't."

David was on his feet now, pacing the room, hands jammed tightly into his pockets. "I know what I saw, Brie. That boy's head was split open. He was bleeding all over the sidewalk and all over

you. There was no way he could have walked away
from that—no way on earth—unless you did something. You can lie to the reporters and the police
all you want, but, damn it, Brie, you can't lie to
me. I *saw* it."

"I'm not going to lie to you. I just don't know
how to make you understand."

"Try me."

Brie took a deep breath and stood up. She walked
over to the fireplace. The stones of the hearth were
rough beneath her bare feet. She couldn't look at
David as she spoke.

"I don't remember when I first realized I was
different. I know it started with animals first:
birds, squirrels, pets. A cat caught a bird in our
backyard. It was hurt. One wing was bent funny.
There was blood. . . ."

She could hear her voice, high, childlike. Her
bare toe made circles on the stone. She could not
turn around and face him. "I picked it up in my
hands. I must have been two, maybe three at the
time. I remember I was crying. All I wanted was
for the bird to be well, for it to be able to fly like
the other birds, for the blood and the hurt to be
gone. My hands got all warm, and when I opened
them what I'd wished for had happened. The bird
was fine again. It flew away."

"My God," David whispered.

Tears were pushing behind her eyes, and a tight
lump had begun to form in her throat. She went
on quickly. "It worked on people, too. All I had to
do was touch them and think magic thoughts and
they got well. 'Magic thoughts'—that's what my
mother called it. She said it was a gift. I don't know
. . . it was just *there*. Some people have blue eyes

and some have brown; some are redheads, blonds, or brunettes. It's like the color of someone's skin, David. I was born with it. I never asked for it or worked at it. It was just there.

"My mom kept it quiet. She said people wouldn't understand." She shook her head sadly. "If what happened today is any indication, I guess she was right. Later, when my parents died and the sisters took me in, they didn't make any fuss about it either. Father Brennan—he's the priest at the church there—he knew. He would take me over to the hospital, to the ones that were dying, ones that really needed it. We'd go in secret, late at night. If the nurses suspected, they didn't say anything."

"That's why you were at the hospital that night."

"Yes." She turned around to face him. Her lashes were wet, and she saw his face through a blur. "When that little boy was hurt today I didn't think, I just acted. He needed help. I was the only one that could help him. I had no idea it would cause such trouble. To be honest with you, David, even if I'd known this would happen I would have done it anyway. With my parents . . . with the sisters . . . with everyone I love, time or distance has prevented me from using my gift to help them. This was somebody I could help. I just couldn't stand there and let him die. I had to help him, David. *I had to.*"

The tears brimmed . . . overflowed. She turned away quickly and leaned against the cold stone mantel, her shoulders shaking with silent sobs.

Gentle hands took her by the shoulders and turned her around. David pulled her against him, rocking her in his arms as though she were a child. Warmth surrounded her, flowing along every nerve, covering her like a second skin, and she felt safe, secure, as if nothing bad could ever come to her within the circle of his arms. There was a rightness to it, a naturalness ... and what happened next came just as naturally.

She looked up at him. His eyes were gentle, tender, and contained none of the revulsion that she had feared to see there. He brushed at her tears with the back of his hand. The motion traveled down her cheek, became a caress. His hand cupped her chin, tipping her face up to meet his lips as he bent to hers.

Without conscious thought, her arms came up to circle his neck. She relaxed into the kiss, her lips softening beneath his. When the kiss had ended she nestled against him, her cheek resting in the curve of his shoulder. There was peace, and something unshakably right in it. She wished that she could make the moment last forever.

"It would be very easy to love you, Brie," he whispered.

She shook her head, feeling an icicle of fear pierce the warmth. "No, David," she said. "Hold me, but don't love me. Everyone who's ever loved me—everyone I've ever loved—has ended up dead."

She pulled back from him. "There's a dark side to this gift, a greedy side." She could see that he didn't understand. She searched for the words to explain to him and to make him take her seriously. "It's as if, where Death is concerned, it's necessary to pay the piper."

"That's silly, Brie. You've had a lot of tragedy in your life, that's true. But there's no reason to believe that those events are linked to your gift. And it's certainly no reason for you to stop loving, or to stop allowing others to love you."

He drew her back into his arms, and she had no will to resist. "There's something special about you," he went on. "I'm not talking about your healing gift. I love *you*, everything about you: your hair, your eyes, your laugh, even that awful gray dress. I love all of you, Brie, and I'll try to understand and love this gift of yours, too."

"Just hold me," she said, shaking her head in denial, clinging to him tightly. "Just hold me. That will be enough."

Samuel Kauffman opened his eyes slowly. The goggles had slipped sideways and were blocking his sight. He pulled them off. Spots swam minnow-like across his field of vision. Someone was bending over him. With an effort he made out the squat, paunchy form of Henry Wright, the security guard. Wright's lips were moving, but no sound came from them. A look of concern molded the guard's jowled face into a frown. Again his lips moved soundlessly. Fears of deafness sent Samuel's hands groping to his ears. Understanding brought a flood of relief as his fingers encountered the headphones. He ripped them off. The guard's gravelly voice was like music.

"Are you all right, Mr. Kauffman? Do you want me to call an ambulance?"

Samuel didn't answer. He sat up carefully, flexing his limbs, checking for broken bones. Everything worked. There was an annoying ringing in his ears, but above it he could hear the roar of the overhead exhaust fans that Wright must have turned on. The air in the lab was hazy with smoke.

Taking the guard's arm and using the edge of the desk as a lever, Samuel hoisted himself to his feet.

"I'm fine, Henry," he said, self-consciously brushing the dust from his trousers. "It was just a little accident, that's all. A small miscalculation on my part." He managed what he hoped was a convincing smile. "You can go now. Everything's kosher."

The guard hesitated. "I'll have to put this in the log, sir. There were no tests authorized for this evening." His voice was apologetic. "I have to report it."

"Of course you do. No problem." Samuel moved in closer to the guard, deftly backing him toward the open door.

"Well, if you're sure you're all right . . ."

"Fit as a fiddle. Good night, Henry. Thank you for your help."

Before the guard could say any more, Samuel maneuvered him into the hall and closed the door. He flicked the lock into place, then leaned against the door for a moment, trying to get his bearings. His vision was clearing and the ringing in his ears had faded to a dull hum, but his head was beginning to pound like the granddaddy of all hangovers. His heart was hammering wildly against his ribs, and it was that, more than the rubbery quality of his knees, that finally made him stagger to the desk and sit down.

The transmitter was still on. He switched it off, feeling a sense of relief as the green light went dark. His nose was running. He pulled a handkerchief from his pocket and dabbed at it, frowning when he saw blood on the white linen. He pinched the bridge of his nose, tilted his head back. In a few minutes the bleeding stopped. As the shock from the explosion diminished strength flowed back into him, and with it came a sense of exhilaration.

It worked.

By all the laws of nature, by all that was rational and sane, it shouldn't have. There were no explosive properties inherent in the combination of chemicals that Isaac had prescribed. Yet, it had worked. He stood up and picked his way to the far end of the lab.

The floor was littered with sand and chunks of brick. Samuel could feel the temperature rise as he approached the protective wall . . . or what was left of it. The explosion had torn open the sandbags, and the firebrick of the rear wall was blackened almost to the ceiling. The vents had blown, as they were designed to do. They probably had saved his life.

The lab table had been reduced to a mixture of ash and twisted metal. It was still too hot for Samuel to get close to it. He surveyed the destruction with awe. If a speck had done this, a tiny speck . . . then the lump of compound lying submerged in the barrel of water, just a few feet away, had the potential to wipe out a city.

That thought sent him staggering back to his desk. He poured more coffee, holding the cup in shaking hands. The world was already balanced precariously on the brink of nuclear disaster. Terrorist attacks had become so routine that only the most heinous ones made the headlines anymore. The last thing humanity needed was a better explosive.

Yet if this worked, what if the rest worked too?

What if all of Isaac's theories were valid? They seemed ridiculous, bordering on the fantastic. Still, many of the world's inventions—things now taken for granted—had seemed preposterous in their day.

He had to know. If it worked—if it *all* worked—the boon to mankind would far outweigh the risks. He would be careful. If Brimstone proved to be nothing more than an explosive, he would destroy the sample of compound he'd made and burn the formula. No one would ever know. No harm would be done.

He stuffed the papers containing the formula into his briefcase and tucked the transmitter into his pocket, then hesitated. The compound had to go with him, along with the ash. There must be nothing left to even hint at what he'd been working on.

There were other considerations, as well. The guard would report the unauthorized test. Disapproval and disciplinary actions would surely follow. He might not find a welcome at Hampton Chemicals after tonight. Any tests he wished to conduct had to be done now. He gathered a sample of the ash and set to work.

Two hours later, his tests completed, Samuel took the plastic bag of Brimstone compound from the water barrel and placed it on his desk top, using paper towels to wipe away the moisture from the outside of the package. Working quickly through the plastic, he pressed at the lump with his hands, leaning on it, using his weight to shape it and force it into a flat gray rectangle, small enough to fit into his briefcase.

He dumped the last of his coffee down the sink and rinsed the stainless-steel thermos well. Returning to the burned-out area of the lab, he used a spoon to scoop up the ash and deposit it through the narrow neck of the thermos. When he had filled it, he put the cork in place and screwed the lid down on top of it. He washed his hands, then took a farewell glance around the lab. He had no regrets. If Brimstone worked—if *all of it* worked—this was not an end, but a beginning, a new beginning for Samuel Kauffman and the rest of the human race.

He left the lab carrying the briefcase, the thermos tucked casually under one arm. He didn't look back.

It was late by the time he got home, and he expected to find the house quiet and David and the young woman long asleep. Instead he found a police car blocking the entrance to the drive. Tradewinds was ablaze with lights, and he had to show his driver's license and explain who he was before the police would let him pass. The front door was bolted from the inside. He was forced to stand and ring the bell until David let him in.

"Do you want to tell me what in hell is going on here?" he demanded, stomping into the living room.

David sat down on the couch next to Brie. Samuel was pleased to see his son's arm go protectively around the young woman's shoulders. The two of them were silent for a moment, each waiting for the other to speak first. At last it was David who answered.

"Dad, you're not going to believe this, but . . ."

As the story unfolded Samuel sank slowly down into a chair, Brimstone temporarily forgotten.

When David had finished, they all sat in silence for a time. At last Samuel got to his feet.

"You're right. I don't believe it." He looked from David to Brie. "You two stay right here."

He hurried from the room and returned with a paring knife. "I don't believe it, but there's one sure way to find out." Before David or Brie could stop him, he took the knife and slashed the blade across his open palm. Blood began to flow, great drops of it dripping between his fingers to the floor.

"Dad!" David protested.

"Damn. I didn't mean to go that deep. Oh, well . . ." He held out his hand to Brie. "Okay, sweetheart. Do your stuff."

Brie said nothing, but took his hand between hers. He felt a warmth grow at the spot and pinpoint on the wound. The stinging pain faded to nothing. A moment later, she took her hands away. The wound was gone. The blood on his hand and sleeve was the only sign that it had ever been. His knees suddenly weak, Samuel dropped heavily into a chair.

"I don't know about the rest of you, but I could use a drink right now."

Brie excused herself to wash her hands. By the time she returned to the living room, David had fetched a bottle of brandy and poured a small glass for each of them. Samuel downed his and then a second, all the while studying his hand. He'd made no attempt to wash off the blood.

"You know, you could make a pretty penny on this gift of yours," he said at last.

Brie shook her head. "I couldn't take money for it. That wouldn't be right."

Samuel studied her face for a moment, and liked

what he found there. "No. I guess it wouldn't be. Well . . . " he said, rubbing his palms together as if to warm them. "Well, it seems this is truly a day for miracles."

Brie understood first. "The formula—it worked?" she asked.

"As far as I've gotten, yes. It works just as Isaac said it would. If the rest of it works as promised, it will make that remarkable talent of yours obsolete."

"What do you mean?" David asked. "I thought it was some kind of explosive."

"It *is* that, but if Uncle Isaac's theories are correct it's a lot more. I don't want to go into that until I've had an opportunity to test it. Otherwise, you're likely to think the old man has gone off his rocker."

He stood up before they could question him further. "Now, in case you didn't notice, it's rather late. I'm heading for bed." He winked conspiratorially at Brie. "The two of you can pick up wherever it was you left off. Just pretend I'm not here. I'm a sound sleeper."

He picked up his briefcase and thermos. Whistling happily to himself, he headed up the stairs.

"So, where was it we left off?" David asked softly.

"I think you were just about to kiss me goodnight."

"Oh, really? Well, then . . ."

He stood up. Taking her by the hands, he pulled her to her feet and drew her into his arms. The warmth of him surrounded her. Brie reached up and took his face in her hands, tracing the curve of his cheek, lightly brushing a fingertip across his lips. She initiated the kiss, drawing his head down to her. The warmth emanating from him grew, became a fire that spread from his lips and his fingertips—from every point of contact—to set her being aflame.

So this was desire.

The sisters had taught her the mechanics of the sexual act, the cold technicalities of copulation and reproduction. But they had not prepared her for this delicious burning that melted her bones and turned them liquid, for the aching need it awakened within her, that only he could fill.

She knew all about the sex act. Her father had taught her all she thought she would ever care to know about it. Her mind associated it with cruelty and pain. But there was none of that here. His touch was gentle, undemanding. She knew that she only had to say no and he would stop.

Instead she found herself pulling him closer, urgently, almost desperately, unable to get him close enough. He drew back from the kiss, his eyes questioning her. *Is this really what you want?*

"Yes," she answered the unspoken question. "Yes, David. Oh, yes . . ."

The robe was a barrier between them. She pulled at the belt, felt it loosen. His lips moved to her throat, to the vee of her breasts.

He lifted her into his arms and carried her up the staircase to his room, leaving the downstairs lights ablaze. She closed her eyes and clung to him. As the robe fell away beneath his hands the lights danced behind her eyes like flames, burning away the last remnant of her fear.

Samuel filled the bathtub three-quarters full with cold water and submerged the plastic parcel containing the Brimstone compound. He knew the precaution was probably unnecessary. The chance of a natural occurrence of the particular set of frequencies that served as a catalyst to explode the compound was so small as to be almost nonexistent. Still, he would sleep better with Brimstone's explosive potential safely inactivated.

Wearily, he sank down on the edge of the bed and pulled off his shoes and socks. He stripped down to his underwear, then sat staring at the thermos on his night table. Though his body was weary his mind was wide awake, so full of what he'd learned at the lab that sleep was impossible.

Before he left the lab, he'd conducted a brief analysis of the ash. A Geiger counter had showed no signs of radioactivity. Chemical analysis had shown the ash to be a harmless mixture of carbon, oxygen, hydrogen, nitrogen, and phosphorus. There was no evident toxicity. Indeed, he'd noticed nothing unusual about it at all until he'd placed a smear of it on a slide and studied it under the electron microscope. Only then had the wonderful, impossible irregularity been revealed.

As stated in Isaac's notes, the chemical components were arranged in chains, the chains intertwining to form a five-strand braid. "Living chains" Isaac had called them, for of course, in 1942, he could not have known of DNA. He had only known that what he was seeing was life.

Life.

Samuel wiped a hand across his brow and found it damp with perspiration. The Brimstone explosion had produced a form of DNA unlike anything he'd ever seen before. Nothing should have survived the heat of the blast, yet the evidence before him was irrefutable.

He pulled Isaac's notes from his briefcase and read through them again—the impossible claims, the ridiculous theories. Thus far, everything had proved accurate. And if the rest of it could be trusted as well . . .

Caution and common sense whispered to him to stop, to wait and test the compound further or, at the least, to try the experiment on animals first, as Isaac had done. Samuel hesitated, but only for a moment. Animals could not speak, could not tell him what they were feeling, what miraculous changes were happening inside their bodies. Only a human subject could do that. Caution and common sense be damned. He had to know. He had to *know*.

He picked up the thermos and carried it into the bathroom. In the cabinet beneath the sink, he found a plastic basin. Opening the thermos, he shook out a large quantity of the ash into the basin. He added water from the tap, stirring the mixture into a gray-black paste.

He hesitated now, scanning Isaac's notes for the mode of administration. Absorption could be achieved either by ingestion or directly through the skin. He looked at the ashy paste. The thought of eating it made his stomach turn.

He scooped up some of the paste, wincing at the cold, gritty feel of it. Feeling foolish, he began to smear it on his body: first on his arms and legs, then across his bare chest, and at last on his face, taking care not to get any in his eyes. Not knowing how much would be sufficient, he continued until the basin was empty.

He reached for the spigot, intending to wash his

hands, then decided against it. As he straightened up, he caught a glimpse of himself in the mirror over the sink. His face—blue eyes peering out of the black flesh—looked like something out of vaudeville. He suddenly felt as ridiculous as he looked. He almost stepped into the shower and washed the stuff away. But if there was a chance . . . even the smallest chance.

He padded back into the bedroom and flopped on the bed, heedless of the dirty smear his body made on the sheets. The excitement was wearing off, and he was terribly tired. He would get a good night's sleep. Tomorrow he would wash away the paste and the silly fantasies that went with it. He chuckled at his own gullibility. Next he'd be believing in fairies and Peter Pan. It was his last thought before sleep took him into a Never-Never Land of his own.

Chapter Twelve

The first light of day woke Klaus Brauer as it crept around the edge of the window shades. In the dim light he made out the slack form of Gunner Hahn asleep on the other bed, his face to the wall, head and shoulders propped up with pillows. From an aging color television set on a rickety stand near the foot of the bed, the morning news chattered softly.

Brauer put a hand up to his face and patted the bandages experimentally. His skin felt tight beneath the wrappings. His mouth was dry.

Moving slowly, he sat up. Pain jabbed needles through his temples, then spread in a dull, throbbing ache down through the shattered bones of his cheek and nose.

"Hahn . . ." he called out weakly. The younger man did not stir. His breathing sounded thick and heavy.

Brauer didn't try to awaken him again. The pain of speaking was too great. He took slow, careful breaths through his mouth until the pain had eased, tasting old blood and the bitterness of what the girl had done to him. Clumsily, he swung his legs over the edge of the bed and stood, holding tight to the headboard for support.

He edged his way along the mattress to the foot of the bed, then staggered the short distance to the small lavatory. He was fighting a losing battle against dizziness, the growing pain in his face, and the echoing throb of the tumor in his belly. Once inside, he used the sink for support and pushed the door closed behind him.

He tried to urinate but nothing would come, and his knees were too shaky to stand for long. At the sink, he raised his head enough for a quick glance in the mirror. That was quite enough. Bandages covered his nose and most of the lower right half of his face. In spots here and there blood and sera had soaked through, then dried. Brauer quickly looked away. The pain in his belly was turning from a throb to a slow burning. He filled a paper cup and rinsed his mouth, watching the brown-tinged water spiral into the drain. His knees trembled, threatening to give way. He leaned on the sink.

He had to get back to the bedroom . . . had to lie down . . . Had to rest. . . .

The room was beginning to swim before his eyes as he tottered back to the bed, the chatter of the television a droning background hum to his shuffling footsteps. Disinterested, only half-focused, his eyes skimmed over the screen, then paused momentarily and widened.

He stared.

Heedless of the pain, he lurched to the television and turned up the sound.

". . . interesting note. In Newport, Rhode Island, the mystery continues today. It centers around a young woman. Yesterday afternoon, eight-year-old Brian Cummings was riding his bicycle when he was struck by a van . . ."

Brauer heard the rest of the report: how witnesses claimed that the child had been critically injured; how quantities of blood on the boy's clothes and the sidewalk indicated a massive injury; how a mysterious young woman had come to his aid, then fled the scene leaving behind an uninjured child and a slew of unanswered questions. Across the screen flashed still photos of the mangled bicycle, the cracked windshield of the van, and a smiling photo of the boy eating an ice cream cone. It then returned to the first picture, the one that had caught Brauer's attention.

It was fuzzy, blurred. The photo had been taken through the window of a moving car, and reflections and the distortion caused by movement made identification difficult. Still, he was almost certain that the woman was Gabrielle Prescott.

". . . and although the mystery lady refused all interviews and declined to reveal her identity, it is known that she is a guest of Newport resident David Kauffman. Kauffman, author of the bestseller *Dark Morning*, refused comment . . ."

Brauer waited until the announcer had moved on to the next item, then switched the TV off.

"We have her, Gunner. Do you see? We have her!"

When he received no reply, Brauer reached across the space between the two beds to shake Hahn awake. His fingers closed around the younger man's arm, his grip tightening in his excitement. Without warning his fingers sank into the flesh—

through the flesh—of Hahn's arm, and into a substance like warm jelly. Hahn screamed.

Brauer pulled away, skittering backward across the bed. His fingers were coated with a thick gray ooze, streaked with blood. Whimpering in disgust, he wiped them on the sheet. His shoulder holster was slung across the bedpost, and he pulled his gun and trained it on Hahn. His hands were shaking.

"What has happened to you?" he demanded.

The figure on the bed stirred slightly. The movement was too smooth. The body seemed to flow beneath the sheets as it turned toward Brauer.

"The gun is not necessary, Colonel. If I had wished to harm you, I had ample opportunity while you were sleeping. I am not a danger to anyone . . . not anymore."

The voice sounded like Hahn's, but there was a thick murkiness to the syllables, as if the speaker were talking underwater. It made Brauer's skin crawl. He reached over to the lamp on the bedside table and switched it on, angling the shade until the light fell across the other bed. He sucked in air in one long, slow gasp.

It was Hahn. The clothes were the same and he recognized the features, despite the changes that had taken place. The familiar blue eyes peered at him from a face creased by lines and wrinkles. The thick blond hair had turned silvery white and had receded back from the broad forehead. Like some modern-day Rip Van Winkle, his young assistant had aged more than half a century in the last twenty-four hours.

"Who are you?" Brauer asked.

"I am Gunner Hahn." The man smiled wearily, and Brauer saw dark gaps where teeth were missing. "I am Gunner Hahn, but in a way you might say that I am something more. In fact, my dear Colonel Brauer, you might say that I *am* Brimstone."

David lay very still and watched Brie sleep. She was curled on her side, knees drawn up close to her body. Her mouth was open slightly. He moved his hand until he could feel the warm whisper of her breath against his fingers.

A lock of hair lay across her face, and he resisted the temptation to brush it back. He was almost afraid to have her wake, afraid he might awaken too and find that last night had been a dream, afraid that the warm reality of her would suddenly dissolve into shadow and mist.

Last night, beneath her shy, childlike exterior he'd discovered depths of warmth and passion he could never have imagined. Brie gave fully and without reserve, reveling in the pleasure she could give him and astonished by the delight her own body was capable of.

He couldn't help but compare her with Marsha. Lovemaking with Marsha had been an exacting and joyless exercise, full of the right moves but devoid of true intimacy. Marsha had never let him get close to the essence of her. She had seemed as much of a stranger to him, after the marriage had run its brief course, as she had been the night they'd met.

How different with Brie! With the secret of her gift out in the open and accepted, it seemed there was nothing more to withhold. She opened herself to him, trusted him. In the short time he'd known her, they'd shared far more than he ever had shared with Marsha.

Last night, on the edge of sleep, he remembered holding her, feeling her body begin to tremble, hearing the trembling turn to a sobbing that brought him fully awake.

"Brie," he whispered. "Brie, what's wrong? Did I hurt you?"

She shook her head and only cried harder, trying to choke out words between the sobs. "Didn't . . . know . . . Didn't . . ."

She clung to him, weeping as if something had broken inside her, crying with a terrible intensity that filled him with dread. At last she quieted and was able to look up at him.

The light from the outdoor floodlights shone in the window, spotlighting her face, making the wetness on her eyes and cheeks shine. The fear must have showed on his face, for she'd kissed him and then caressed his cheeks as if he were something delicate and fragile that would break.

"Nothing's wrong, David. Everything is right . . . so very, very right." Her fingers were like butterfly wings against his skin.

"I didn't know. I never dreamed it could be like this. . . . Could be good, I mean."

"I don't understand, Brie."

"The police didn't tell everything about my parents, about my father and what happened . . . what he did to me."

What she had told him then made him love her even more—had showed him the courage and the trust it had required of her to allow him to get close to her, to touch her, to know her.

"I didn't realize, David. The only thing I had to

go by was when my father hurt me. Mother Margarethe never said much about sex, except that it was a wife's 'marital duty.' She always believed I would enter the order, so I guess it was something she thought I would never have to deal with. I came to the conclusion that lovemaking was something you endured because you loved someone."

"And you loved me."

"Yes."

Beside him Brie stirred, drawing his thoughts quickly back to the present. As he watched, she opened her eyes. She smiled.

He loved that smile. Remembering the oh-so-serious young woman in the gray dress, he longed to hear her laugh. He leaned over and kissed her forehead, then her nose.

His hands traced lightly over her shoulders, trailed down the outer curves of her breasts to the firm, flat plane of her belly. His fingertips walked playfully along the base of her rib cage.

"David, what are you doing?" she laughed. "Stop it."

"No."

"Stop." Giggling, Brie tried to push his hands away, but his fingers pressed more firmly into her ribs.

"You're ticklish! I'll bet nobody's ever given you a good tickling. No one should reach adulthood without once being tickle-tortured. There are experiences in life that people simply should not miss. I would be neglectful of my duty if I didn't—"

She wriggled from his grasp and snatched up her pillow, pummeling him with it before she scrambled to the foot of the bed.

"So, the lady wants to fight." He grabbed his own

pillow and stood up unsteadily, the mattress heaving beneath him. "Take this!" He launched himself across the bed and plowed into her, pillow-first.

Kneeling on the bed, they rained blows on each other, Brie squealing with delight, until he finally managed to wrench her pillow from her and pin her to the mattress.

"I have you now, my pretty!" he screeched in his best wicked-witch voice, straddling her, his hands loosely encircling her wrists.

But he did not go ahead with the tickling. The sight of her lying there, smiling up at him, eyes bright with laughter, her hair spread like a dark fan beneath her, called forth all the tenderness in him and pushed any thoughts of tickling from his mind. He gave no resistance when she slipped her hands from his grasp and brought them up to encircle his neck. He shifted his weight to his elbows, lowered himself gently between her legs as she opened them in invitation.

"I love you, Brie," he whispered huskily, just before his mouth closed on hers.

"What do you mean, you *are* Brimstone?" Brauer asked. "What has Brimstone to do with you?"

"What has Brimstone to do with me?" Gunner chuckled. The laugh became a liquid gurgle that drowned in his chest. He fought for breath. "I haven't much time, but I will tell you my story, Colonel—if only so that you will give up this obsession with Brimstone and let it go back to whatever heaven or hell it came from."

He licked his lips and drew in a ragged breath. "I was born Ivan Hahn, to a Jewish family in Breshkov, Lithuania, in the year 1859."

"Rubbish."

Hahn had the satisfaction of seeing Brauer flinch, and wondered briefly if it was due to his race, the name of the village, or the seeming impossibility of the date. "No interruptions," he chided Brauer weakly. At the other man's silence, he went on.

"My life was fairly uneventful. I worked the farmland around the village with my parents and brothers and sisters. After a minimum of schooling, I married a village girl. She bore me two sons and three daughters. We farmed the land and, though we were not rich by any means, we were happy.

"The First World War claimed one son, and in 1923 my wife succumbed to pneumonia following a measles epidemic that swept through our village. Drought and epidemics were the two things we feared most—of course, no one knew about Brimstone then. . . ."

Abruptly, a fit of coughing took him. He turned his face into the pillow. Deep within his chest, it felt as if his lungs were being wrenched from their fragile moorings. When the coughing had quieted and Gunner was able to lift his head, he saw that the pillow was dotted with flecks of blood. From the other bed, Brauer was staring at him with disgust. Gunner cleared his throat.

"By 1942, there was something new to fear. The Nazis had invaded Lithuania. Jews were at the top of their list of undesirables. Still, what could we do? There was no place to go, nowhere to hide. Breshkov was a small village, far out in the countryside. We minded our own business and were a threat to no one. We counted on our insignificance and our remoteness to save us. We deluded ourselves into thinking that we were so small that the

Nazi war machine would overlook us. But we were wrong, eh, Colonel?

"How were we to know that our smallness and our remoteness would make us a perfect target for the test of a new Nazi superweapon?" He shook his head sadly, then fixed his gaze on Brauer.

"I was always known for my sharp eyes. In my youth I received the nickname 'Gunner,' because I could shoot the eye of a rabbit from one hundred yards. I was eighty-three years old that autumn of 1942—crippled with arthritis and ready to die— but my eyes were still good. I saw you, Colonel Brauer, you and your short, fat friend. I saw you on the hill overlooking our village, and I knew that all our hopes of coming through the war unnoticed were in vain. . . ."

He stood in the shelter of the woods and watched the two men emerge from the long, black car. He did not recognize them, but he did recognize the uniform that the tall one was wearing and the danger it represented. As one, their gaze turned toward the village and he felt his heart leap with dread. Dropping the load of firewood he was carrying, he hobbled down the brush-covered side of the hill and struck off through the woods toward the town.

Warning. He had to give warning. His heart thudded in his chest and he fought for each breath as he ran. The dense underbrush seemed to clasp at his legs, snagging on his clothes and slowing him down. The toe of his boot caught an outcropping of rock. He fell.

The fall shook him to his bones. When he tried to rise, his knee joints seemed on fire with pain. He whimpered softly. Too late. Too late. If he did not hurry and warn them, it would be too late.

Sobbing, tears of frustration running down his face, he raised himself on one knee, caught hold of a bush, and used it to pull himself up. Just as he gained his feet, the woods suddenly lit with a blinding brilliance. The image of tree branches, like black lace against the dazzling white of the sky, seared itself upon his retinas. He fell backward.

A terrible wind, hot as the breath from a blast furnace, ripped through the forest, knocking trees aside as if they were matchsticks. With a hiss, the rain turned to steam. Then that small sound was swallowed up by a thunderous roar, unlike anything he'd ever heard before. It pressed down on him, threatening to crush his skull like an egg. His last thoughts, before the brightness dimmed and the sound faded to silence, were of his family, of his village. As his skull compressed his thoughts narrowed down too, to one word:

Gone.

Samuel Kauffman awoke at mid-morning with last night's coffee an ache in his bladder. The remnant of a headache pulled at his temples.

He itched.

Memories of the night before surfaced slowly, bouyed by the sight of the pillowcase. The crisp, white percale was smeared with gray. A glance down at his body showed that the ash paste had dried to a thick gray crust. As he sat up it cracked and crumbled in the folds of his skin, sending avalanches of soft gray powder cascading down the slight paunch of his belly to come to rest at the waistband of his briefs. He grimaced in disgust.

"Samuel, Samuel. What an old fool you are to believe in fairy tales."

He stripped off his underwear and trudged into

the bathroom, not bothering to switch on the light. The dimness was soothing. He relieved himself, then stepped into the shower. In the dim stall he lathered himself by rote, like a blind man. The hot water was a warm cocoon, sluicing away the dry, scratchy later of ash. With it gone he felt light, refreshed. By the time he'd stepped out of the shower, his headache was gone.

The rough terry of the towel set his skin tingling as he dried himself off. He felt good—no, better than good. He felt wonderful. Whistling softly to himself, he flicked on the bathroom light.

"I don't know how long it was before I regained consciousness."

Gunner closed his eyes and concentrated on the words. In his lower back pain flared briefly, then faded altogether. The lower half of his body simply went numb, as if it had ceased to exist. He tried not to think about it and focused his thoughts, instead, on that long-ago day in 1942.

"Even though it wasn't cold enough for it, the sky was sifting down a strange gray snow. It covered everything: the trees, the ground. It was in my hair and on my clothes, in the very air I breathed. It was only as I began to make my way toward the village that I realized it was ash. . . ."

He staggered through the wood. Nothing broke the profound silence, not even the murmur of the wind through the leafless trees. The only sounds were his own crashing footfalls, the harsh rasp of his breathing. The gray ash fell silently, brushing his cheeks like warm down. It clogged his nose and mouth, and he was coughing and snorting by the time he reached the place where the village should have been.

One old tree stood like a ragged sentinel. The explosion had stripped it of its leaves. Its bare branches had the appearance of arms reaching frantically toward the sky. The first house should have stood just beyond it, but there was only black, scarred earth and rubble. Even these were beginning to disappear beneath the anonymous coating of ash.

Gunner's feet carried him onward. There was no way of distinguishing one house from another, where the main street might have been . . . the synagogue . . . the village square. He picked his way between heaps of charred brick and slate. A mass of blackened, twisted steel that might once have been an automobile blocked his way. He skirted around it and kept moving, his numb mind focusing in on the task of putting one foot before the other, for to think beyond that was to flirt with madness.

He spent the remainder of the day going in circles, picking among the rubble for some sign, some small familiar bit of the life and the people he had known here. But there was nothing but silence and ashes. He said the ritual prayers for the dead. The grayness absorbed the words, and it was as if they had never been uttered. At last, he sank down on the still warm ground and closed his eyes in exhaustion. The soft gray around him darkened to black. Night came, silent and starless, and he lay amid the ashes of his life and his loved ones and waited for death.

"How about some breakfast?" David stood up and shrugged into his robe.

Brie nodded silently. She pulled on her own robe, then stepped to the window and pulled the edge of the curtain aside just enough to give her a clear view of the front lawn and the drive. The police car was still there, blocking the entrance from the street. Fear trickled into Brie's veins like ice water, a drop at a time, slowly displacing the warmth that lingered after the lovemaking.

She had promised herself that she would never love anyone again. Now she saw how foolish that promise had been. Love was not something that could be planned for or prevented. Whether she wished it or not, it had happened. That put David at risk. Though he'd dismissed her fears about the dark side of her gift, she knew better. Death stalked anyone she loved.

Her picture was in the newspapers and on the television news. The men who'd killed the sisters would see it and come for her, but it would be David that death would try to claim. She could not allow that to happen.

She thought of leaving, but quickly rejected the idea. That would not help him. With both of her parents and the sisters death had come when she was apart from them, as if to prevent her from using her gift to save them. Maybe the trick was to stay close to David, close enough to shield him from whatever was to come. It *was* coming—something dark and terrible. She felt it, in the same way an animal can sense an earthquake before it happens.

Without warning, David's arms came around her from behind. She jumped. Playfully he spun her around to face him.

"I didn't mean to startle you." He kissed her forehead, then held her at arm's length, studying her. "You've got your serious-young-lady face on again. What's troubling you?"

She couldn't meet his eyes. "Nothing that concerns you," she lied. "Anyway, if I told you everything I was thinking I'd soon lose my air of mystery, and you'd become bored with me."

"Never," he declared solemnly. "Not in a million years." He cupped her chin in his hand and turned her face up to his. "You're still worried about those men, aren't you? You shouldn't be, you know. They're probably half a continent away by now. The police are guarding the house. Don't worry, Brie. Nothing's going to happen—not to you, not to me. Everything's going to be fine. You'll see."

"You're right, of course. Nothing will happen." She forced a smile and tried to keep her voice light. "Did someone mention breakfast, or was I just imagining things? I'm starving."

"After you, my lady."

He ushered her ahead of him through the door and down the hall. Sunlight poured through the window at the head of the stairs. She paused for a moment, feeling its warmth surround her. A silent prayer formed within her, and she didn't know whether she prayed to God or to death or to both: *This time, if You have to take someone, let it be me.*

As in all the other times she'd tried to pray she felt no sense of comfort, no reassurance that Anyone had heard or was even listening. David came between her and the window, his body blocking the sunlight. The hallway suddenly went dark. Then he passed her and was pounding on ahead down the stairs.

"Last one to the kitchen is stuck with the dishes!" he called over his shoulder, as he rounded the bend in the stairway and disappeared into the cool dimness of the downstairs.

The sunlight surrounded her again, but she saw only the shadows that had claimed him and felt only the chill of premonition.

Slowly, she followed him down the stairs.

The brightness of the bathroom light dazzled Samuel Kauffman's eyes. He closed them and toweled his hair, cocking his head to drain the water from his ears.

He bent to dry his feet, whistling "Song of India" softly between his teeth. He'd never been much of a singer but he was an adequate whistler, and the confined, tiled space of the bathroom picked up the sound and amplified it. He opened his eyes.

The whistle stopped abruptly, as his mouth went dry.

The body he was staring down at was his own—yet not his own. He ran a trembling hand down one arm, then held the hand up to the light, flexing the fingers, watching the play of the tendons beneath the pale flesh.

His fingertips traced wonderingly across his chest, trailed down over the rise of his belly, through the bush of pubic hair that sprouted beneath it. His penis came erect, a rarity since the prostate surgery he'd undergone four years earlier.

Some part of his mind registered the sound of footsteps passing his bedroom door. He heard David say something, recognized the soft lilt of Brie's voice, but the sounds seemed light-years away from whatever universe it was he now existed in.

He stumbled across the small bathroom to the mirror and rubbed a circular hole in the fog that steam had made on its cool surface. The face in the mirror looked frightened. He watched his fingers touch its brow and nose and lips the way a dealer in antiquities might touch a priceless Ming vase, as if touch alone would shatter the fragile illusion.

It was all too much. He staggered back into the bedroom and sat on the bed, hunched forward, his arms dangling between his knees. His mind slipped its gears for a time, freewheeling until it could cope with the magnitude of what had happened to his body. At last, his thoughts began to reorder themselves. Sanity returned.

He took clothes from the closet and found comfort in the normal, mundane activities of fastening buttons and tying shoes. By the time he'd finished dressing his hands had stopped their shaking.

He had to tell David, but how? How could he ever begin to explain? Perhaps showing would be enough. Yes, that probably would be best. He opened his bedroom door and headed downstairs.

Chapter Thirteen

"I hoped to die that night, but of course I didn't."

Hahn laughed bitterly. Beneath the sheets something let go with a wet, popping sound that made Brauer's stomach churn. The sickly-sweet reek of decay filled the room. Hahn didn't seem to notice it. His eyes were far away.

"The next morning I awoke feeling full of energy. After a night sleeping in the open on the damp ground, the arthritis should have been raising hell with my joints, but there was no pain, no stiffness. I was afraid that the Nazis—that *you*, Colonel Brauer—would return and find me, so I fled into the woods.

"I walked for days, skirting the towns and villages, except to steal what I could to eat. There was precious little of that. I should have sickened and died. Instead, I grew stronger. At last I found shelter with a farmer and his family. They took me in, fed me, gave me water to wash with ... and that was when I discovered the change. I washed away the ash, and with it it seemed I washed away half a century of living. Beneath the ash, my body was that of a young man in his prime—thirty or thirty-five. All signs of aging, all the afflictions and ailments that go with it, were gone.

"The family hid me there for the remainder of the war. I fell in love with one of the daughters and married her. We were happy. We had a family. I was a man reborn.

"Only as the years went by did the curse reveal itself. My wife and my children, all those around me whom I loved grew old—but I did not. At first they joked about my eternal youth, then, as more years passed and I still didn't age, the jokes changed to jealousy and finally fear. At last I left.

"I nearly went mad from the loneliness. Finally, in desperation, I tried to drown myself. That is when I discovered the true horror: I could not die. Brimstone has a will of its own, an overpowering will to live. After three days, my body washed up on shore. Sharks had been at it. They put what was left in the local morgue. Within forty-eight hours, the cells had repaired themselves. I woke among the dead, early on the morning when they'd planned to bury me. I ran away."

His voice had risen to a hysterical pitch. The gnarled fingers gripped the edge of the sheet, twisting it in anguish. "After that, I didn't try to kill myself again. I was afraid that I would wake in my coffin—underground."

His eyes focused on Brauer. Their blue had muddied to gray.

"Do you have any idea what it is like, Colonel: to wish to die and be unable to do so; to be condemned to an everlasting hell of loneliness and loss?" A sigh escaped him. His body seemed to settle deeper into the bed. His voice growing weaker, Hahn continued.

"I became a drifter, a loner. Not by choice, but of necessity. Every few years or so, before my lack of aging became noticeable, I would move on. Around me the world moved on also, became a place of noise and congestion, a place where fresh air is only a memory. I grew weary of the moving, weary of life. Slowly, the idea grew in me."

The dull gray eyes became animated for a moment, but Brauer realized that Hahn was looking beyond him, at something that only he could see. Curious, Brauer reached out and waved a hand before the other man's eyes. There was no response. The hand holding the gun had begun to cramp, so Brauer set the safety and let the revolver drop to the bed beside him. It was no longer needed. Hahn was blind.

"I knew that the explosion had somehow caused my condition. I thought that perhaps, if I found the source of it, I could find a means to counteract it— a means of release. I began a slow search, full of false leads and dead ends. It went on for years, but, after all, I had the time. Eventually, Colonel Brauer, it led me to you."

The wrinkled mouth curved into a semblance of a smile. Hahn laughed, the sound barely recognizable as coming from a human throat. Brauer saw two yellowed teeth fall from the wrinkled maw and roll down the slope of the sheets. At the same time, Hahn's breath washed over him with the stench of an open grave.

"Under your tutelage, I became a murderer. Now I'm on my way to Heaven or Hell—it matters little. Anything is preferable to this half-life that Brimstone has condemned me to."

"But why?" Brauer asked, thinking aloud. "After

all these years, why did the process reverse itself now?"

The blind eyes turned toward him. Brauer flinched. The irises had gone liquid, and were leaking a cloudy gray slime down Hahn's shriveling cheeks.

"I've thought about that a lot in the last few days. I have no answers. Maybe Brimstone has a set life span, or maybe whatever Brimstone is has grown tired, too—that is what I think with my head. But in my heart, Colonel, I *know* it is the girl."

"What?"

Without warning, Hahn's arm snaked across the space between them with uncanny accuracy. His hand closed around Brauer's wrist. Brauer tried to pull away, but the fingers clung to him like a leech, drawing him closer, until his face was only inches from Hahn's.

"Let me go!" Brauer shrieked, frantically trying to pry the fingers loose. The skin peeled away from the bones in long gray tatters, but the hand still held firm.

"The girl is what you want, Colonel," Hahn went on, heedless of Brauer's cries and struggling. "I've been listening to the news and thinking. There's something strange about her. When I caught her in the woods that night, she sensed that something was amiss inside of me. She *saw* Brimstone within me, saw the unnatural evil it was, and in touching me, whether she realized it or not, she made it right again."

Empty of their contents, the blind eyes had sunk deep into the sockets. The lids came down over them, like shades closing. The skeletal fingers tightened convulsively on Brauer's wrist. "Don't you see? She's the answer for you, Colonel—not Brimstone. She gives life, like she did for that boy. Brimstone . . . gives . . . only . . . death."

The last word was like the whisper of escaping steam. Hahn's body fell forward, muscles contracting involuntarily and drawing the two men together, as if in a lover's embrace.

With a scream Brauer jerked backward, dragging Hahn's body with him. The dead man's arm came off at the shoulder, with a wet, tearing sound. The body fell back onto the bed.

The fingers around Brauer's wrist were like bands of steel. With the strength of pure terror Brauer tore at them, bending the joints backward and snapping the bones. Blood coated his fingers, making them slip. More blood, mixed with a thick gray fluid, spurted from the torn vessels of the upper arm, spraying the wall and the bed sheets. At last the dead fingers gave up their grip. The hand fell away. Brauer scrambled away from the bed, rubbing at his wrist, where Hahn's fingers had left deep purple grooves in the flesh.

The thing that had been Gunner Hahn lay still. Something gray and glistening oozed from the shoulder wound and fell onto one of the pillows. It seemed to shudder for a moment, then all movement ceased. The gray turned dark and dull, as if a light deep beneath the surface had gone out.

As Brauer watched, Hahn's body diminished. The shriveled flesh collapsed inward, folded in upon itself, the body shrinking to a dried husk. Then even that began to lose substance, until all that was left on the bed was a sprinkling of gray dust.

Brauer fetched his gun from under the bed, then snatched the car keys from on top of the television set. He paused for a moment in the open doorway and looked back. A breeze was sweeping through the room, ruffling the sheets and making the blinds on the windows thrum. It lifted a swirl of gray dust into the air.

Brauer slammed the door behind him.

"Close your eyes."

"Dad, don't you think we're a little old for this?"

David rolled his eyes at Brie and shook his head in exasperation. He finished pouring milk into a small pitcher, then replaced the carton on the shelf and nudged the door of the refrigerator closed with his hip. He set the pitcher on the kitchen table, next to the coffeepot. The smell of fresh-perked coffee mingled with the aroma of the bacon that crackled in a skillet on the stove, making Brie's mouth water.

From the dining room, Samuel laughed. The sound was high-pitched, almost hysterical. "We'll just see who's too old. Now close your eyes. You too, Brie."

Brie spooned scrambled eggs onto a platter and popped it into the oven to keep it warm, then switched off the burner under the skillet of bacon. She stole up on David from behind. Straining on tiptoe, she reached up and placed her hands over his eyes.

"Humor him," she whispered, kissing David's neck. She closed her own eyes, pressing her cheek into the warm hollow between his shoulder blades.

"I heard that. She's right. Be a good son, David, and humor an old man."

"Okay," David conceded. "Come on in, Dad. Our eyes are closed."

"No peeking." Again the hysterical giggle.

"Come on, Dad, before the coffee gets cold."

Brie heard the sound of footsteps.

"Ta-daaah! Presenting the new Samuel Kauffman!"

Brie let her hands fall away from David's eyes. At the same moment, she felt his body stiffen. He made a small sound and took a step backward, almost knocking her off balance. Curious, she peered around the curve of his shoulder. Her hand came up to her lips to stifle a gasp.

Samuel laughed, obviously delighted by their consternation. Hands on hips, he struck a jaunty pose, then did a slow pirouette.

"Well, what do you think?"

What could they think? The voice was Samuel Kauffman's, but the man who stood before them was not. A thick new growth of black curls had begun to crowd out the thinning gray hair on his head. His back was straighter, his body trimmer. The skin of his face and neck had firmed and tightened, nearly erasing the lines that age had etched at his eyes and mouth. He looked like a shorter, *slightly* older version of David.

David's hand found hers and gripped it tightly. She could feel him trembling. "What's happened to you, Dad?" he asked hoarsely.

"This is your Uncle Isaac's secret. Brimstone isn't a bomb. It's a fountain of youth."

Samuel placed his hands on David's shoulder. "Do you see why I couldn't have explained it to you—why I was so mysterious? I couldn't believe it myself until I saw it with my own eyes. But it's real, David. I feel like a kid again. Isn't it wonderful?''

"But . . . how?"

Samuel released him and began to pace the room, nervously running the fingers of one hand through his hair, over and over again.

"Even I don't completely understand it—not yet. Brimstone is essentially a reaction between a precise chemical mix and sound. This produces the initial explosion. The Nazis saw the explosive potential as the end, but it is really only one step in the process. The explosion is a catalyst that fuses and activates the chemical mix to produce a new life form. This has the capability to combine with existing life forms in a sort of symbiosis that results in cell regeneration and longevity in the host."

"It's a parasite?"

"In a sense, yes. It can't live unless absorbed by a host body. Unabsorbed, it dies within twenty-four hours."

"What if it doesn't stop? What if you keep getting younger?" David asked.

"You're worried that you'll end up changing my diapers and feeding me pablum? According to Isaac's notes, that shouldn't happen. Whatever life form Brimstone is, it tends to stabilize the host subject at an optimum age. Isaac theorized that for humans that would be approximately the mid-thirties. Already the process seems to be slowing down."

" 'Theorized'—didn't he test it?"

"On animals. He didn't have the time or opportunity to move on to human subjects. He was trying to keep the secret from the Nazis. I think he did remarkably well, considering the circumstances."

"So you're the first human subject."

"Yes. But I'm fine, David. Really."

Samuel sat down at the table and poured himself a cup of coffee. "Look, if it'll put your mind at ease, I've already made an appointment to have a complete physical. I'm curious to see just what the doctors will find." He pulled out the chair beside him and patted the seat, looking imploringly at Brie. "Now stop gawking at me and sit down. Have some breakfast before it gets cold."

Brie brought the bacon and eggs to the table and sank into the offered chair. She sipped at the cup of coffee that Samuel poured for her, barely tasting it. Mother Margarethe's voice filled her mind:

"In the beginning was the Word . . ."

"What?"

Brie started. Without realizing it, she'd spoken aloud. Both David and Samuel were staring at her questioningly. She felt a hot flush creeping up her neck to her face.

"It's the beginning of St. John's gospel," she explained. "Scholars take the Word to be Christ. But what if things did begin with a word spoken by God—not just a word, but a shout—the Big Bang that scientists speak about?"

"You mean an explosion—like Brimstone," David said.

"Maybe Brimstone is a small part of it."

"Who knows?" Samuel picked up a piece of bacon with his fingers and nibbled at it thoughtfully. "In the Pentateuch, God begins the process of creation with the words 'Let there be light.' The release of light energy is undeniably part of the

Brimstone explosion. Come to think of it, the patriarchs lived to ages that now seem incredible. Abraham was one hundred and seventy-five when he died, if I remember correctly. It's an interesting line of speculation."

Brie shook her head. "I find it a little frightening. Maybe we're starting to tamper with things that are better left alone."

"That's in the same line as 'If man were meant to fly, God would have given him wings'. Yet air travel is taken for granted now."

"What we're dealing with here is far bigger than airplanes," David said. "The moral implications . . ."

Samuel wiped his hands on a napkin and got up from the table. "Anything new is always a bit frightening." There was a note of annoyance in his voice. "I had hoped that you would share my enthusiasm."

"David's trying to," Brie assured him. "It's just such a shock. I've only known you a few days, but every time I look across the table at you I feel a little dizzy, as if my senses are playing tricks. David has a whole lifetime of perceptions to readjust to. Give him time."

Samuel reached out and laid a hand on her cheek. "You're right." He winked at David. "If you don't hurry up and ask this young lady to marry you, I'm liable to give you some competition."

He put his empty plate and cup on the counter by the sink. "Well, I'll be off." He hesitated. "What are you two planning for today?"

David looked at Brie. She shrugged, forcing a weak smile, one hand rubbing absently at her cheek where Samuel had touched her.

"After what happened yesterday, the press will be staking out the house," David said. "It's probably best that we just stay put and hope this whole thing blows over. I've got the book to catch up on."

"In that case, let's plan to eat in. I'll pick up steaks, champagne . . . some dessert. We'll have a celebration."

He looked at Brie. "Don't look so glum, young lady. There's nothing to worry about. Tonight I'll explain everything to you: the formula, Isaac's notes—everything. Once you understand, once you see what a miracle this is . . . what it can mean for humanity . . ."

His voice broke. He shook his head in wonder. Before either David or Brie could say any more, he had hurried out the door. Brie got up from the table and stood at the sink, watching through the window until he had disappeared around the side of the house. From the driveway a car door slammed and an engine roared to life; tires crunched on the broken shells. Then there was only silence.

Brie remained at the window, staring out at the ocean, her face furrowed into a frown. Instinctively, her hand still rubbed at the spot on her cheek where Samuel had touched her, as if in an effort to wipe away all trace of the contact.

"You really don't like the book, do you? Tell me the truth. I can take it."

David's voice startled Brie from her reverie. She was curled in a large arm chair in a corner of the study, *Dark Morning* open across her drawn-up knees. On the other side of the room David had been working at his word processor. Now she saw that his back was to the screen. He was staring at her instead. Slowly, she grasped what he'd said.

"Of course I like it. Why do you think I don't?" It was the truth. David was a fine writer. She had started the book just yesterday and was already three-quarters of the way through it. The story was a compelling one.

"I've been watching you. You haven't turned a page for fifteen minutes."

Brie closed the book and came to kneel by David's chair, taking his hands in hers.

"The book is wonderful. I would like it even if I wasn't in love with the author. It's a fine story, but right now I just can't seem to get your father out of my mind."

"I'm worried about him, too. I don't like this whole Brimstone thing."

Brie's hand strayed to her cheek. "When he touched me today, I felt something . . . something so wrong. I've only felt that wrongness one other time, in one of the men that killed the sisters. He grabbed me, and the feeling was the same. I don't know how to explain it. It's not a feeling of good or evil but of something foreign, something totally alien that just doesn't belong, that doesn't *fit*. It's like seeing a red juicy apple. It looks like an apple, smells like an apple—but when you bite into it, it tastes like an onion. It's not what it seems. It doesn't fit. Do you understand?"

"Yes. I think so."

"Whatever this is, I don't trust it—not the thing itself or people's reactions to it. Those two men wanted it so badly they were willing to kill a dozen innocent people to get their hands on it. What's your father going to do with it—turn it over to the government? And if he does, how will it be used? Who's going to control it? Who's going to decide who has the right to the miracle and who doesn't? It frightens me."

"I don't have any answers, Brie. I can only tell you that my father's a good man. He wouldn't knowingly do anything that would harm people. He's always been a person who's willing to listen to reason and to look at something from all angles before making a decision. Before we decide that this Brimstone whatever-it-is is evil, we should give it a chance. He said he'd explain things tonight. Let's try to keep an open mind 'til then and hear him out."

Brie laid her head on his lap. He stroked her hair gently. "I'll try, David," she promised. "But I *know* what I felt. I'm afraid for him, afraid for us."

Afraid for you, she thought, but she didn't say it aloud. David continued to stroke her hair. She knew he meant the action to be soothing, but she took no comfort from it. The alien feel of Samuel's hand against her cheek remained with her, overpowering all other sensations. She knew that as long as Brimstone existed, she would never feel truly at peace again.

In the failing light of evening, Klaus Brauer crouched among the bushes on Newport's famed Cliff Walk. Beach roses pressed thickly around him, making pink and white splashes of color in the gathering darkness and filling the air with their sweet scent. At his back, far below at the base of the cliffs, breakers thundered a continuous crescendo and diminuendo. The sights and sounds were lost on him. He hunched over, head almost resting on one bent knee, aware only of the nagging pain in his belly.

The cancer was growing, aggressively invading new tissues. Twice during the drive to Newport he'd had to pull the car over to the side of the road to vomit. There had been fresh blood mixed with the bile, in frightening amounts. He didn't have much time left.

He raised his head and looked toward the house. There were lights in the windows now, warm and beckoning. The girl was somewhere inside—and Brimstone. Soon he would have both.

Locating the house had not been a problem, and the police car blocking the driveway had proved only a minor inconvenience. He'd expected the house to be guarded, though perhaps not so openly. A tourist map of Newport, purchased for a few dollars at a local bookstore, had showed him how to get to the Cliff Walk. From there, gaining access to the house had been an easy thing. Moments ago, a bolt-cutter had made short work of the chain holding the rear gate closed. Now it was only a matter of waiting for full dark.

Along with the map, he'd also purchased a copy of *Dark Morning*. He'd not bothered to read the book, but had studied instead the black-and-white glossy on the back of the dust cover. He would know David Kauffman when he saw him.

A stiff breeze blew in from the ocean, sending a spray of sand hissing against the toes of his shoes. Brauer shivered. The long drive had given him plenty of time to think about Hahn—of what Hahn had become. Ashes to ashes. Dust to dust. For the first time in all these years he was uncertain of

Brimstone, uncertain of what he wanted. There were suddenly more options than death or revenge.

Over and over again, he found his thoughts returning to what Hahn had said: "The girl is what you want." What if the news reports were true? What if she did possess some miraculous healing power?

His hand moved to touch the bandages that covered his face, and he remembered the way the people in the bookstore had stared at him. In anger he tore at the gauze, pulling the taped end free, unwrapping it until he could feel the evening breeze against his cheeks. Lightly his fingers traced over the rough stitching, where the edges of the wound were drawn together. He could only imagine how he must look. He remembered his younger self, blond and blue-eyed, handsome, so very confident of his destiny. The pain of the memory was far worse than the wounds on his face or the cancer in his belly. A sob escaped him.

Without warning, the nausea overtook him again. He swallowed hard, taking deep gulping breaths of the salty air until the feeling had passed. All that was left of the sunlight was a pink glow on the horizon. In moments, even that would be gone. He slowly unbent from his crouch and stood up.

His eyes studied the dark, brooding shape of the house, as if trying to probe its secrets. If the girl could heal—if he could be made well—then all his plans would change. There would be time to study Brimstone, to test it and assess the possibilities. With the power of eternal life in his hands, the opportunities were limitless.

The girl would have to die, of course—she and

any others who knew of Brimstone's existence. He alone could possess the secret.

Somewhere over the water, a seagull gave a screeching cry. Brauer looked for it, but saw only darkness. The fence before him was now just a shadow among shadows. He took his gun from its holster and screwed the silencer in place. Noiselessly, he pushed open the gate, then slipped through the narrow opening and became one with the night.

"Sit still. I'll get the dessert and coffee."

Samuel bustled away to the kitchen with an armload of dishes, and some of the tension in the room seemed to leave with him. Brie let out a silent sigh of relief. Beneath the table, David's foot nudged hers. He gave her a reassuring smile and reached his hand across the table toward hers. Their fingertips brushed. The warmth of him flowed into her, but it was short-lived. She quickly drew her hand away as Samuel beetled back into the room, a plate of cheesecake in one hand and a coffeepot in the other.

"Let me help you." She started to get up.

"No. This is my treat tonight. You lovebirds sit still. I'll take care of everything." He set down his burdens, then scurried back into the kitchen.

He had taken charge of the whole meal, single-handedly preparing steaks and a huge tossed salad to the accompaniment of whistled Sousa marches. Brie and David had little choice but to stand back out of his way and simply marvel at his energy. They had been quiet during dinner, a bit overwhelmed by Samuel's presence, and had allowed him to do most of the talking.

He returned from the kitchen balancing a stack of cups, saucers, and dessert plates. Somehow, the crockery made it to the table in one piece. In a flurry of activity, Samuel poured coffee for everyone and dished out large slices of the cheesecake. He looked from Brie to David and frowned.

"What's with you two? You've said three words between you all evening. A man gets tired of hearing himself talk."

Brie lowered her eyes. She chased a bit of cheesecake around her plate with her fork, unsure of what to say. Across the table, David cleared his throat.

"Frankly, Dad, we're worried about you, about this Brimstone compound and what you plan to do with it."

"Still worried about me? Look at me. Take a good look. I feel wonderful."

He did look wonderful, Brie had to admit. Since this morning, the last of the gray had vanished from his hair. His complexion glowed with good health. The level of energy he exhibited made her feel exhausted just watching.

"My body's like new. There's not a trace of damage from the heart attack, not the slightest sign on the EKG that it ever occurred." Samuel laughed. "I told the doctor that I'd had a heart attack just last year and he wouldn't believe me. Reflexes, blood pressure, lung capacity—everything is perfect for a man of thirty-five." He beamed at David and Brie.

Despite her apprehensions, Brie couldn't help but return his smile. Samuel's excitement was contagious. So long as she didn't touch him it was possible to believe that this was just Samuel Kauffman, the same man she'd met just a few days before. His warmth, his sense of humor, his personality remained unchanged. Only his physical appearance was different.

At the same time, she knew that if she touched him it would be like touching something from another world, something foreign and cold and unfeeling. Something that neither loved nor hated, laughed nor cried, but simply existed. Something whose only purpose was to be.

"Did they find anything unusual?" David asked.

"You mean did they find Brimstone? The answer is no. Brimstone isn't something that lives inside me, separate but equal. It's part of me, David, part of my very cells. It wouldn't show up in a normal blood test or a urinalysis. You'd have to go much further—down to the level of DNA. If the doctors did that, they'd have a paper to write for their journals that would set the whole scientific world on its collective ear."

He looked from David to Brie and threw up his hands in exasperation. "Doubting Thomases, both of you. Maybe you'll feel more comfortable if you understand things. Eat your dessert. I'll be right back." He strode purposefully from the room. Brie heard his footsteps on the living room stairs.

Soon he was back again, with an armload of papers and paraphernalia. He swept his coffee and dessert aside and arranged his things on the table. With the attitude of a professor lecturing, he picked up the first item.

"Uncle Isaac called this Brimstone, but the compound is only the precursor." He opened the plastic bag, tore two fist-sized chunks from the gray mass, and handed one to David, the other to Brie.

"Don't be squeamish about it. It can't hurt you. You can mold it, punch it, shape it. I'll explain the formula later."

He let them examine the compound, then held up the next object. "This is where Brimstone begins: the transmitter. As I explained this morning, Brimstone is produced by a reaction between chemicals and sound. The switch on the left activates the device, and the switch on the right transmits the desired combination of high-frequency tones. This interacts with the compound, producing an explosion. I would estimate that the amount of compound here on the table would yield an explosion that would destroy everything within a ten-mile radius."

Brie flinched and quickly handed back the ball of compound she'd been holding. It was difficult for her to even think of such destruction. Her inner sense sent cold shivers of fear along her arms, set the hair at the base of her neck prickling a warning. She shuddered and tried to concentrate on what Samuel was saying.

"The explosion gives birth to Brimstone. The life form can enter the human body either by ingestion or absorption through the skin. I achieved synergy by spreading the ash on my skin and letting it absorb overnight. When I woke up in the morning, the change had taken place. The process is safe and absolutely painless."

"Painless, yes. But safe—it's too soon to know that for sure," David objected.

Brie pushed her plate of cheesecake away, her appetite rapidly dwindling. "Samuel," she said, "whatever this is, however it works, whether it's truly safe or not is beside the point. What do you intend to do with it? A dozen people whom I loved died because two evil men wanted to get their hands on that formula. There'll be others who'll be willing to kill for it, once the secret is out."

"Even if you make the formula universally available, think of the problems it will create," David added. "Overpopulation is already of global concern. If you suddenly double or triple the normal life span . . ."

"Mankind has always risen to challenges," Samuel interrupted impatiently. "Brimstone will cause tremendous change and create some problems, that's true. Man will have to change his short-sighted way of thinking. Perhaps if we know we're going to be on this Earth for a long time, we'll begin to take better care of our world."

He took the chunk of compound from David and returned it and Brie's sample to the plastic bag. "I've thought it all out. No one individual, no company or country can have a monopoly on this. It must be made available to everyone. I'm going to give the formula to the world. It's the only way."

"I don't think so."

Three heads turned to face the doorway leading to the kitchen. Brie gasped. A man stood there, gun in hand—the older of the two men who had killed the sisters. Before any of them had a chance to react he took a step forward, leveled his gun at Samuel's chest, and fired.

Chapter Fourteen

The gun spit twice. The bullets caught Samuel just as he'd begun to stand up, burrowing into his chest with the dull non-sound of a baker kneading dough. The force of the impact spun him from his chair and sent him reeling. As he fell, bright gouts of arterial blood began to spurt from the twin wounds, fountaining in an eerie, steady rhythm with each beat of his shattered heart.

For the space of a breath shock kept Brie and David in their chairs, then simultaneously they both started to get up. The gun swung around and centered between them.

"Sit down," the man ordered.

Brie hesitated. David sat, slowly, his eyes fixed on Samuel's bloodied body. He reached his hand across the table toward her and caught her arm, pulling her back into her seat. "Listen to him, Brie," he said tightly.

"A wise move, Mr. Kauffman."

The man strode to the table. In the candlelight, he was even uglier than the first time Brie had seen him. Her blow with the crucifix had done more damage than she'd realized. A jagged wound now divided his face in two. Dark stitches spliced the edges together, and the flesh around them was puckered and discolored. His nose was nothing but a mass of shapeless tissue. Without taking his eyes from the two of them, he quickly pocketed the transmitter and stuffed the sheaf of papers down the front of his jacket. He smiled crookedly at Brie.

"We have never been formally introduced. My name is Klaus Brauer." He nodded toward Samuel. "Your friend's lecture was most informative."

"Let me go to him," she pleaded.

With his free hand Brauer hefted the bag of compound, then set it back on the table. "He's quite beyond help."

"Not beyond her help," David said.

Brauer tried to conceal his eagerness. "What are you saying?"

"I . . . I'm able to heal him. I know it sounds crazy, but it's true. Please let me help him."

Brie saw that Samuel's body had gone ominously still. The bleeding was slowing. Soon it would be too late.

The man grabbed her arm and yanked her to her feet. Eagerly she started toward Samuel, but Brauer jerked her back, pulling her against him. "Your talents are wasted on a dead man. You'll heal me instead."

"No, please."

Brauer put the gun to her head. "The tumor— you *will* heal it now."

"No."

"Brie . . ." David whispered.

"I can't, David. You know he's going to kill us both anyway."

She felt Brauer's body tense against hers. At her

temple, the gun shifted slightly. Her eyes met David's through a blur of tears. She wasn't afraid to die. The only fear death held for her was the parting from him.

Abruptly the gun fired, making a loud *whump!* beside her ear. David's body lifted off his chair. He tumbled to the floor and sat up, slowly, his left hand clutching the opposite shoulder. Blood began to ooze between his fingers.

"David!" Brie screamed his name. She struggled, but Brauer's arm was unyielding.

"You'll heal me or I will kill him—a little at a time."

"Don't do it, Brie," David said through clenched teeth.

The gun went off again. This bullet caught David in the left knee. He screamed from the pain. Around the neat hole the bullet had made, the blue denim of his jeans began to darken with blood. He doubled over. Brie could see him trembling.

"Let me go to him."

"All in good time. You heal me first; then you may take care of him. Make your decision quickly, before I change my mind."

"No, Brie," David said weakly. Somehow he managed to sit up, his right hand a prop for his body.

Brauer made an impatient sound. The next bullet ploughed through David's hand. His wrist seemed to explode in a shower of blood and bone fragments. Brie's scream blended with his as he went down. He lay helpless, his body twitching slightly. A red pool of blood from the severed artery began to spread rapidly beneath him.

"David!" Brie was sobbing now. She struck at

Brauer repeatedly, heedless of the gun, but he easily avoided the blows and held her fast.

"The cancer first. Then you can go to him."

David was still now. His eyes were closed, his face deathly pale. There was blood everywhere—soaking his clothes, forming a lake on the hardwood floor, sending out small rivers of red along the cracks between the boards. The air of the small dining room was thick with the heavy, metallic smell of it. *How much blood can a person lose and still live?* Brie wondered. She made her decision.

"All right—I'll do it."

Brauer didn't respond, and she realized that he was waiting for something to happen, waiting for her to act.

"I can't work this way. You'll have to sit down. I need to place my hands on you. Hurry . . . please."

He shifted his weight and released her. She turned around. He was watching her, tense, wary, the gun still pointed at David. "If you try anything, the next bullet will be in his brain."

With his free hand he pulled over a chair and sat down, all the while keeping the gun trained on David. Brie knelt on the floor beside him. She put the palm of one hand flat against his injured face and clasped his wrist loosely with the other. Her inner sense could feel the cancer in him. Tumors were ripening like dark fruit in his stomach and bowels, shooting out probing tendrils through his lymph system. She had the power to banish them. She tried to fill her mind with the magic thoughts, but they wouldn't come. Around her, time seemed to slow down. Her mind was racing, examining and discarding a hundred alternatives and always circling back to the same inescapable conclusion.

Brauer had to die.

She could not heal him, could not let a monster like him loose on the world to kill more innocents, especially now that the Brimstone formula was in his possession.

And yet . . .

The sight of David's still form created an ache in her worse than any physical pain. She couldn't let him die, not if there was even the smallest chance that she could save him. She knew that Brauer would never allow them to live. If she cured him she would be his next victim, and David would be lost as well.

An idea came. Just a few days ago it would have been unthinkable. Now it was the only way, but she didn't know if it would work. She only knew that it had to.

Her face hardened. She allowed herself a last, longing look at David, then closed her eyes. She blocked out all thought of him, of the gun . . . and the blood. She concentrated only on the magic thoughts. Her breathing quickened. As her thoughts cleared and sharpened, her grip on Brauer's wrist tightened involuntarily. Power gathered in her and flowed like a white-hot current down her arms and into her hands.

Brauer felt the girl's slim fingers tighten on his wrist. His body tensed with anticipation. Soon, his victory would be complete: victory over the miserable Jew who had destroyed his future, victory over all those who had kept Brimstone from him, victory over the cancer that was eating him alive, and yes, even victory over death itself, the ultimate enemy. In moments he would be well. He would kill the girl, and then Brimstone's secret would be his alone.

A tingling began, first in the wound on his cheek, then at his wrist, where her fingers pressed against his pulse point. Her hands grew perceptibly warmer.

Brauer searched inside himself for the first inklings of change. Deep within his belly, the tumor still throbbed like a second heartbeat. Hardly daring to breathe, he waited for the pain to fade, but was conscious only of the increasing heat coming from the girl's hands. It was more than warmth now; her flesh was becoming uncomfortably hot. He shifted nervously in his seat, careful to keep his gun hand steady.

Something happened. Inside him, he could feel a strange squirming sensation, as of organs shifting. Abruptly, the girl's hands began to burn him, and deep within his belly the tumor seemed to burst. Pain flared inside him. He tried to get up, to pull away from the searing touch of her hands, but her grip on him was unshakable. He could feel her palm melting the flesh of his cheek. The smell of burning meat filled the room. Smoke began to curl in slow tendrils from his wrist, where her hand clutched him like a white-hot band.

A strange noise began, thin as the wisps of smoke that filled the air. It was several seconds before Brauer realized that it was the sound of his own desperate screaming.

Pain.

It coursed down Brie's arms and sparked from the nerve endings, as if every nerve fiber and dendrite had been stripped raw. Tears ran down her face, but she was not aware of them. Eyes tightly closed, she held fast to the struggling Brauer. She ignored the pain and channeled every ounce of concentration she had into making magic thoughts.

Magic thoughts—but a dark magic this time. From memory she called up every disease she had ever cured, every injury her gift had ever healed. Her imagination, fueled by anger, supplied what memory lacked. Determinedly, she took every scrap of suffering and misery she could think of and willed them into the body of the murderer.

The gun . . . Brauer's tortured mind struggled to reach beyond the cauldron of pain that bubbled in his belly. He had to turn the gun on her, to destroy her first before she succeeded in destroying him. He managed to swing the gun around, to bring the hand holding it up to the level of his face. But that was as far as it got.

His arm seemed to freeze in that position. The hand holding the gun began to change. Of its own volition it bent inward, to the limits of the normal range of motion and beyond, until the heel of his palm had curled back against his wrist. Still clutching the stock of the gun, his fingers began to reshape themselves. Joints cracked and popped, as arthritis sculpted the bones into impossible shapes. The gun slipped from his grasp and clattered to the floor.

The pain moved into his shoulders, then flowed down his spine. His neck twisted sideways, until the stump of his left ear had come to rest on his shoulder. He could see the girl now. Lines of concentration etched the taut skin of her face, and her hair hung in damp tendrils. Her eyes were closed.

"Please . . ."

Never once in all the years of imprisonment had he begged, but he begged now. It did no good. She seemed unaware of him.

Beneath the cloth sleeves of his windbreaker, something new began to happen. The skin on the back of his hand suddenly raised up into pustules. These burst open. Blood and a thick, yellow exudate ran down the twisted fingers and dripped from their tips. The skin of his back, chest, thighs, and buttocks rippled into a roiling boil of putrescence. Brauer resumed his screaming.

He struggled frantically against the girl's grip. The flesh of his wrist was charred black now, and he could only guess at what was happening to his face. The girl remained immovable as stone.

Then, abruptly, a shudder went through her body. The terrible heat of her touch began to lessen and, around his wrist, her fingers loosened ever so slightly.

Effort sent rivulets of sweat coursing down Brie's face, turned her breathing to a ragged gasping. But with it came reward. His struggles were growing weaker. Deep in one small corner of her mind, she dared to hope.

Suddenly, somewhere along the nerve path between her hands and brain, something short-circuited. The power started to drain from her, dissolving away. Her strength faded with it. She gave a soft cry of despair, as Brauer pulled free of her grip.

He staggered to his feet, his only thought to get away. The thought proved easier than the deed. She had done something to the bones of his legs.

His right foot now twisted inward and dragged uselessly, while his left knee was locked. Somehow, he managed to stay erect.

His bowels felt as if he had swallowed molten lava. Without warning he doubled over and vomited, spraying the floor and wall with black blood and bile. The pain moved into his chest, clamping a viselike hold around his heart and lungs. That was when he realized that whatever she had set in motion inside him was still at work.

He was a dead man.

Fury cleared his mind, gave him the strength for one last desperate act. The package of Brimstone compound was still on the table. He lurched to it and scooped it up, cradling it against his body with the clawlike thing that had once been his right hand.

The girl was still on her knees by the chair. Her eyes were open, but unseeing. There was no telling how soon she would summon her strength and come after him again. He gave her a last hate-filled glance, then staggered for the doorway to the kitchen.

She would pay for this. He would make them all pay.

The first thing that Brie noticed was the pain. Her arms and hands were on fire with it. Every muscle and joint throughout her whole body throbbed with it. Her limbs were heavy, unresponsive, and she was more tired than she had ever been in her life.

With a great effort of will, she opened her eyes. The room was a blur, and it took precious seconds before things came into focus. To her dismay, Brauer was gone.

David . . .

She tried to stand, but her legs would not hold her.

She crawled to him.

His body was limp. Calling his name brought no response, and when Brie felt for a pulse she found none. Sobbing, she took the shattered ruin of his hand between her palms. She filled her mind with thoughts of healing. They came easily.

But the power that usually came with them, the wonderful power that turned thought to reality, was gone.

Samuel lay face-up on the floor, his eyes open and unseeing. The pain in his chest had come and gone. There had been a brief moment of fear, a few seconds of horror at the sight of the blood pumping down his shirt front, then . . . nothing.

Life returned slowly. Though he could neither hear nor see nor move, he became conscious of a frenetic activity inside his own body. Cells were rebuilding at a fantastic rate. The torn walls of his still, bullet-shredded heart were reforming, new cells replacing the destroyed ones. Broken ribs repaired themselves. Rips in muscles and connective tissue closed seamlessly. Over it all skin cells wove and intermeshed, until all sign of the terrible wound was erased.

He felt his new heart flutter. It stopped for a moment, stuttered into an arrhythmia, then settled down to a steady, pounding rhythm. With a wheezy sigh, his diaphragm came to life; the bellows of his rib cage expanded. An intense burning sensation spread through his chest as air reinflated his collapsed lungs.

Hearing returned before sight. The first thing he heard was someone screaming—a man, by the sound of it. The darkness around him lightened to a dense gray fog. The room slowly swam into view, but still he was unable to turn his head or move his eyes to see who was doing the screaming. It was terribly frustrating.

His hand moved first, the fingers flexing and extending involuntarily. He raised his arm. It came up in a series of awkward jerks, like the limb of a marionette. Indeed, something inside him was pulling the strings, something still unfamiliar with the way a human body moved ... something that he sensed was deadly tired.

The screaming stopped. Samuel could almost hear his neck muscles groan as he forced his head to turn. The movement brought Brie into his line of vision. She was kneeling by an empty chair, hands raised, eyes closed. For a moment, Samuel thought she was praying.

At the edge of his vision, something moved. He turned his head in time to see Brauer stagger out the door toward the kitchen and the rear of the house.

Brie crawled past him. He tried to call out to her, but his throat muscles were still unresponsive. By a sheer effort of will, he sat up. Her back was to him. She was kneeling beside someone else.

David. The thought registered in his death-fogged mind, along with the sight of the blood—far too much blood. Brie put her hands on his son, and Samuel realized what she was doing. A warm flood of relief washed through him, then turned to ice water in his veins as another thought surfaced.

Shaky as a newborn colt, Samuel staggered to his feet. A glance confirmed his worst fears. The compound, the transmitter, the formula—everything relating to Brimstone was gone.

The German.

Tottering, bouncing from table to door frame like a drunk, Samuel made it across the room and through the doorway. The kitchen was empty. A trail of blood led across the linoleum to the back door. The unlatched screen door swung gently in the night breeze, making a soft, creaking sound.

Without hesitation, Samuel lurched through it into the night.

Brauer shambled along, stopping only long enough to shove the bag of compound into his windbreaker.

He was bleeding, both inside and out. Blood dripped down into his eyes, blurring his vision, and he used his good arm to wipe it away. His insides had gone to jelly. Still he kept moving, his legs functioning by will alone to propel him across the dark lawn to the open gate.

As he stepped through it, his foot came down on empty space. His twisted arms and legs pinwheeled uselessly. Like a broken doll, he tumbled down the short embankment onto the hard-packed earth of the Cliff Walk.

The fall knocked the wind out of him. Precious seconds ticked by before he managed to roll from his side to his stomach, gather his legs under him one at a time, then push up to his knees. Fluid bubbled in his lungs with every breath. Using his good arm for support, he made it to his feet.

He looked back to the house, the fingers of his hand reaching inside his jacket to caress the cold, hard slab of compound, where it lay against his heart.

Brimstone . . .

Tears mixed with the blood that was streaming down his cheeks. A scream of rage shook him. His left hand fumbled along his side, searching for the pocket that held the transmitter. When death took him, he would not go alone.

"No . . . Oh God, please no . . ."

Brie heard her voice babbling the words aloud, over and over. Her fingers dug into the torn flesh of David's wrist, but there was no power in them, no healing. Her hands were cold.

"It's not fair."

All her life she'd used her gift for good, bringing healing to countless strangers. Now, as with her parents and the sisters, when she needed it most she was helpless.

"Please," she whispered. "Please . . . just this once. I'll never ask for anything ag—" Her voice broke. She pulled David's limp body into her arms and cradled his head on her breasts. Weeping with despair she rocked him, pressing her lips to the cold, clammy skin of his forehead.

A tingle.

For a moment she thought she'd imagined it, then it came again—stronger—a prickling along the curve of her spine. A strange sensation began in the core of her and spread rapidly. She felt like a reservoir filling . . . filling. Power suffused her, reaching down to the tips of her toes, spreading upward into her head then out into her shoulders, her arms, her hands.

The strength was not her own. It was a Power far beyond anything she had ever known before. Light grew around her, until her eyes were dazzled by it. She closed them, only to find that the light came from within her as well. She was vaguely aware of Something—*Someone?*—guiding her hands.

Her inner sight opened up. Her eyes were still closed, but she could see David. He was walking down a long, dark tunnel toward a small point of light. His back was to her. She called out his name, but he did not respond. She started after him.

Immediately, the whole atmosphere around her began to change, become threatening. All sound was cut off. The silence of the grave closed around her. She knew nothingness, emptiness ... fear, knew what this place was and where David was going. Beneath her feet the floor of the tunnel transformed itself into a soundless, churning morass of mud and sand. It swallowed her shoes and sucked at her legs, threatening to drag her down. Thorny, branchlike tendrils sprouted from the walls and ceiling to catch in her clothing and tear at her hair, further slowing her progress. David continued to move farther away.

Desperately, Brie forced her way forward. The thorns raked the skin of her arms, sent needles of pain jabbing into her scalp. Spears of rock pushed up through the unstable floor.

She was gaining, but so slowly—each weary step reducing the distance between them by only a tiny fraction. The point of light at the end of the tunnel was closer also, and she knew that if he reached it the battle was lost.

"David!"

She screamed his name, and this time he heard. He turned in slow motion, a look of astonishment on his handsome face. She reached out her hand. A white aura surrounded her splayed fingers, like a glove of light. David reached for her, and as their fingers touched the light flowed from her flesh to his. In moments it had surrounded them both in a brilliant cocoon.

Brie pulled David close and turned. Their arms around each other, they started back the way she'd come. She could see the dining room. It was far away and small, as if viewed through the wrong end of a telescope. Two tiny figures huddled in the center of the image. Determinedly, she led David toward them.

A wind kicked up around them, driving waves of stinging sand into their faces, pushing the two of them back. The ground heaved and Brie fell. This time it was David who helped her. He pulled her to her feet and they continued on, heads bent against the silent onslaught of the wind. The silence pressed in around them, heavy, almost suffocating. The air itself seemed to thicken in an effort to hold them back. It was like trying to run underwater.

Brie was growing weaker. Her limbs seemed heavy and uncooperative. Time had slowed, but she knew that if they did not leave this place soon it would be too late. The silence was crushing her chest, the wind sucking away her breath. The darkness pressed down on them, threatening to snuff out the light. Then she was falling . . .

falling . . .

falling . . .

into herself. Her own body closed around her. Sound returned. The normal quiet of the old house was blessedly deafening.

In her arms, David stirred.

He opened his eyes and reached up a shaky hand to touch her face. The skin of his palm and wrist was bloodstained, but whole.

"I had the strangest dream, where—" he began, then broke off when he saw in her eyes that it had not been a dream at all.

Brie held him close, kissing his eyes, his forehead, his mouth. She was exhausted, physically and emotionally too weak for words.

Except for two.

"Thank you," she whispered, too softly for David to hear. Someone in the peaceful quiet of the room accepted the words. A warmth surrounded her and David. She closed her eyes and buried her face in the soft, damp tangle of David's hair.

Samuel squinted through the darkness. Moonlight cast a pale luminescence across the black expanse of the lawn and tipped the tops of the trees with silver. Nothing moved. He cocked his head, listening. Cricket song mixed with the distant susurrations of the tide, but his ears did not pick up anything unusual. The man might have gone around to the front of the house. Samuel started to turn, then caught the ghost of a movement, black on black, at the property line near the gate.

Of course. That was how the intruder had gotten to the house without alerting the police. Samuel willed his leaden legs into motion and headed across the lawn. Feet planted wide apart, arms raised for balance, he felt like a toddler learning to walk for the first time. Indeed, was he not newborn? His foot hit a slight depression and he nearly went down. Determinedly, he pushed any other speculations from his mind and concentrated only on the chase. There would be time for speculation later.

It seemed to take an age for his legs to carry him to the fence. The gate was open wide. Samuel used it to swing down the short drop to the Cliff Walk. He regained his balance, then straightened up to find himself face-to-face with his quarry.

The man's appearance froze Samuel in his tracks. The killer's face was a mass of pustules and running sores. Strange growths sprouted, wartlike, along his jaw and clustered on the bald, shiny dome of his scalp. Blood oozed from hundreds of small cracks in his tortured flesh.

The stranger seemed just as startled as he was, but he recovered more quickly. One hand had been cradled across his chest, the other buried in the pocket of his coat. Before Samuel could react he'd pulled his hand out of his pocket. Samuel made out a dark shape clutched in his fingers.

The transmitter.

The man grinned, obviously delighted with the horrified look of realization that came to Samuel's eyes. With his thumb, he flipped the first switch on. The amber light lit up like a flare in the darkness. The second switch was more awkward for him, and he shifted the small device in his hand, trying to get at it.

Samuel charged him, inwardly cursing the clumsy slowness of his limbs. He flung one arm awkwardly around the German and used the other to try to get a grip on the man's wrist, but the ruptured flesh was slick and kept slipping from his grasp. Locked together, they struggled on the edge of the cliff. Through the stranger's jacket Samuel could feel the flat, hard lump of the Brimstone compound, pressing against his ribs.

They staggered back and forth, like a couple in the last minutes of some bizarre dance marathon. Samuel's strength was rapidly failing but he hung on, sensing that his opponent was weakening also. If luck was with him, if he could hold out just a little longer, he might be able to exhaust the other man and get the transmitter away from him.

His luck ran out.

The German managed to wrench his good arm free and brought it smashing down across Samuel's face. Samuel's neck snapped back. Vertebrae crunched in protest as they were stretched to the limit. The man pulled free and kicked Samuel's legs out from under him.

On his hands and knees, Samuel tried to raise his head. The movement sent the sprained muscles of his neck into spasm, but it was enough to make out the amber light of the transmitter pulsing like a warning beacon and the other man's hands fumbling for the switch. There was no time. He knew what he had to do.

From a half crouch, Samuel sprang at the madman. Every last ounce of strength he had went into the rush, as he launched himself across the short distance between them. He caught his enemy around the waist. The force of his momentum drove them both forward.

He heard the other man scream.

Then there was only empty space and the rush of the wind, the sound of the water drawing closer . . . closer . . . the water that would, hopefully, neutralize the compound before it could explode.

His last thoughts, as the white froth of the breakers seemed to rush up to meet him, were of David and Brie. He wondered what their children would look like, the grandchildren he would never see.

Epilogue

Five years later

A seagull flew low over the beach, its klaxon-like cry shrill on the hot air. Brie sat up and stretched. The sun was warm on her skin. The baby growing within her responded to the change in position, sending a butterfly flutter of sensation along the base of her ribs. She rubbed affectionately at the spot.

On the other side of the blanket, David looked up from the book galleys he was busy correcting. He peered at her over the bridge of his sunglasses.

"Everything okay?"

"Yes." She rubbed at her ribs. "I think this one's going to be a football player."

David grinned. He waggled his pencil in front of her nose. "You never know—maybe she's just flexing her writing arm."

A pair of young women strolled by, clad in two of the skimpiest bikinis Brie had ever seen. She glanced at David, but his attention was back on the proofs. She smiled and reached out to brush a smudge of sand from his temple.

He looked up questioningly. "Did you say something?"

"No. I was just sitting here thinking about how very much I love you."

He put the galleys aside, sat up, and put his arm around her. "The feeling is mutual," he said, giving her a peck on the lips. He looked at his watch and frowned. "It's getting late. We ought to be going."

Brie nodded. She picked up a towel. "You get the things together, and I'll go play the heavy."

David raised an eyebrow, looking pointedly at her bulging stomach. Feigning outrage, she stuck her tongue out at him and swatted him with the towel.

"You writers can be so literal-minded."

Moving with awkward grace, she got to her feet and walked to where a group of children huddled by the water's edge. A sand castle was under construction. Two little girls were dribbling spires of wet sand into its top, and another was decorating the sides with bits of shell. A boy was energetically digging a moat around its base. Brie spoke to one of the spire-makers.

"Ellie, it's time to go."

The child paused in her work. From mid-chest down she was covered by a dark, gritty layer of sand. More sand clung to her arms and to the suntan lotion on her face, adding to the light sprinkling of freckles across her small, upturned nose. Her lower lip thrust out in a disappointed pout. "Do we have to?"

"Grampa's coming for dinner. You want to see him, don't you?"

Ellie's face brightened. She nodded her head vigorously. "I love Grampa."

"I do too. Now hurry and come here, so I can rinse some of that sand off before we get into the car."

Brie knelt in the shallow water and washed the child down. Grampa ... The roar of the breakers brought back memories of that night, five years past, when she and David had clambered down the cliffside. They had shouted Samuel's name until they were hoarse, but their only answer had been the mocking rush of the waves. At last, they'd given up in despair.

As they turned to begin the long climb back up to the house, a small sound carried above the crash and boom of the water. Far down the rock-strewn shoreline, a dark figure emerged from the surf.

Samuel staggered to the shore and collapsed into their arms—an old man, silver-haired and weary-looking, but blessedly whole. When Brie held him, she felt only the loving warmth of the man. His body was empty of anything else. He later theorized that resurrecting him twice within such a short period of time had been too much for the parasite. Even so, its brief sojourn within his body had left him healthier, stronger than before. Even the heart disease was gone. No trace of Brauer—or Brimstone—was ever found.

"Mommy, I cut myself!"

Ellie was standing, stork-like, on one foot, clutching the other one tightly in her hands. On the pink ball of her foot Brie could see a small cut, oozing blood.

"Come on. We'll fix it up." She bundled her daughter into a towel and carried her back to the blanket. Cradling Ellie to her, she sat down beside David.

"It hurts, Mommy."

"What happened?"

Brie gave David a reassuring smile. "She must have stepped on a bit of broken shell." To Ellie she said, "It's going to be all right. Let Mommy kiss it and make it better."

And she did.

And it was.

SPELLBINDING THRILLERS

☐ **NIGHT OVER WATER by Ken Follett.** This national bestseller is an explosive thriller of spiraling suspense, romance and intrigue aboard the high-flying Pan Am clipper, bound for America from war-torn Europe.

☐ **THE KEY TO REBECCA by Ken Follett.** A #1 nationwide bestseller! Alex Wolff, "The Sphinx," must send ruthless Nazi agent Rommel the secrets that would unlock the doors to Cairo and ultimate Nazi triumph in the war. "Brilliant adventure by the most romantic of all top thriller writers!" —*Time* (163494—$5.99)

☐ **PAPER MONEY by Ken Follett.** Felix Laski is a powerful corporate raider who built an empire and shook the stock market. Ambitious moves led him to an affair with a bored wife and to masterminding for a professional criminal. (167309—$4.99)

☐ **EYE OF THE NEEDLE by Ken Follett.** His code name was *The Needle*. He knew the secret that could win the war for Hitler . . . and Lucy Rose was the only one who could stop him. . . . (163486—$5.99)

☐ **LIE DOWN WITH LIONS by Ken Follett.** Two men on opposite sides of the cold war—and the beautiful Englishwoman torn between them—caught in romantic adventures from Paris to Afghanistan! "Rivals his Eye of the Needle for sheer suspense."—*Washington Post* (163508—$5.99)

Prices slightly higher in Canada

There's an epidemic with 27 million victims. And no visible symptoms.

It's an epidemic of people who can't read.

Believe it or not, 27 million Americans are functionally illiterate, about one adult in five.

The solution to this problem is you... when you join the fight against illiteracy. So call the Coalition for Literacy at toll-free **1-800-228-8813** and volunteer.

Volunteer Against Illiteracy. The only degree you need is a degree of caring.